THE STRAY SOD COUNTRY

THE STRAY SOD COUNTRY

A Novel

PATRICK McCABE

B L O O M S B U R Y

NEW YORK · BERLIN · LONDON · SYDNEY

Published by Bloomsbury USA, New York

All papers used by Bloomsbury USA are natural, recyclable products made
from wood grown in well-managed forests. The manufacturing processes
conform to the environmental regulations of the country of origin.

LIBRARY OF CONGRESS CATALOGING-IN-PUBLICATION DATA HAS BEEN APPLIED FOR.

ISBN: 978-1-60819-274-8

First U.S. edition 2010

1 3 5 7 9 10 8 6 4 2

Typeset by Hewer Text UK Ltd, Edinburgh
Printed in the U.S.A. by Quad/Graphics, Fairfield, Pennyslvania

1

Who says a policeman's life is not a happy one?
Certainly not PC Jimmy Upton of Margate who had just scooped £252,984 on a Littlewoods first dividend payout.

– O isn't he the lucky beggar! gasped Happy Carroll, replacing the folded pools coupon in his pocket, as an ear-splitting scream left him sitting there dumbstruck. It had come from the café directly across the street.

– *Jesus, Mary and Joseph!* cried Patsy the barber – already halfway out the door.

Nobody ever got to know what exactly happened that day – the owner Mrs Ellen Markey certainly wasn't known for hysterics. But it wasn't very long before rumours began to circulate. With a significant number of individuals professing themselves convinced that the devil had somehow been involved, citing the dramatic appearance of the priest on the scene as strong evidence to this effect. There had also been talk of a sighting of some kind – in the vicinity of the lake.

– However, in my opinion there's no need to worry, suggested Happy Carroll, for even if it does turn out that His Nibs influenced things in some way, Father Hand won't be long softening the saucy rogue's cough.

Most people tended to concur with this assessment – concluding that, as always, Father Hand was there when you needed him.

The parish priest was a big, blustering fellow with a shock of silver hair and an enormous set of dandruff-dappled shoulders, who now, at this very moment, was on his way back home – in spite of his success with Mrs Markey, regrettably finding himself turning irritable once more. No matter how he tried he just could not seem to rid himself of the thoughts which had been plaguing him obstinately since early morning. Why did he have to go and read the stupid paper, he asked himself. For if he hadn't then he would never have come across the photo of Patrick Peyton. A man he loathed profoundly and there really is no other way of putting it.

– Father Patrick Peyton, he hissed, stumbling awkwardly over a stone as he added bitterly:

– The hateful lickspittle, that useless good-for-nothing!

He was aware, of course, that as a clergyman he ought never to swear – either in public or private. But now he had gone and done it again – succumbed to those base, unworthy urges. Grinding his teeth as he climbed the presbytery stairs, closing his fist as he struck the newspaper yet another resolute blow.

– Very well then – damn it to hell, I swore! he growled, but if it's the last thing I do, I'll best that infuriatingly smug Mayo toady!

Beneath the sober black-and-white image of Father Peyton, the caption proclaimed proudly: IRISH PRIEST IS FRIEND TO THE STARS.

*   *   *

Father Patrick Peyton, originally from the West of Ireland, had in recent times been forging a reputation in the world of show business – in both Hollywood and the United States of America generally. This displeased Father Hand immensely. Which was why he was endeavouring again to suppress profanities – and with no great deal of success, it has to be admitted. Gradually becoming aware that Mrs Una Miniter, his housekeeper of many years, was standing directly on the landing behind him – and making no secret of her displeasure. Father Hand was mortified. For he was extremely fond of Una Miniter, and would not wittingly have done anything to upset her.

– I'm sorry, he said, fumbling for his hat, making his way back across the landing in a state of complete confusion – before finding himself in the street once more. Tentatively extending his large red hand – for the purpose of inspecting some raindrops. At which point he heard his name being called – quite loudly. As he turned to look across the street, descrying there, in his tea cosy hat, none other than the bedraggled figure of James A. Reilly, who was in the process of hurling a torrent of abuse in his direction.

– Yes, there he is, ladies and gentlemen, the parish priest of Cullymore – I hope you know that you're a bastard, Father Hand.

The consensus in the town was that it was a pity about James Aloysius Reilly – and all such unfortunate delusionals, indeed – religious or otherwise.

2

Laika the dog hadn't been long in space when Golly Murray decided to go up the town. As she donned her headscarf, she found herself thinking about James A. Reilly and the speech he had made outside the church gates the previous Sunday.

– Isn't space fierce big when you think about it, all the same? he had said.

With his scruffy navy-blue belted gabardine raincoat, not to mention his shapeless old woolly hat, there was little dividing James Reilly and the average scarecrow, the house-wife found herself thinking bemusedly.

– A right-looking sketch and no mistake! she smiled.

Before seeking out a small pencil to note some items on her shopping list. Tugging her scarf underneath her chin she professed herself pleased with how presentable she looked. For a fleeting moment she thought that she'd forgotten her fur-backed gloves. But then she remembered: they were in her handbag.

The handbag Patsy had given her for a present. Unlike Golly, her husband was a Catholic. But, being so fond of him, she had gone ahead and married him anyway.

Seven years before, in 1950. She checked on her shop book one more time. For although she might be married to a Catholic she had not abandoned her thrifty Protestant ways, making sure to clear her bill without fail every Friday. Then out she went and gently closed the door.

Now as she proceeded along the street, Mrs Patsy Murray, the barber's wife, continued to repeat in sing-song fashion the various items which she intended to purchase in a variety of retail establishments.

– I have a postal order to get and chicken-noodle soup. And a jar, of course, of *Fruitfield* marmalade – anything except *Robinson's*, that's for sure! And when that's all done it'll be off to the butcher's to buy ribbed steak. And maybe some eggs – yes, I think half a dozen. For Boniface, that little rascal of mine – there is nothing he likes better than his *guggy egg*! So I'll have to make sure not to forget those.

– Thank you, Barney, she heard herself say.

Barney Corr was the name of her favourite victualler. A long-standing friend of the family's was Barney, belonging as he did to that august band of brothers – the *great old Cullymore gang*, as they called themselves. Which was a little family in itself, or at least that was how they thought of it, with its number including a great many of her husband's dearest friends – among them Jude O'Hara the schoolteacher, Happy Carroll the carpenter and Conleth Foley the artist. Not forgetting Dagwood Slowey, dedicated racer of champion pigeons, and snooker-hall manager for many a long year.

Emerging from Corr's, quite unexpectedly she encountered Blossom Foster.

– *Golly!* What do you make of all this talk about space? enquired Blossom, quite animatedly.

Golly's immediate response was that she didn't really have any hard or fast views on the subject. But by now her interlocutor had already moved on and was enquiring as to what Golly's opinion might be of *Italy*. Golly replied by explaining that, regrettably, she'd never been.

– O have you not? That's interesting. My husband and I are going there.

– Are you really? How nice, replied Golly.

Then Blossom said that she had to be on her way – that she still had a number of outstanding purchases to make.

– Goodbye then, said Golly, I'll probably see you at church on Sunday.

– Of course, dear! Blossom called back, steadying her hat against a sudden gust of wind.

When Golly returned home, she stood for a moment in the quiet of the kitchen. Behind the wavering coloured strips that led into her husband's barber's shop, she could hear the muffled drone of voices – and the familiar and steady hum of Patsy's electric shaver. For no particular reason she found herself thinking about the subject of space again. Or more specifically, *Laika* the Russian dog. Who right at that particular moment was drifting some-where in the galaxy's spectacular immensity. How huge it did indeed seem, she thought – with a little shiver. What must it be like for *Laika*, up there all alone?

She had seen his picture in the *Daily Express*. A poor

unfortunate mongrel harshly plucked off the streets of Moscow, and left abandoned there inside his fishbowl helmet, looking hopelessly lost behind the letters *CCCP*.

Then the sound of laughter rose faintly in the shop, the thin plastic strips of the partition shimmering anew before settling, at last.

As Golly Murray released a small peal of anguish, hot tears leaping sharply to her eyes.

3

At five past three one Saturday afternoon in the middle of January James A. Reilly kicked a collie in the face. But nobody paid the slightest attention. Why should they? It was just the kind of behaviour they expected from him, releasing his frustrations by ill-treating dumb and defenceless, quite innocent animals. For its part, the poor unfortunate canine had just scuttled off, whimpering – as though aware in its heart that it warranted no better.

However, it must be said that James A. Reilly hadn't always been the object of such trenchant and all-pervasive public derision. In a former life, indeed, had been one of the most respected teachers in Rathwilliam College. Where he had been employed as a teacher of Latin and English – was something of an authority on *Horace* the Roman poet, in fact.

Coincidentally, Father Hand had also worked there – in the post of Senior Dean of Discipline. For this reason the parish priest harboured a special loathing for James A. Reilly – perceiving him to have brought disgrace upon his revered Alma Mater. It was a fact which was indisputable – he had. When, one morning right in the middle of Junior 3 Latin class, he had apparently undergone some kind of episode and manhandled a student by the name of Jerome Brolly – brazenly kissing the boy on the lips, in fact.

– *God, how I love you, Dorothy McGuire!* by all accounts, he had whimpered.

The affair became the talk of the country, as well as being the subject of an investigative tribunal after which *Satan's henchman*, as one woman had christened him, found himself summarily dismissed in disgrace.

Life in Rathwilliam College had been demanding in those days. It was wartime. Sugarless tea and black bread were the order of the day. The highlight of the school week was the half-day on Wednesday, with a special news-paper-reading session in the common room on Friday evenings. The bombing raids which were proceeding in London and other provincial towns in England seemed far away. Days crawled past with a crushing tedium. So the *Reilly* incident provided something of a respite for the excited students. What had taken place, they consid-ered, was truly beyond belief, when compared with the normal procession of unremarkable events in the college. This was how it happened.

Master James Reilly had just left his Latin book down on the table. The text in question was *Horace's Odes*. The teacher had been intensely considering its contents for some time. Before his manner had begun to manifest what might be described as an exceedingly agitated and alarming aspect. Already his countenance had grown quite pale. In response, hardly surprisingly, various little pockets of nervous laughter had begun to form around the classroom – but dissipated almost as dramatically. For the boys had become unsettled too. But it was only when their custodian began to tremble violently – the whiteness of his knuckles was plain for all to see – that all attempts at levity were suspended. Their teacher's forehead was moist and seamed with anxiety. There was a rational and explicable reason for this, however – and it is highly likely that if, in an effort to distract himself from the inevitability of his mother's impending death, James A. Reilly had not visited the cinema the previous evening – events that day might have proceeded somewhat differently. In his fraught and exceedingly emotional state that night, he had willingly surrendered himself to the events which unfolded in the film *The Spiral Staircase*, in which a beautiful deaf-mute, played by *Dorothy McGuire*, is terrifyingly preyed on by a loathsome, psychotic killer. *Dorothy*, as an actress, was generally regarded as a model of sincerity, bringing dignity to all the roles she inhabited, possessing a passive quiet beauty, with a soothing quality to her open-faced looks. She had literally taken the teacher's breath away. Whenever she appeared onscreen, as seen through the predator's eyes, her luscious mouth was hidden by a small, hovering, vaporous cloud.

– *Dorothy McGuire*, I really must see your lovely lips! the Latin master found himself crying tearfully as he stood in the middle of the Junior 3 classroom, before gripping the astonished student tightly by both arms – passionately crushing his lips to his, in front of the whole class.

In the one hundred and fifty years of its existence, nothing comparable to it had ever occurred in Rathwilliam College.

At the subsequent tribunal, in a less than impressive attempt at mitigation, the teacher had audaciously claimed that *something* had made him do it – that an inexplicable foreign influence had subordinated his will.

– Left to my own devices, I promise you, I never would have dreamed of doing such a thing. It would have been entirely abhorrent to my nature. There was something else in the room that day – mastering my desires. I know you won't believe me, but it's true. I couldn't see what it was, but I could *feel* it – standing there. Watching me. I could hear it breathing – keeping perfect time with my own.

For many years afterwards, he would steadfastly hold to this version of events.

– Whether it was *Nobodaddy* or not, I cannot say. All I know is – whoever it was – they entered my mind through a gap in my defences, and consequently ruined me. For no other reason, perhaps, than that of their own amusement.

– What a headcase, laughed the barman in the *Yankee Clipper Bar*, as Patsy Murray ordered another whisky. James Reilly was alone at the end of the bar, relating the same old tired and familiar story.

– The *Fetch*, he whispered, maybe it was him. Have you heard of him, he tracks you like a shadow. Maybe it could have been him. And not *Nobodaddy*.

– *Nobodaddy?* Who the fuck's that, asked the barman, tossing his head back as he emitted a loud guffaw. But James A. Reilly wasn't laughing. His face was chalk white.

– He's the father without a body, at least according to William Blake.

– William Blake, asked Happy Carroll, does he drink down in Billy McNeill's?

As the barman once again erupted uproariously, but eliciting no reaction from the stony-faced loony James A. Reilly.

4

Cullymore was a border town with an equal number of Protestants and Catholics, numbering two thousand in total. It had always been a source of pride for the community that, by and large – unlike so many other places – somehow everyone got along together. Which made it all the more regrettable that the ongoing feud between James Reilly and their parish priest showed no sign of subsiding. In fact, if anything, it appeared to be getting worse.

One ordinary and otherwise quite unremarkable evening, Father Hand was bending down in front of the fire and getting himself ready to rake some coals when he was seized by an uncomfortable sensation – that someone was standing at the window, gazing in. Discarding the tongs sharply, he hastily made his way across the room. Only to discover, despairingly, that it was a most familiar countenance that was pressing its flattened features against the glass. No sound was heard to pass James Reilly's lips. Not unjustifiably, the clergyman found himself deeply aggrieved – and was on the verge of erupting violently, in fact, with all manner of obscenities crowding to his mind.

But when he opened his mouth with the intention of releasing them, to his surprise, he saw to his amazement that there was no one there. Maybe he had imagined it, he began to think. But still remained puzzled. He craned his neck – no, there was nothing. Just young Jenny Cartwright in her bottle-green blazer, swinging her bag, making her way home from school.

Such incidents, regrettably, had become commonplace over the years. Indeed, not long after the flattened-countenance incident, the disgraced teacher had flung the massive oaken doors of the church wide open and burst in roaring like the lunatic that he was, shouting and threatening to assault Father Hand – right there and then in the middle of morning Mass. On another occasion he had brought a billy goat into Benediction, and rounded aggressively on the parish priest when challenged.

– I thought Our Saviour was supposed to love animals, you stupid bollocks! And anyway it wasn't me who kissed Jerome Brolly. He made me do it – whoever he is, the *Stranger*! O so you don't believe me? But you just wait. You just wait till he decides to turn his sights on you. Maybe we should wait till he opts to come for you, or some of the other shitehawks in this town. We'll see how smart you are then, Father Fuck.

It was inevitable that eventually James A. Reilly should find himself prohibited from entry into the church or daring even to approach any part of its grounds. However, he soon made it clear that no illegal edict had even the slightest hope of succeeding.

The waters of the baptismal font were contaminated the following week – and it soon became public knowledge that James A. Reilly had shamelessly urinated in them.

And if that wasn't bad enough, turned up that same evening in the presbytery garden, paralytic drunk – with a flinty-eyed fox squatting defiantly on his shoulder.

– Beneath that *Stray Sod Sky* you will all live and die, he snarled, and I ought to know, for now it's all clear – he told me last night. I have been chosen to be his messenger.

As he chuckled and grinned inanely, feeding a handful of nuts to the fox.

5

I mean, honest to God – did you ever in all your life see as
funny a character as *Francis the Talking Mule* – he was the
most hilarious character on the telly by far.
. But Patsy Murray the barber wasn't really interested in
what *Francis the Talking Mule* was doing. At least not right
now, being much too busy leafing through his paper.
– *Boo!* his wife squealed suddenly, leaping out of nowhere
as the barber placed his hand instinctively on his heart.
– Jesus Christ almighty, Golly – you put the fear of God
in me, so you did!
But the giddy abandon of his wife's girlish laughter began
to amuse and excite him then, as it so often did, when she
swung her bag gaily, tossing back her lovely blonde curls.
She had just been shopping in Enniskillen, she informed
him.
– Would you like a sandwich? she asked. I was just going
to wet a fresh pot of tea.
– There's nothing I'd like better, her husband replied, for
as you can see there's damn all stirring in the shop at the
moment.
Some Protestant ladies would have objected to the word
damn. But such public stances on morality would not have

been in Golly Murray's nature. Certainly she would have considered herself a committed Protestant but perhaps the most defining thing about her was that she had always loved a good laugh.

It was one of the reasons that her husband had been attracted to her. They had met at a dance in the *Masonic Hall* ten years before, in 1948.

And now, as *Francis the Talking Mule* gave way to the news, Patsy entertained a vivid recollection of that special and long-treasured night. His wife had been wearing a dress with forget-me-nots all over it, cinched in at the waist with a thin white belt. He remembered nearly collapsing when he realised that she had actually consented to dance with him. The reason for this was that she was generally regarded as one of the finest-looking girls in the town.

– Is there much stir about Balla these times? he had asked her, holding her hand gently as they waltzed and he looked away.

– Och sure you know Balla, she had replied, there never be's much stir around there, about anything.

Her home place of Balla was a village just five miles away, across the border. The *Tony Farmer Orchestra* had been playing that night. The song they had ended with had been called *Goodbye Lover*. But it hadn't been goodbye for Golly Phairs and Patsy Murray. Who, in spite of certain murmurs of disapproval, from that night on had begun to keep company with his lovely Protestant girlfriend, as he thought of her.

One night she had allowed him to touch her *tit* – or *breast* as he preferred to think of it, at least whenever he was thinking of his Geraldine.

The emotions she had released in the wake of her agreement to dance with him, overwhelming though they had been, would soon be as nothing to those he experienced while unbuttoning her white blouse and cupping her soft flesh in a darkened alley not far from the hall.

That had been in June 1949, a year before they made the decision to publicly seal their union in marriage. Mixed marriages at the time were extremely rare – vigorously discouraged by both traditions.

– Marrying one of them, Blossom Foster had declared coldly, is of no advantage to anyone and she ought to have known that.

– You know, Protestants have it in them sometimes to be very hard, Patsy Murray heard his wife murmur when they found themselves lying in bed one night, so quietly cruel that it can be difficult to accept.

Eventually she and Blossom became reacquainted. But Golly was never to forget what had happened between them, what had been said about her and her husband.

– When you're in love with someone, Patsy had told her one night after the pictures, you're prepared to do almost anything for them. Golly hugged his arm warmly and told him she thought it was the loveliest thing she had ever heard.

*   *   *

Then, another time, Patsy Murray found himself being awakened – at first he thought he had imagined what he had heard. His wife had been moaning bitterly in her sleep.

– If only she could be disfigured – maybe in a road accident, then we'd see who's the great Blossom Foster.

And he thought to himself how he never wanted to hear the like again. What had made his wife say such a thing, he wondered. It was as if a stranger was lying there, whispering.

However, all of that was quite forgotten now, or seemed to be – as Golly stood in front of him brandishing a plate of sandwiches on a cloth, toying with one of the buttons on her housecoat.

– You know that I love you, don't you, Patsy? he heard her saying. I was wondering would you mind awfully if I sat down on your knee?

This was a most unusual development, for as a rule Golly was anything but demonstrative. But her husband found himself gamely patting his thighs, delighting now in the smooth softness of his spouse's warm buttocks. Then she looked at her sandwich and repeated that she loved him. He loved her too, the barber told her – and not just a little, but a lot. It was at this point that Golly put down her sandwich, placing both of her hands on his shoulders, gazing directly into his face. She said that it did her heart good to hear that.

– I could listen to you saying things like that all day.

– I'm glad, he replied.

– It's what us girls want, I really think, in the end. We just want to *know*.

– Know? he replied – choking a little.

– I was reading in *Woman's Way* that there are some husbands who love their wives so much that there is absolutely nothing they will not do for them. Anything in the world that they ask, they'll do it. That's what it says.

The announcer on the telly said that the news would be back tomorrow at the later time of 5.15.

Patsy Murray was somewhat taken aback – realising that his wife had grown cold all over. Not only that but, in fact, was trembling a little. There was definitely sweat all along her back. Or *perspiration* as he liked to think of it when it was her.

– You know, she continued, turning a blonde corkscrew curl around her index finger, when we got married and I agreed that if we had any children. When I agreed that they'd be brought up as Catholics – in your religion?

– Yes, of course, I remember that well. How could I forget? It was a hard time.

– Indeed it was – it was a very difficult decision to have to make. I mean I could see the way they all looked at me in the street. My own kind.

– I know that, Golly. I know how hard it must have been for you. I really do understand.

– I know I shouldn't even be bothered with them – but it's hard even yet. I overheard them saying the most terrible things.

– I want you to believe me that I really do appreciate it what you did – and always will.

Her hands rested demurely in her lap. Like little birds, he found himself thinking.

As she jerked again, fiercely rigid and pale in his embrace.

– I'm glad, she said, because then I know what it means.

– What does it mean then? he said, giving her a little smile, as he lifted one of the little birds in his hand.

Outside, a car backfired suddenly – and this time it was the barber's turn to jump.

– That it'll be just like the men in the magazine. *Woman's Way*.

– *Woman's Way?* stammered Patsy, with some beads of perspiration appearing on his forehead.

– The men who agreed to do anything for their loved ones. For their women, their wives – that they love more than anything.

– Of course, dear, I see. Now I understand.

– I want you to do something, Patsy – just for me.

– I'll do anything you want, all you have to do is ask.

As, rising from his lap, his wife turned her back and stood staring through the window – at the needles of rain which were now attacking the glass.

Would you do it, Patsy – interfere, with the brakes of her car?

Such was the nature of the thoughts that were proceeding through Golly's mind. But she never got a chance to give voice to them for just at that moment Happy Carroll the carpenter came waltzing in – with a hopelessly optimistic grin on his face, as always.

– Effing bucking nag with three crooked legs! he complained, *I thought I was away with it today at Newmarket!*

– Ah sure, there you are, isn't it always the way, never seen a poor bookie yet! chirped Patsy, plucking out his scissors and elevating the padded black chair.

6

Bodley Foster had been walking his dog by the shore of the *Stray Sod Lake* when out of the corner of his eye, to his astonishment, he had observed the gunmetal grey of the water suddenly changing colour – ever so slowly turning crimson, in fact. It occurred to him that, in spite of his best efforts at refutation and profound scepticism, the water had taken on the consistency of what seemed like actual blood. But when he looked again, feeling rather foolish, the quite unremarkable character of the lough had once more returned to its former state – seeming as grey as the sky above it, with scarcely a ripple upon its surface.

Perplexed though the bank manager had been by this uncharacteristic deviation from his normally phlegmatic appreciation of the quotidian, he made a solemn resolution to summarily dismiss the incident from his mind.

It was the sort of occurrence, he realised, often reported by those who were of the Catholic persuasion – those who were by nature excessively credulous and at times quite hilariously superstitious. He resolved not to mention what had happened to anyone. They would probably attach all sorts of premonitory significance to it, he felt. Which was laughable. So he just did his best to shake off the feeling of embarrassment which succeeded this rather unsettling occurrence as he sauntered onward with the family pet, distracting himself by considering what his wife Blossom might be preparing at that moment for tea.

Ah Blossom Foster, my lovely wife, thought the bank manager.

The distinctive figure of his spouse Blossom Foster in her pleasantly voluptuous amplitude disported itself routinely throughout the district with a not inconsiderable assertiveness. Her voluntary work included collecting for the *Salvation Army* band, presiding over any number of fund-raising church socials, bazaars and concerts. Not to mention her dedication to the task of learning Italian, and the crochet and needlework classes she conducted on weekday evenings.

Not for her the drudgery of so many of her neighbours, the endless tedium of emptying chamber pots, the tiresome cooking and laundering and dusting and scrubbing – and perhaps the savagery of a drunken husband to contend with in the evenings.

Why, even ladies whose own dwellings were scrupulously clean and painstakingly maintained perceived themselves somehow diminished in her wake. They had often been invited into her home – finding the interior with its hallway bathed in the smell of *Mansion* polish and the parlour with its *VAT 60* table lamps, the bookcases with their neatly arranged *Reader's Digests* and the shiny coronation plate on the wall quite breathtaking. Her garden too was legendary

– fastidiously manicured, almost to a fault. In this she was ably assisted by her husband Bodley, who had served as an RAF pilot during World War II but on cessation of hostilities had been appointed to the position of deputy bank manager in the *Midland and Ulster*.

Before rising to the rank of general manager – which he now was. Bodley Foster cut an imposing figure – there could be no mistaking his military credentials. Striding ramrod-stiff down the main street, with his umbrella rolled and his moustache tidily trimmed. One could have been forgiven for assuming it was his intention to imperiously inspect every inch of the town. On occasion, Bodley Foster and his wife could be seen holding hands – a sight rarely witnessed in Cullymore, certainly among married couples – of either religious persuasion.

Golly Murray had once remarked on this.

– Why do you never hold my hand when we're out, like that? she had asked Patsy.

– I'd be just that wee bit embarrassed, her husband had, somewhat tentatively, explained, now that the two of us are that little bit older. But I do love you. Don't ever think that I don't, Golly Murray.

Blossom Foster even wore trousers – tight-fitting black ones with straps on the ends. And when they drew disapproving comments, had nothing more than this to say:

– *Pooh pooh*! As though I care, dear Bodley! she had giggled dismissively, with her coronation chime tinkling musically on her wrist, her husband closing his hand around hers.

*   *   *

Golly had met Blossom outside Corr's.

– That's a nice dress, she had said with a smile, plucking a full stop of fluff with her finger.

It had been located, almost invisibly, underneath the collar of Golly's coat.

– I'm searching for a nice piece of lamb for Bodley's tea, she had told her.

Golly once more began to feel uneasy. She could not bear to look at Blossom's dress – knowing how expensive it must have been.

But it was more the older woman's rigorous composure and assuredness which, as always, comprehensively succeeded in getting under her skin.

– Excuse me, love – if you could just step out of the way. I think I see a nice little piece over there.

The older woman's hand was now firmly resting on Golly's shoulder – ever so subtly edging her out of the way. Suddenly, Blossom released a small cry.

– *Ecco!* she shrieked, leaping up and down in almost childlike fashion. *What a lovely cut of meat!*

She had at last found her cut, she triumphantly declared.

To her dismay, Golly found herself becoming hopelessly tongue-tied – with her shoe describing shapeless patterns in the sawdust. As Blossom smiled and took her by the hand.

– My garden! You really must come around and see it, yourself and Patsy. You could perhaps take some cuttings – for your own garden, I mean. Is that something that might appeal to you, Golly? You'd be more than welcome, as I'm sure you well know. It was only after she had fingered the silver half-crown on to the marble-topped counter that Blossom Foster was seen to hesitate. Before pressing her gloved hand in mock awe against her lips – as though quite affronted by her own insensitivity.

– But then, of course: *you don't have a garden!* she pealed.

She looked away and began conversing with Barney Corr behind the counter. Not that it mattered, for Golly now could hear nothing, making a few half-hearted attempts to rally herself, galvanise herself in some way towards making a reply. In this, however, she did not succeed. It was only after a period of some minutes had elapsed that Golly realised she was again being addressed and that Blossom Foster, in fact, had left the shop.

– What an elegant lady, an old woman was saying to her. I don't suppose you knew that she speaks Italian?

– Does she, replied Golly, no, I didn't know that, wondering would she make it to the door without fainting. Before – making a supreme effort – hurling herself blindly into the street.

7

Father Patrick Peyton, known internationally as the *Rosary Priest*, was a man who could inspire the fiercest of loyalties. Of course there were clergy who, in private, did not hesitate to indicate their disapproval of his many fundraising activities. They considered them unseemly, they said, feeling that the word of God, and the sacred prayer of the rosary in particular, ought not to be disrespected in such a vulgar and populist manner. But, carp though they might, they could not argue with the extraordinary success of the Mayo priest's most recent campaign. Indeed, so productive was it becoming that they were often found wondering, in spite of themselves, might their objections find their roots in something much less laudable than they might care to admit – the vice of envy, for example?

But, inevitably, they would find themselves wholly humbled – disarmed entirely by the effusive and generous personality of Father Patrick Peyton, when they met him.

Finding him a veritable powerhouse – a man gifted with the most prodigious of energies. And who appeared, in these days of the late 1950s, to be practically everywhere at once. One minute on the cover of *Picturegoer* magazine, clasping *Frank Sinatra's* hand, then the next delivering a little homily on the wireless, or laughing maybe at some funny little story – before leading a group of believers in prayer, specifically for the conversion of Russia.

– *I'd love to kick his stupid Mayo teeth in!*

This was how Father Hand related to such broadcasts – in private, of course.

– Parading around like a cock in the farmyard, thinks he's the holiest of the holy, thinks he's St Peter himself, I swear to God! Which, at times, did indeed seem to be the case – for in almost every single photograph Father Patrick Peyton appeared delighted with himself. Thinking that, through nobody's efforts but his own, he had managed to muster a galaxy of stars – all of whom had pledged their talents and services. *Guy Mitchell* had already committed to performing at his forthcoming *Rosary Crusade* in *Madison Square Garden*, he said, and there was a possibility that *Johnnie Ray* might be there too. But top of the bill had to be *Old Blue Eyes* himself – yes, the one and only *Frank Sinatra*. He had vowed that it would be the *Rosary Concert* to end them all. And so it had proved, in the world-famous location in *Madison Square*. Where Father Peyton had made it his personal business to entertain the legendary star in his dressing room.

– How are you holding up, Frank? he had said to the singer who was now lighting a cigarette.

– I'm doing good, Frank had replied, just kinda glad that the show is turning out to be such a success.

– It sure is, Frank, it sure is, replied Peyton (or so the parish priest of Cullymore persuaded himself) in a markedly pronounced American accent.

– You really wowed them out there, so you did. I sure did like you singing *It Happened in Monterey*. Guess that's one of my favourite tunes, Frankie boy.

– That's real good to hear, for nobody enjoyed singing it more than me, padre!

The more he pondered this plausible, however imaginary, exchange, the more incensed Father Hand became. Indeed, eventually growing so livid that he actually found himself striking the brass fireguard.

– You'd think he had been born in Manhattan to hear him, instead of some hole in the stupid West of Ireland. *Prut!*

But try as he might, he could not banish his rival from his mind. The Reverend Patrick Peyton quite simply and obstinately refused to be dismissed. Father Hand tossed the copy of *Picturegoer* aside. He was sorry he had ever purchased the worthless rag. Anyway, he thought, it was time for him to go to bed. He yawned and laughed aloud. A bit of a sleep would soon put paid to all that Father Peyton nonsense, he reflected now as he climbed the stairs. Then, out of nowhere, he fancied he overheard a suppressed but mischievous chuckle. And thought for a moment that Father Patrick Peyton was laughing at him. His cheeks flushed scarlet as he pushed the door of his bedroom open. And saw him large as life there before him – rubbing his Mayo hands as he chortled.

– There must be at least thirty thousand souls here in *Madison Square Garden*, thirty thousand noble Catholic souls who have suspended their ordinary working lives and come here today to demonstrate solidarity with my worldwide campaign to save the rosary. Yes, with Father Patrick Peyton's *Rosary Crusade*.

Father Hand groaned as he tried to get some sleep, now in spite of himself entertaining an idea which even the most petulant child ought to have scorned.

– I could beat you hands down in any contest or competition, sniffed Peyton, because I know you're just not of my quality, Hand. That's the long and the short of it, Father – whether you like it or whether you don't.

– That's what you think! hissed the parish priest fiercely. I'd take you on anywhere, Peyton – I'm not afraid of you, so don't you go starting to think that I am!

Then he snorted derisively in the bed, as a delicious ripple of defiance coursed through him.

– It'll be just you and me, Father Peyton, he bawled, just you and me, in a fight to the death. *Haw!*

He closed his eyes and twisted a corner of the sheet as he mumbled:

– I'll soon settle you, you arrogant Mayo donkey!

At which point in our modest little narrative, I must declare some small degree of interest – for the priest's antics on this occasion genuinely did amuse me, to such an extent that I was prompted to encourage him further, ever so mischievously presenting the seductive image – of Patrick Peyton *in flagrantè delicto*. With none other than *Jane Russell*, if you can possibly conceive of such a combination. A sight which had the effect of wringing desperately confused tears from the eyes of the hopelessly vulnerable parish priest. Not to mention the overpowering waves of remorse the following morning.

When he awoke some moments just before dawn, feeling quite worn out. Hoarsely crying in the fragile light of early morning:

– *The family that prays together stays together fuck! The family that prays together stays together fuck!*

Afraid that he might be becoming possessed, consequently saying three rosaries – before dressing, and finally bustling down the stairs to enjoy his breakfast.

8

It might reasonably have been described as an almost exclusively Protestant form of conveyance – the *Vauxhall Saloon* in which Albert Craig and Bodley Foster were now motoring along merrily, making their way to the Methodist church on this pleasant Sunday morning. Or at least had been in the process of doing so until a sharp and dangerous-looking stone hit Bodley Foster a glancing blow to the side of the head. With both occupants turning just in time to catch a glimpse of the perpetrator. Who was none other than James A. Reilly, hiding his face as he scuttled off down an alleyway, his greasy blue gabardine flapping out behind him.

– *Freemason cunts!* they heard him bawl as he turned again. *Youse have it coming, youse no-good superior Black Preceptory bastards!*

They decided to give pursuit – but their efforts proved to be of little avail. As they stood now, frustrated, at the back of the cinema – beside some crates of old rotten cabbages.

– They're all the same, Catholics! growled Albert in disgust, as his colleague set about dabbing the small flesh-wound with his handkerchief.

Bodley made no reply – but it was plainly evident that he was equally aggrieved.

– It's him who'll get what's coming to him, pledged Albert, and the sooner the better. I've said it once and I say it now again – you can't trust any of them.

– *Queen of England West Briton cur-dogs!* the harsh voice returned anew. May the whole cursed lot of you get venereal disease!

Still fuming, both men reluctantly returned to the *Vauxhall*.

Later that day, there were reports of further trouble – this time with the *Scrawkey Dawes*, a noted family of urchins from the terraces, who apparently had fed a concoction of *Jeyes Fluid, Bextartar, Milk of Magnesia* and sundry other liquids to a stray tabby cat they'd found wandering the country roads. By all accounts its cries had been unbearable – and if that hadn't been bad enough, they subsequently took it out to the lake – and hung it from the *Stray Sod Tree*.

– It just kept on screaming, one of them had explained, we didn't know what to do, you see.

– In any other country, Patsy Murray remarked, nobody would have got away with it. Doing the like of that – it's barbaric. They ought to have been charged, every man jack of them.

– There are times when I wonder about that policeman, I really do, fumed Jude O'Hara, after all it's his civic duty!

– What kind of a town is it going to be, if he just sits there in the barracks, squatting there on his big fat . . . grumbled Conleth Foley, abstractedly sketching on the back of an *Afton* packet.

– He ought to try laying off the drop for a wee while, suggested Patsy darkly.

– I'll tell him myself – that he ought to have arrested them *Scrawkey Dawes*, complained the schoolteacher.

But the police officer said he had enough to be doing, and that anyway the screeches and the yowls of the abject urchins had been enough to put any man astray in the head. So, for the sake of peace, he had let them go, he said.

Some people had seen what they had done to the helpless animal – as it walked around in circles with its pathetic pale body covered in tinker's tartan – like the marks a fire'd leave on a woman's bare legs.

– We don't care what youse say – it was the devil who made us do it, they continued to claim, nodding their shaved heads in unison – it was him who put the idea in our heads. We're sorry, so we are – we really are!

But no one believed them, or their convenient placing of blame on outside forces.

Or at least said they didn't, publicly scorning the idea in the bars, particularly in the *Yankee Clipper*.

But late at night in the privacy of their own beds, there were few of them who were all that certain. For Cullymore – like so many towns, still tended to believe in its ancient superstitions.

9

There was nowhere in the town like Patsy's barber's – if you wanted yourself a good lively argument. Besides getting their hair cut, that was the main reason people went there.

– I'm off to Enniskillen now, said Golly, planting a little kiss on her husband's cheek, at which point all present modestly averted their eyes.

But just as soon as the door of the barber's shop closed behind her, Jude O'Hara once more resumed his conversation. As he patrolled the streets swinging his ebony, brass-topped walking cane, Jude O'Hara cut a distinguished-looking figure. He had a fine, commanding voice, and had been the co-director, along with Father Hand, of the *Cullymore Drama Guild* now for many years. The numerous varieties of confectionery available in the town was the subject which had been under discussion.

– You can say what you like, gentlemen, continued Jude, and I'm not disputing your right to your opinion. But for my money, the *butternut* will always be superior to the *clove drop*.

Patsy traced an even line across the centre of the primary teacher's scalp with the shaver but as he tilted his subject's head he made it quite clear that he was not entirely in accord with this assertion. To the point of wincing, in fact.

– *No*! he declared vehemently. The clove drop would be more of the type of thing that a woman might go for – the sort of fellow she might pop in her handbag. To take with her to the pictures, maybe.

Barney Corr pronounced himself in agreement with this view. Like a lot of butchers Barney was extremely popular, being of a markedly sunny disposition.

Conleth Foley the postmaster changed the subject, looking over the top of his *Amateur Painter* – as always neatly attired in his crisp white shirt and dicky bow.

– I was wondering did youse see *Wagon Train* last night? he enquired, and if youse did what the verdict might be?

The topic of westerns was one which could be relied on to elicit all-round good humour and pleasant consensus. Which was the reason why Happy Carroll the carpenter, who up until now had taken little part in the discussion, at this point leaned forward eagerly, giving himself a shake like a spaniel after a swim.

– Boys, he said, but it'd break my heart to miss that programme. Can you beat that Matt Dillon? That's what I'm asking!

– Unfortunately, groaned Barney, I didn't get to see it last night. The wife's mother was over and we had to go to devotions.

– Damn its soul then but he missed it, eh Patsy? It was the best episode yet, no word of a lie. What about youse boys – did youse happen to see it? Conleth? Jude?

Before either individual could rise to a reply, the shop bell tinkled and Father Hand poked in his head, smiling and blustering as he arrived in, and shook his umbrella. Jude was the very man he was looking for, he announced.

– I was wondering if it might be possible to have a word?

– Indeed and you can, as a matter of fact I'm nearly finished, the barber informed him.

– Powerful, splendid. Then I'm just in time. We'll repair inside, if that's all right with you, my bold Patsy.

– It is indeed, replied the barber, smiling. Five minutes more and you can have *Joseph Cotten* here all to yourself.

The comparison to one of the greatest screen actors did not displease Jude O'Hara at all, a fact to which his broad grin attested as he reclined in the padded leather chair, tapping two giddy thumbs beneath the cotton cape.

While he was waiting, the parish priest flicked through the pages of the paper, blowing his nose sharply as he lifted his head.

– It says here that the red devils are a cert for the match this coming weekend, he announced, with a not insignificant murmur of contentment.

At the mention of Manchester United's name, an unmistakably proprietorial ripple of pride ran through the shop.

– They had better! laughed Patsy, for I have them down in my coupons to win!

The priest smiled broadly and brought the tips of his fingers together. As Patsy finished and began briskly brushing Jude O'Hara's shoulders.

– *Dah-dah!* laughed the barber, replacing his comb in the breast pocket of his nylon jacket.

– I won't keep you a second, the clergyman assured Jude. All I want is a few words in your ear.

– No bother at all, replied the newly clipped schoolmaster, as he followed his parish priest into the kitchen.

– Tattybye, men, shan't keep you long!

Which was good news, thought Patsy and Happy Carroll at exactly the same time – for in confessions the priest had been known to keep people for hours. But on this occasion, as it happened, Father Hand proved to be as good as his word – for it seemed that no length of time had elapsed at all before Jude O'Hara had emerged once more – followed by the red-cheeked, good-humoured clergyman.

Who now revealed that he had been concocting a *little plan* – yes, that he had a certain important scheme in mind.

– You are aware, gentlemen, he began, that in the town of Cullymore we have what you might fairly describe as one of the most active and talented drama guilds in the country, with two of its finest talents right here in this shop. It is in this regard that I'd like to have your attention, if I may.

– So are we to assume you have another show up your sleeve? asked Patsy approvingly, vigorously rubbing some hair oil into his hands.

The priest stroked his chin and considered for some moments. Then he nodded and raised his head.

– I'll not beat about the bush, Patsy – I'll tell you what I've just been saying to Jude. Yes, you are correct in what you say – this very Easter, as it happens. I have given it a lot of thought over the Christmas period and I have come to the conclusion that 1958 is to be the year when our humble *Drama Guild* will distinguish itself above all others in this country. We'll leave everyone standing in this glorious year. This coming March I intend to pull out all the stops, to humiliate our competitors once and for all. My choice this year will be the play to end them all. Of that let there be no doubt. And I am now at liberty to reveal to you its title.

– We're all ears, interjected Happy Carroll. I wonder what it's going to be?

– *Tenebrae*, Happy, the drama is to be called *Tenebrae*, and it is one which will be specially written to mark the holiest feast in the liturgical calendar – that of Easter.

– *Ex tenebris Lux* – out of darkness cometh light, sighed Jude O'Hara, somewhat knowingly.

– *Tenebrae*, mused Happy, I like the sound of it.

– It has a nice learned ring to it, Father, I have to say, offered Barney Corr – now also stroking his chin.

The parish priest said that he could not agree more. As he went on to explain:

– It's the time of year when we remember the hour that Christ Our Saviour expired on the cross, when darkness enfolded all four corners of the earth. Obviously, as you are aware, it will mean a lot of work. But if someone like Peyton can do it, then by golly so can we. So can *we*, men!

– *Father Patrick Peyton*, now there's a man! exclaimed Happy Carroll all of a sudden, finding himself taken aback by the severity of the parish priest's reaction. For there could be no mistaking Father Hand's displeasure.

– Ah, for the love of God, will you give me peace! he snapped abruptly. Hasn't Peyton any amount of halfwits queuing up to help him – hundreds! Why wouldn't he be able to put on a show! Would you go away out of that and don't be annoying my head, Happy Carroll!

The carpenter, quite astonished by the unexpected nature of the parish priest's response, thought it best to retreat then into silence. Which was what he promptly did. There was a definite tremor in Father Hand's voice. As he mopped his perspiring brow with a large hankie.

– This past couple of nights I've been giving the matter a great deal of thought, he continued falteringly, and come this Easter our town will attain the status of legend. Can I count on you, do you think?

He craned forward eagerly, with almost a suggestion of faint terror in his voice.

– On our band of brothers, the old gang from Cullymore, who have been together through thick and thin? *Eh? Eh?*

– We won't let you down, was Happy Carroll's answer.

– Absolutely, confirmed Patsy Murray.

– One hundred per cent, assented Jude O'Hara, the highly respected schoolteacher.

As Barney the butcher took his hand and boomed:

– For *definite!*

– *Fantastic!* cried Father Hand.

And with that, the beaming parish priest bade them all

goodbye, all his old pals from the *great old Cullymore gang*, floating ecstatically out the door.

As the radio spurted and a newsflash erupted.

– *So far we know there are twenty-one survivors after Manchester United's air crash this afternoon. These are the names of the people known to have survived . . .*

– Everyone present in that instant turned white, and Patsy's barber's might have been tenanted solely by spectres.

10

Sharing a hovel with a fox by a filthy landfill near a lake was hardly where one expected to find a former Classics master. But that was where James A. Reilly had been domiciled ever since his dismissal – spending his days by a dump near a lake, in a hovel made of wooden railway planks and corrugated iron.

It was a beautifully crisp January morning and he wasn't long up – having been awakened by the sound of an approaching motorbike, still somewhat distant. He waited in the doorway, yawning and rubbing the sleep from his eyes. He wondered would he bother concealing his firearm.

– No. There's really no need, he persuaded himself.

Which was probably true. For nobody, least of all Ralph Foster, considered his stupid old ancient *Lee Enfield* rifle a threat.

– Sure that old crock of his doesn't work, he had often heard them saying, and even if it did he'd be hard-pressed to hit an elephant in the arse with it.

Which was an amusing way of putting it, thought James. As Ralph Foster came chugging alongside him on his bike, the gleaming chrome frontage of the B & A machine *phut-phutting* to a halt by the edge of the landfill. It stood now before him like a beautifully polished sculpture, with its engine plaintively groaning into silence. Its rider in his helmet sighed as he coolly observed the wheeling seagulls. Before swinging his leather-strapped leg across the saddle and removing his helmet, cradling it beneath his arm as he said:

– Good heavens, what a racket.

Ralph Foster removed his goggles and good-humouredly observed to James:

– I thought we were going to get a spell of good weather, Mr Reilly. I'm sorry I have to say that it appears that I was wrong.

James A. Reilly looked at him and nodded.

– Yes, my dear Ralph. It would seem that you were. As soon as you see our old friends the gulls you can be assured the rain is on its way.

Ralph Foster was well known in Cullymore. Which was not surprising – considering he was the eldest and only son of the highly respected manager of the *Midland and Ulster Bank*, Bodley Foster. Although for some years past he had no longer resided in the family home, having left town at the age of eighteen to become a member of the *Royal Ulster Constabulary*, the young policeman made it his business to return home regularly. At the astonishingly young age of twenty-five, he had already attained the rank of Sergeant. But no one in the town was ever heard to speak of subjects such as that – you couldn't afford to, not when you were living along the border. There were certain topics which might be deemed sensitive, and any casual discussion of them could, without a doubt, be dangerous. Not that the young Sergeant allowed that to bother him to any great degree – for as far as Ralph was concerned, there were infinitely more interesting subjects which he would have preferred to discuss – subjects more important than politics or the so-called *troubles*. For Ralph Foster for some time had been a world-class TT rider – had won the Isle of Man Prix three times, in fact.

He was tall and extremely handsome, well built with finely chiselled features and fair hair like his father. His eyes were of a striking glassy blue and he was a man on whose shoulders authority rested easy. Why, even to the extent that when he happened to walk past you, disinterestedly, on the street, you almost felt like confessing immediately to some crime – however small. This was even the case with those who had known him all their lives. But not, however, with James A. Reilly, for the simple reason that, as far as he was concerned, he had nothing left to be afraid of. And Ralph Foster knew that, and found himself relieved to be appreciated in the manner to which he had become accustomed on his friendly visits to James Reilly's hovel. He also tended to respect and admire the older man's learning. However eccentric he might be.

– What are you at all, James, he said, indicating the *Lee Enfield* rifle slung beneath his arm, fidding about with that old thing. Sure I'm sure it hasn't been fired in years. And can't you see there's going to be a downpour soon? Toss away that toy and hop up here on my bike – I'll drive you to the *Yankee* for a pint.

45

James laughed and shook his head.

– I suppose it must look like a broken-down old wreck of a thing all right, Ralph. But in point of fact it's not a bad little weapon at all. It's an SMLE Mk. 3 .303-calibre Enfield pattern, made in 1916 and regarded in its day as a really good rifle, quite accurate, reliable and suitable for rapid and accurate firing. It belonged to my father, as you probably know, and if nothing else oiling and cleaning it keeps me busy – for time can hang heavy on my hands out here.

The policeman grinned and tugged his leather gauntlets. As he looked all around him and drank in the scene.

What, he wondered, on God's earth could anybody be expected to make of such a place – not to mention this downcast, bereft-looking figure, in his scruffy belted gabardine and scarecrow's knitted cap. You never knew what he was going to come out with next.

– It won't be long now before the time comes, he was continuing now, but you know that, Sergeant. I've told you before. You know all about that time which is approaching – when, to a man, we're to find ourselves in the *Stray Sod Country*. It's going to be terrible. I think you know what I'm saying and that you believe me – don't you, Sergeant?

– I do indeed, laughed Sergeant Ralph Foster, as James A. Reilly fed his fox some hazels.

– Funzel likes his dinner, he told the Sergeant.
Before adding gravely:

– Some people think I'm joking, Sergeant – you don't think I'm joking, do you, Ralph?

46

– Of course I don't, laughed the policeman unconvincingly.

– It's all right, Sergeant – I don't expect you to believe all my stories. I don't even know who it was that night. It might have been *Nobodaddy*, I can't say, or the *Fetch*. All I know is that he was standing right over there – not moving a muscle, breathing in time the very same as myself. My heart stood still in my chest when I saw him – but he was in no hurry, it was as if he had all the time in the world, just standing there. He told me more or less everything, Ralph. The way it's going to be – how it's our destiny to live side by side for all eternity – in a homeland of strangers where all our names will have vanished. O the town as we know it will still seem to be there – but it will just be an illusion, a simulacrum – a cruel trick. The loneliness of strangers – that's to be our lot for ever and ever.

– And it was *who* you say that told you all this?

– I didn't see his face. He was standing over there, right over there, in under that tree.

Funzel's jaws rotated and he made a face as he crunched a nut.

– I forgot to tell you that you're to be murdered too. In front of your wife and children, he said. But don't worry, it won't be for a good while yet, Ralph.

– Yes, James – but of course it won't, nodded the Sergeant.

Having decided, as usual, that the best course of action was to humour poor James. Placate the unfortunate fellow as best he could. But in spite of how pitiful the Latin master continued to sound, nonetheless Ralph Foster still did genuinely enjoy his company – that of the former Classics

47

and English teacher at Rathwilliam College, who had now moved on to the poetry of *Horace*. Which Sergeant Ralph Foster knew precious little about. Much to the amusement of James A. Reilly.

– The only Horace I know is Horace King that breeds the horses! he had laughed.

Just before departing, Ralph had reached into the pocket of his leather breeches and produced a gleaming two-shilling piece.

– Here, James, he said, I got some overtime this week. Take this, will you, and treat yourself to a drink. It was great to meet you again, as always. But now, I'm afraid, I really must go. They'll be waiting for me at home in *Dunroamin*.

Then he hopped up on the saddle and turned the shining machine around, wildly scattering the seagulls and roaring off into the clouds and the haze, leaving a white hoarse riot in his wake. As a result not hearing the regretful laughter of James A. Reilly. Who, levelling the stock of the *Lee Enfield* against his shoulder, remarked bemusedly to his adoring pet fox:

– What's saddest of all is that in his heart he doesn't believe me. He doesn't believe what I saw that night – or just how deceptive appearances can be.

As, to prove his point, he raised the stock of the 'ancient wreck' of the *Enfield* up against his shoulder, firmly pulling the trigger – watching the head of a seagull completely disintegrating.

11

Dean Harry Gribbins was a narrow-faced man with thin, light-grey hair and delicate effeminate gestures which belonged to an age not quite so coarse as their own – or so it seemed to Blossom Foster and her husband. The Dean was a regular visitor to *Dunroamin*. Perhaps unexpectedly for a mild-mannered clergyman, he displayed a keen interest in military history, and with Bodley Foster, who was of a similar cast of mind, would happily debate various conflicts and engagements for hours. Serious disagreement over decisions taken in the North African campaign or the Peninsular Wars were far from uncommon in the parlour on the Enniskillen Road. As were their regular musical soirées, for both the clergyman and the businessman were devotees of the German tenor *Richard Tauber*, and it was not at all uncommon to hear the operatic strains of *Don Giovanni* or *Die Fledermaus* drifting through an open bedroom window.

Blossom Foster adored Dean Gribbins – always had. She had known him all her life, chiefly through his work as their pastor – but also because of the fact that she was a founder member of the Methodist church choir – a commitment which would see them, twice a week, winter and summer, lifting up their voices in their humble little church – not three minutes' walk from their home. The hymns which she favoured most included *When I Survey The Wondrous Cross, Praise The Lord From Whom All Blessings Flow, Lead, Kindly Light* – and, of course, the perennial standard *Abide With Me.* It remained the habit of Dean Gribbins' congregation – as it had been that of their fathers and mothers before them – to assemble each Sunday morning after service on the lawn, in the company of their neighbours, the *Chapmans* and the *Mooreheads* – and a number of other Protestant families who resided close by.

They posed a quaint, perhaps, but deeply respected gathering, as their aspirational harmonies were discharged into the fragile quietude of those early Sabbath mornings.

– If each day of the week is a dull dim stone then Sunday morning is a jewel brightly polished and we must remain assiduous, vigilant in our efforts to ensure that this sacred day ever remains thus, Dean Gribbins would smile as the page-turning choristers nodded with unthwartable conviction.

Golly Murray, or *Golliwog* as some people had unkindly christened her, even though she had married a Catholic, had continued to remain a dedicated member of the Protestant choir. Thus it was not at all uncommon for her to find herself, on Sunday mornings, standing in church side by side with Blossom Foster. That Blossom had retained her youthful looks, her tendency towards a certain rotundity notwithstanding, could not be denied. Her singing voice was also the subject of much admiration and comment. For she alone could attain the uppermost note of the octave in the notoriously difficult *Lead, Kindly Light.* A fact of which she was more than aware and her extravagantly contented, self-assured lips had, more than once, been turned in the direction of her manifestly cowed neighbour Golly Murray – in particular on those embarrassing occasions when she would identifiably fail to sustain the same notoriously elusive note.

In the grounds of the Catholic church at the other end of the town, there was a large metal shamrock painted green which bore the legend: PLEASE KEEP OFF THE GRASS.

No such admonition was evident in Dean Gribbins' Methodist churchyard – for the very simple reason that it was not deemed necessary. It being generally acknowledged, not least by the Catholics themselves, that there was something so innately law-abiding and ordered and civic-spirited about the Methodist nature – that any stern strictures in this regard would have been wholly superfluous. It was no wonder, some said, that such was the level of their self-respect and organisation that they could simultaneously excite self-loathing and envy in those of the Catholic persuasion.

– They're not like us. They have self-respect. We won't even pay our bills, were sentiments which were privately, and indeed bitterly, entertained.

This particular Sunday afternoon seemed a more brightly polished jewel than usual. The bells rang out, lingering resonantly in the air, with the shoots of the crocuses bending over garden borders – as though straining to perform as might the subjects of some particularly ambitious and gifted versifier. There were cars parked here and there, and through lowered windows a near-delirious falsetto bleat was heard to deliver a scene-by-scene account of a Gaelic football match. Of which the Fosters, being of the opposing tradition, knew little or nothing. By the looks of things – certainly if the hysteria of the commentator was in any way indicative of proceedings – at this advanced stage of the tournament, both stalwart teams were now neck and neck. Blossom Foster sighed and placed her right hand upon her bosom, having just become aware that the Murrays were approaching along the road.

– *Dearest!* exclaimed Blossom, as the couples met. How lovely to see you – and you too, Patsy, sweetheart, of course!

She pecked the younger woman ever so lightly on the cheek. Golly was wearing a pillbox hat.

– O! I'm sure you bought it in *Heaton's* of Enniskillen, did you, dearie? cried Blossom.

– No, replied Golly, actually I bought it in *Vera Brady's*.

As a consequence of this seemingly innocuous exchange, the remainder of their conversation grew somewhat strained – *Vera Brady's* being the haberdashery habitually patronised by Catholic customers.

By this point, however, Patsy Murray's attention had been diverted and he was much more concerned with the progress of the match. When sufficient time had elapsed, Blossom committed herself to a discussion of the recent good weather. Then there was further talk regarding the forthcoming summer – and where both couples intended to spend their holidays.

– Yes, as I told you, it's Italy for us again this year, mused Blossom, for as you know, Geraldine, we go there without fail. And what about yourselves, yourself and Patsy – have you made any plans?

– I think we're going to Bundoran again, replied Golly, unecessarily adding, by way of explanation, it's in Donegal.

– But of course it is, sweetheart, do you think I don't know that! laughed Blossom. I really think I ought to be aware of that!

– *Yuh-yuh*-yes, Blossom, *buh-but* of course, Golly heard herself reply – as her cheeks slowly, steadily began to turn crimson.

– But now that we're on the subject of Italy, it's time for us to turn our attentions to thoughts of the eternal city itself, Geraldine. For I've been meaning to tell you this for weeks. Do you know my dear friend Hope Fairleigh-Warburton from Dublin? Of course you do – she's a fashion buyer of considerable note. Well, for some time she and I have been considering mounting a fashion show spectacular. Yes, right here in Cullymore, believe it or not. And the theme we have chosen is that of the eternal city. *Roman Holiday* we're going to call it. Hope, she really is so excited. And when she heard about you, she couldn't wait to meet you. Do say you'll come – on our little *Roman Holiday*! My daughter Verity will be modelling, of course – and we really would love you to assist us in whatever way you might care yourself to choose. Dearest Geraldine! *Roman Holiday, Audrey Hepburn* – O my goodness, but it's going to be wonderful! The hotel will have seen nothing like it – ever. Now don't say you can't! No excuses, lamb, I implore you.

– *Come along, dear!* called Bodley Foster.

As Golly Murray stammered and tried to think of something – *anything.*

Already, however, Blossom and her husband were on the verge of departure – the older woman raising her hand to give them a little wave.

As Golly stood, trembling – releasing a scarcely audible, helpless cry of perplexity. One to which everyone, including her husband, remained oblivious.

– *O boys, by the jamity!* Patsy Murray cried sharply. *Did you hear that, Golly – Down's in the lead by seven points to five!* squeezing her arm with such ferocity that it hurt. Her husband's eyes at that point were so wide with enthusiasm that he might have been no more than ten years of age.

As he turned away and went back to his transistor, Golly Murray could have sworn she heard someone calling her name. It seemed to have come from somewhere behind the hedge. Or so she had thought. But when she looked, there was no one there.

Later on, after church, her husband was having himself a whale of a time in his favourite pub the *Yankee Clipper.* Sometimes he drank in Billy McNeill's but he preferred the *Yankee* because you nearly always found some of the boys. Why, even now, on account of the game that had just been played a good few of them were in, and, like Patsy, they

were having themselves a rare old time. As Conleth Foley
had put it:

– We're as well to enjoy ourselves now, gentlemen, for
before we know it the annual retreat will be upon us and
then, after that, Holy Week and Easter. So drink up there,
boys, and don't stop till we reach Mountnugent!

No one, of course, was going anywhere near Mountnugent
– it was just another of Conleth's *rare old spakes*, as they
liked to call them. And there were plenty of those. Such as
the time Jude O'Hara, a little tipsy, had referred to Happy
Carroll's head being so narrow:

– That one single eye would have been more than sufficient for the gentleman's needs!

There were all sorts of plans for the coming summer.
Patsy intended to go to Bundoran and, if God spared him,
attested Happy Carroll, he might get across to visit his
brother in Leeds.

As, just at that moment:

– *Speak of the devil!* chuckled Happy, and in trooped
Dagwood with two pigeon boxes under his arms.

– We were just saying! began Happy. The day we went to
Omeath, do you remember?

– Do I remember? Didn't I scoop twenty guineas on a
nag by the name of *Water Sprite?*

– Was that how much? gasped Happy incredulously.

– Now I remember. Twenty guineas is what it was!

The pub became as a hive of the busiest bees. Manus
Hoare arrived in selling copies of the *United Irishman*, looking as broody and serious as ever.

– Cheer up out of that, urged Patsy as he bought a paper, it might never happen – receiving no reply as he turned back to his conversation.

– This pair of rascals, Khrushchev and Bulganin, Dagwood was observing – between the pair of them they'll blow up the world.

– You have to hand it to the *Yankee Clipper*!

– There's damn all wrong with the *Clipper* now, let's face it.

– The best wee pub in the whole of Cullymore!

– The best wee pub in the best town in Ireland!

As off they sailed home, on that happy Sunday night, underneath the approving, sleepy orb of the moon, doing their best not to ponder on the tragedy of Manchester United. But pledging to 'storm heaven' with prayers at the retreat in order to save the souls of the 'faithful departed'. Which included some of the greatest players that English soccer had ever known.

12

The religious retreat turned out like no other. For two days the public houses remained closed and public entertainments of any kind were expressly prohibited. All day long a steady stream of people made their way towards the church in order that they might give themselves to silent contemplation and committed adoration of God the Father. The missioners had taken the town by storm. With the congregation gasping in awe as the chief Redemptorist howled and bawled and delivered great ferocious thumps to the pulpit. When it came to delivering sermons there was serious consideration given to the possibility that he might even be better than Father Hand. The man was enormous – well over six foot five, it was estimated.

– Youse had better watch out when our new missioners come, Father Hand had cautioned his congregation, for they've put the fear of God in better towns than this! But when it's all over your efforts will be rewarded and we'll find ourselves renewed and more fighting fit than ever – more than capable of facing the coming challenge – that which is to be our performance of the glorious *Tenebrae* this coming Easter. May God help anyone then who gets it into their head that they are capable of competing with the famous *Cullymore Guild*!

By *anyone*, of course, the parish priest could mean only one person – Father Patrick Peyton. But very few parishoners, apart from his housekeeper Una Miniter perhaps, would have been aware of this fact. Indeed, for the greater proportion of his congregation, the world-famous Father Patrick Peyton was just another faceless individual who had set off on the emigrant trail from a humble rural background in order to seek his fortune in the USA. And after making a miraculous recovery from tuberculosis, which he attributed to his receipt of a cure from none other than the Blessed Virgin Mary herself, had devoted his life to the Ministry of Christ. For the great majority of people, he was a good man who had been fortunate to survive such a trial. However, as it transpired, this was not quite how the missioners viewed it – especially not the head Redemptorist. No, he did not prove to be quite so tolerant of Father Patrick Peyton's unsanctioned enthusiasms. Peyton belonged, he attested, to that category of untrustworthy individuals – emigrants who had arguably let the country down – in his case by being a priest drawing attention to himself when he ought to have been preaching the word of God. The lights dimmed as pale faces shrunk back in the gloom. The missioner descended the steps of the pulpit, hooking large thumbs in his wide brown belt as he paced the stone floor in front of the altar – after the manner of a giant only recently liberated from its chains.

He had little time, he continued fiercely, for members of the clergy who shamelessly thrust themselves forward. It was a form of simony, he contended, and as such was to be wholly and utterly condemned.

– I think I'll find you in agreement when I suggest there was no *Frank Sinatra* in the stable at Bethlehem. Our Lord Jesus Christ was born amongst humble people. I didn't, for example, see *Perry Como*, there.

Father Hand shifted delightedly in his chair. Realising that, up until that very morning, the head Redemptorist had shown scant interest in the likes of Patrick Peyton – hardly even knew he existed, in fact. Not until Father Hand had produced his ledger of newspaper cuttings. This had changed everything. The missioner had turned every page with mounting fury, encouraged by the irate displeasure of his host. Now he waved his arms in the transept. His massive voice rolled boomingly through the vaults and over to the gallery.

– O yes, you'll see their pictures in the magazines and newspapers. Those very same periodicals and magazines and English rags which I've seen here on sale in your very own town. Yes, my dear brethren – the *News of the World*! That's what these emigrants have done to our country – encouraged filth and alien ideas. Of course they'll deny it. But I've seen them – I know all about them. Yes, off they'll go to England with their suitcases, where they'll billet themselves in boarding houses and fraternise with strangers in all manner of lower-class public houses. Disdaining, the very first chance they get, the faith of their fathers that sustained them through the generations, turning their back on the Saviour who died for their sins, and whose loving heart bled for them and their likes – now bowing and scraping any chance they get, fawning over the invader at any opportunity that presents itself, willingly purchasing their newspapers and filthy magazines. Coming back home then to laugh at their neighbours, those law-abiding folk who are doing their best to keep body and soul together, and haven't turned their backs on Jesus and His Blessed Mother. O yes, I've seen them, with their fancy cars and shoes and hats, firing around money and doing their best to impress decent people. But we're not impressed, friends, here in Cullymore or anywhere else. We're not cowed by their Dagenham twangs, their cheap, embarrassing Manhattan drawls. And may that be the subject of our retreat here today, my dear people. Let us proclaim loud and clear that with pride we shall wear the sacred cloth of humility – that for the duration of these three days of private contemplation, naught but sackcloth and ashes shall cover our humble backs. During Father Hand's days of private contemplation we shall haughtily scorn the blandishments of those who would have us cheapened by the wiles and treacheries of slick foreign ways. I have seen what they're capable of in Father Hand's ledger – *Frank Sinatra, Mr Johnnie Ray*!

– *Prut!* hissed Father Hand as both he and his visitor swooned to their knees.

With Una Miniter descending upon the organ keyboard as her powerful chords began to swell in the western gallery.

The service, in total, had lasted for three hours and had been so emotional that all of those in attendance remained stunned for the rest of the evening. There wasn't a sound as they made their way home.

It was Jude O'Hara who came up with the idea of establishing a private, separate lay confraternity – which held its first meeting in the parochial hall.

– You have to hand it to Jude, said Happy Carroll, there's times when he puts me to shame he's that holy.

– I would say he's the holiest man in the town, suggested Dagwood Slowey, not once has he darkened the door of my snooker hall.

– Never saw him take a drink in my life, said Patsy Murray – and mind you, I've known him a very long time.

– He lives for the *Drama Guild*, so he does, nodded Patsy, a man like that reads and studies the way he does, he'd have no need for a drink or a smoke.

– A sherry at Christmas or maybe a puff of a *Capstan* when Lent is over – that'd be more than enough for him.

It was just after eight when the man in question arrived.

– Gentlemen, said Jude O'Hara, shaking the drops off his folded umbrella, I'm sorry I'm late.

Immediately he began reading from the *Imitation of Christ*.

The gang were all proud to know someone of the stature of Jude O'Hara. And had a speaking voice that was second to none.

– Small wonder the Abbey Theatre was looking for him, said Happy Carroll. He could have been on the stage with *Barry Fitzgerald*, they say.

– I'll never forget him in *Oklahoma*, so I won't – cripes but he was great! Golly never shuts up talking about it! enthused Patsy Murray.

– What we all as God-fearing Catholics must do, began Jude O'Hara, clearing his throat, is to promote as best we can self-denial and renounce all evil appetites.

– Not always so easy when you've a bit of a thirst on you after a hard day's work, smiled Happy Carroll.

Jude O'Hara frowned disapprovingly.

– Please, Happy. If you don't mind . . . !

– Jasus, I was only joking . . ., came the response.

As the door opened and Barney Corr blustered in.

– The fucking rain it'd . . . !

– Barney! chided the schoolteacher – as the butcher remembered where he was, falling immediately to his knees.

– Beware vain and worldly knowledge, gentlemen, continued Jude, and bear your temporal sufferings patiently, after the example of Christ.

When Jude had departed, Conleth Foley produced a *Baby Power* whisky.

– By rights, you know, we shouldn't be drinking it, ventured Patsy.

– At least not after what we've been saying, agreed Dagwood.

– But don't you think Jude maybe sometimes goes too far?

– Aye! cried Happy, with surprising eagerness. Why didn't he become a priest if that's how he feels – eh, lads?

– Did you see him looking at me when I came in? said Barney Corr – reddening.

– Here, wait a minute, men, don't you see what we're doing, we're letting ourselves down! cautioned the artist, taking back the bottle.

They lowered their heads.

– You know what, you're right, Happy Carroll said, if we drink that we're letting Jude down. And our lay confraternity.

– Give me the fucking thing! rasped Barney Corr – before pouring its contents down the sink.

– Now let us say a decade of the rosary! he demanded.

As all there present sank to their knees, pleading forgiveness for their disloyalty and momentary weakness, and to be given the strength to *imitate Christ*, as Jude had urged them. At least for as long as the missioners were in town.

The Redemptorist retreat was proclaimed without peer – and one must definitely acknowledge the extraordinary degree of committed involvement.

The storm troopers of Christ, as Father Hand had christened them, appeared to be almost everywhere at once. If they weren't lurking furtively in the alleyway behind the cinema, they were brazenly flitting through the streets of the town, or surveying it from the vantage point of elevated ground – in search of any transgression, no matter how minor. Father Hand's countenance had assumed an expression of the most extreme gravity. His homilies also had grown more intense – he resembled nothing so much now as a politician of the old school. There was evidence also of this development within the privacy of the confessional where penances of an almost unsustainable severity were now being routinely administered. There could be no doubt there but that the professionalism and determination of the more worldly experienced practitioners had left their mark on the heretofore casual Father Hand. On a number of occasions there had been rumours of penitents reduced to tears by his voluble reprimands. And reports had circulated of *unfair* and *inappropriate* sentences being handed down for the most inconsequential of moral lapses.

As the missioners' black sedan cruised noiselessly through the cowed streets – as though unswervingly committed to the execution of some grisly, soul-taking vendetta.

Jude O'Hara also seemed to be everywhere, grimly clutching the *Imitation of Christ*.

He had prevailed on the *Cullymore gang* to study the text – which they now had, feeling cleansed.

– It really is a terrific book, said Conleth Foley, I took the liberty of making some drawings from it.

– Father Hand was asking me if we'd go up and give him a hand at Benediction, said Patsy Murray, he says the missioners would be very impressed.

– Maybe you could read a little bit from it, Happy, now that our rehearsals for the play have got under way?

– O jakers, not me, I wouldn't be fit to read it – would you not ask Patsy? protested Happy.

But Patsy wasn't too enthusiastic either, so in the end they decided to approach Barney Corr. Who said that he'd be more than delighted to have a go. When they told Father Hand he was over the moon.

– The missioners will think it powerful! he said.

And so they did – with Barney's selection from the *Imitation* proving a terrific hit. No one would have dreamt that he'd had it in him. He was even privately congratulated by the missioners in the sacristy afterwards. Much to the chagrin of Happy Carroll.

– He wasn't that good, he was overheard muttering.

The comment was immediately intercepted by Jude O'Hara.

– Now now! he chided. We all got our chance.

– What's he saying? enquired Barney Corr, instinctively sensing that something was amiss.

– Oh nothing, replied Jude, we were just saying how you did us all proud.

Emboldened by such successes the town's citizens continued to apply themselves with a rigorous, uncharacteristic discipline. There were crucifixes, banners, shrines and painted statues on display – and an enormous, elaborate tapestry in gold – specially woven by Una Miniter and other members of the *Legion of Mary*. It read: CULLYMORE CALLS ON KHRUSHCHEV TO ADMIT THE ERROR OF HIS WAYS.

— I've never seen anything to rival it, the head Redemptorist was heard remarking to their parish priest, it's a credit to you and your flock, Father Hand.

In the evenings the missioners took tea in the *Cullymore Hotel*, with their giant silhouettes stooping on the dining-room blinds and their laughter reverberating like claps of majestic thunder. There had also been rumours of miracles having been performed – but no sustainable evidence was ever produced. All copies of the *News of the World* newspaper, as had been suggested, were ultimately destroyed. With the shopkeeper who stocked them publicly vilified. A returned emigrant himself, to his astonishment, he now found himself reviled at almost every turn, turned into a laughing stock in the course of otherwise normal conversations. When he had brought up the subject of how *great* he felt the city of Liverpool to be, one individual had attempted to physically assault him – threatening to kick him all the way back to *pagan England*!

In conjunction with Father Hand, it was the missioners, everyone agreed, who had succeeded in conferring this kind of courage and pride in themselves upon the town. The mettle, at last, to insist that, whatever the Protestants might think, not only was the ordinary Irish Catholic civilian equal to all others – but superior, in fact, in almost every conceivable way.

On the final evening of the Redemptorist retreat, the polished black sedan led a victory parade through the bunting-lined streets and people wept helplessly as the missioners waved goodbye. At a farewell service in the square, Father Hand found it difficult to hold back his tears.

– Throughout the course of this glorious week, he told his people, you have consistently demonstrated just what you are capable of. Well done, my children. There are many so-called leaders in the World Church today who would give anything to be blessed with a congregation as devout and dedicated as yourselves! People who think they have to go to Hollywood to find it – to hire out halls paid for with ill-gotten gains, from the pockets of go-boys, and bobby-dazzlers!

It was, of course, a veiled allusion to his nemesis, Father Patrick Peyton of Mayo. But Father Gus Hand had better things to do than be bothered with the likes of that egotistical Western donkey. He raised a clenched fist and delivered an almighty thump into the air. As his voice, just like theirs, boomed out resonantly across the town square.

– Roll on *Tenebrae*! Hurrah for this coming Easter! When we will be as a beacon upon the border!

At rehearsals, everyone was about to burst with enthusiasm.

– *We have no king but Caesar!* cried Patsy Murray.

– *That's right!* responded Happy, *we have no king but Caesar, so we haven't!*

– *No, no, no!* interrupted the director, there isn't any *so we haven't* at the end. Now take it once more from the top.

Happy Carroll looked away, somewhat sullenly – stung.

– *We have no king but Caesar!*

– *What would you have me do with this man?* asked Barney Corr, sweeping around in as yet invisible robes.

– *Crucify him!* cried Patsy Murray.

– *Crucify him!* demanded Conleth Foley.

– That was our best rehearsal yet, suggested Jude O'Hara afterwards.

But when he had gone to the toilet, Barney Corr had growled darkly under his breath:

– Aye but O'Hara'd want to watch his lip sometimes, the way that he often talks to people. Him and his fucking *Imitation of Christ.*

But after a few jars, all of that was completely forgotten – for the time being, at least.

It was a proud, if physically exhausted Father Gus Hand who stood outside the church at the end of the retreat, making his last goodbyes to his equally exhausted but contented counterparts. He blessed them all and stood there, immobile, waving his hand sadly. As the sleek sedan glided on spoked wheels – rounding the corner and disappearing for ever.

There was a red-crowned rooster which made its home near the *Stray Sod Lake*, just a stone's throw from James Reilly's hovel. It often came strolling, without a care in the world, to peck and forage along the shore – making an unholy racket as it did so. There it would stand making its comical staccato gestures, effeminately raising its right leg as it prepared to release yet another unmerciful ululation. Right now it was on the verge of doing that very thing. Just as a rifle report rang out.

– *Ka-boom!* it thundered, as the *Lee Enfield* jerked, and a misty flurry of blood fountained over the head of the unfortunate fowl – which was completely atomised.

James A. Reilly sauntered over to inspect his handiwork – deriving, it must be accepted, no special pleasure from his efforts.

– She's working perfectly, he mused to himself, fondling the gun which had belonged to his late father, fingering a few little nuts for Funzel, it'll take his head off, that white-haired philistine, that execrable, most contemptible of clergymen. When the time finally comes for him to meet his end.

Meaning, of course, his old enemy, Father Hand.

Quite coincidentally, at that moment, Sergeant Ralph Foster happened to be at home with his parents – having tea in the drawing room of *Dunroamin*, in fact. His mother and father, as always, were in the throes of professing themselves eager to hear any stories he might happen to have about poor old James Reilly. Poor old James Aloysius, God help him. The Sergeant left down his cup and laughed, clapping his hands softly as he brought up his knees.

– The latest, apparently, is that I myself am to be murdered. Can you believe it? laughed the policeman.

– He really is the most dreadful case, mused Blossom, lifting the teapot, attempting to conceal the pride in her eyes as her gaze accidentally met that of her son.

– More tea, dear? asked Blossom with a smile, as the bone-china stand clinked forebodingly on the sideboard.

13

Albert Craig the dentist was always going on about *Douglas Bader* – the decorated airman who had been blasted out of the skies by the Hun. The dentist liked to suggest that, on account of his own disability, a certain kinship existed between the two men – of the humblest bravery.

In actual fact the dentist's injury had been incurred by a late-night collision between his *Ford Prefect* motor and a dry-stone wall, his navigational miscalculation no doubt assisted by the excessive consumption of numerous *Tuborgs*, the popular lager which for some time past had been his preferred tipple.

Albert Craig was a somewhat taciturn man, well known to be essentially good-natured – and generous to charities, even Catholic ones. By way of dress, the dentist favoured greenish plaid jackets and there was a mole located directly above his right eye, from which leaped a brace of agile hairs. He smoked a twirly pipe and lived alone but spent a great deal of time in the company of his two best friends, who were also Methodists – the Fosters. He dined every day at the *Cullymore Café* – a habit which he had maintained for years. And in which establishment – where he would enjoy his meal of mince and mashed potatoes, followed by stewed apple and custard – he would always be formally addressed as *Mr Craig*.

The proprietor, Mrs Ellen Markey, was extremely fond of him – considering him to be a mild-mannered, inoffensive soul – his only failing, perhaps, being that he could be considered just a trifle dull. A perception which, more than any other reason, led Mrs Markey to believe, just as she was passing the dentist's table one day, that she was simply imagining things again. But the creeping sensation would not seem to go away and she remained convinced that the person seated at the table was no longer, in fact, the inoffensive dentist Albert Craig – but was, in fact someone else – someone quite *awful*. She remained there right in the middle of her own café, terrified she might take leave of her senses. Then she heard, suddenly:

– Better for them had they not been born, the wretches.

As he uttered the words, Albert Craig's lower lip twitched – but only ever so slightly, his countenance once again assuming its familiar state of passive repose. Immensely relieved, now that she was returning to herself, Mrs Markey realised that Mr Craig was now smiling over at her. And it was only later on when her eyes fell on the newspaper which he had been reading, with its banner headline: RENEWED TROUBLE ALONG THE BORDER, that she was reassured that this explained her guest's quite uncharacteristic outburst and the consequent intimations of dread which it incurred. She threw back her head and folded up the paper, wiping the table surfaces, relievedly.

– *And here was me thinking . . .!* she laughed, without even bothering to finish the sentence.

Before waltzing breezily into the kitchen, smiling once more, quite happy and content. Considerably grateful that a repeat performance wasn't in the offing – of what had happened that previous awful day. When she had emptied Patsy's barbers with a scream, her new *Hotpoint* mixer showing no signs of abating as the motor continued to malfunction, dispensing its gluey contents in a profusion of sparks.

– *Help me, please, I can't stop, I can't stop it, I can't stop it!* Mrs Markey had wept as the machine continued to cover her in glutinous brown liquid, a group of familiar figures hastening across the square.

Far from the excitement of *Nagasaki*, say, or *Verdun*, I will acknowledge – but given the indistinguishability of decades and places across the flat and motionless sea of what is called *Time*, the quite comical importance which the natives of Cullymore have always attached to such unremarkable incidents – they have always managed to divert me, I must say.

14

I would like to emphasise, however, that whether *Serbia* or Cullymore, my position remains essentially one of restraint and indifference – inscrutable chronicler, call it what you will. That there will be virulent testimonies to the effect that it is simply not in my nature to be otherwise, I have no doubt – a nature which has remained reassuringly constant throughout history, being one which tends to derive considerable satisfaction from the misfortune of blameless individuals in the extremity of their weakness. It will also be contended that my only purpose is to avail of yet another opportunity to impair the judgement of vulnerable innocents, and coolly, blithely undermine their resistance. This, I must insist, is an ill-informed and groundless prosecution, one entirely unworthy of its proprietors. For there were – as will be seen – many occasions in which I could have effortlessly exerted my influence, choreographing an almost unspeakable pain – and chose not to.

For instance, take the example of Golly Murray in the aftermath of Blossom's *Famous Roman Holiday* fashion show. She had been so confused and out of sorts emotionally that she might easily have crashed the car on her way home that night. But I made sure to guide her *Volkswagen* home, as carefully as though I had been leading her by the hand. You see, Blossom Foster had been so *nice* to poor uncomprehending Golly that she now regretted ever having gone near the fashion show – ever darkened the door of the hotel, indeed.

– It's a trick, that's all it is, Blossom Foster pretending to be nice. I know what she thinks of me, deep down you see – I *know*.

Hope Fairleigh-Warburton had met her at the entrance, taking her by the arm and trilling excitedly as she led her across the floor of the ballroom with its specially built catwalks, potted palms and Italian murals, trilling excitedly to all her friends from the industry:

– *You really must meet Geraldine! A long-standing friend of Blossom's, you know.*

It had taken her breath away, the whole experience, and she had to admit that Blossom had acquitted herself magnificently once again. Having literally *tormented* Happy Carroll, by all accounts, prevailing upon him to build her a replica of the world-famous *Trevi Fountain*. Which now sat proudly in the middle of the floor, and behind it Conleth Foley's breathtakingly beautiful representation of the Colosseum.

– *Geraldine darling, how good of you to come!* Golly heard Blossom call, as she came sweeping towards her with two white-gloved hands extended.

The band she had engaged, Blossom explained, had come all the way from Belfast and were much in demand for such occasions. Golly didn't know what to say – she had never been treated so thoughtfully in her life. As she sat in between Hope Fairleigh-Warburton and Blossom, leafing through the glossy printed programme.

– Hello, I'm Austin Fry, declared the young man beside her, it really is nice to make your acquaintance.

She smiled as he informed her that his girlfriend Verity was one of the models. Just as she appeared, in fact, with one of the buyers delivering an approving commentary in clipped, refined vowels.

– *Observant ladies will notice that her bag is the Hermès brand, of the type favoured by none other than Grace Kelly. Now we have the lady of the moment, yes, none other than Verity Foster herself, who is wearing a lovely dress made from Californian cotton. Note its classical simplicity and the unusual strawberry design. Ideal for those all too brief hours of sunshine.*

During the interval, as the band played *Three Coins in the Fountain*, they had tea and sandwiches and Golly got talking to Blossom's husband – who told her he was absolutely delighted to see her.

– The only time I get to see you these days, Geraldine, is when I pick Blossom up after choir practice.

– It really was the most wonderful idea of Blossom's, Golly said, but then of course you both know Rome very well.

– Oh I wouldn't say that we know it well, but whenever we get a chance we like to visit. Verity of course also is a big fan of *Roman Holiday* – the film, I mean.

Which was why she played the part so well – of the gamine princess going incognito in the eternal city – actually delivering a few lines from the picture as she paraded, attired in her tight-fitting slacks and Polaroids.

– Doesn't Verity look gorgeous! sighed Golly, feeling somewhat drab in her own A-line dress.

Which she had agonised over for hours, earlier on. Pointlessly, she now told herself, for she had actually overheard Blossom and Hope admiring it. She swallowed with shame. But that wasn't all. When the models had all finished, Blossom made a speech in which she specifically mentioned Golly. Complimenting her on her wonderful fashion sense. But which Mrs Murray, once more, had interpreted as a ruse. For Blossom Foster – she could be so wily. But it didn't stop Golly from being ashamed. Why did she think such things, Golly asked herself.

– I just can't tell you how delighted I am that you made the effort to come, darling Golly! beamed Blossom when they were leaving.

As Hope Fairleigh-Warburton nodded and smiled. For no reason that she could name, Golly's heart was pounding and she was waiting for Blossom to add something about her son Boniface. Or *Little Bonnie*, as people often called him.

– Was it difficult to get someone to mind *Little Bonnie*? she expected Blossom to say.

But she didn't. She just waved goodbye and called chirpily:

– *Toodle-oo!*

*   *   *

76

Now piloting the *Volkswagen* homeward, Geraldine Murray wondered anew how she could have ever thought such a terrible thing? What could possibly have made her entertain such unfair and ill-founded considerations?

Of such confusions is my life's blood constituted.

Hmm, I thought, *hmm,* as Golly Murray climbed into bed.

– Is that you, love? asked her husband as she pulled up the covers.

And she tried to respond – but she couldn't find it in her, her soul contaminated by a most grievous sin. It was even worse when in her mind's eye she trembled as she watched Blossom taking pains to forgive her. She could see her plainly as she fell asleep. Taking both her hands and gazing into her eyes.

– But of course I forgive you and I know Hope does too. Don't you, Hope?

– Of course I do, my dearest Geraldine! Don't be so silly!

As Golly left, Blossom cupping a white-gloved hand and whispering:

– Poor little thing. It must be so hard, you know, for her, at home. Herself and Patsy – they wouldn't get out much socially. But, darling Hope, I really must show you this fabric I bought in *Heaton's!*

Of course this episode may well be interpreted as yet another example of self-interest on my own part – and that Geraldine Murray's experiences at the fashion show were just another example of me yet again enjoying her little confusions – directing her febrile mind every which way for no other reason than that of self-gratification, cruelly fogging her perception and judgement, increasing her already dormant paranoia.

But I really must refute such a nefarious charge. Honestly, the things credulous people can get into their heads.

Why, it's nearly as bad as what happened to poor Hughie Considine, while working on the roads – back in what they call a few *generations* ago. Ah yes, poor old Hughie – yet another vulnerable Cullymore figure, loping across the sweeping expanse of *Time's* ocean – of which he had no comprehension at all, as he stumbled onward without map or compass.

It was a cold sharp morning in the year 1896. I was routinely referred to as the *Fetch* in those days. During a period when such concepts were rarely questioned. They wouldn't dare.

– The *Fetch*, they murmured in choked, awed whispers, once you see him coming around you're finished.

The *Fetch*, like *Nobodaddy*, inscrutable director of souls and motivation.

A labourer by the name of Hugh Considine had been working with some colleagues, building the new road that would lead from Cullymore into Balla. Hugh Considine had lived in the district all his life. He was twenty-seven years of age. Hugh was a quiet sort of individual and well disposed towards work or physical exertion of any kind. Not that he was big – was quite slight, in fact – pale, angular and thin. He wielded his shovel on the *tar road* from dawn to dusk. This notable enthusiasm had the effect of prompting his somewhat less enthusiastic colleagues to have fun with him on occasion. To *take a hand out of him*, as the colloquial expression went, at the time.

– Considine, they'd say, you're showing the rest of us up, so you are. If you don't let up we'll have to do it – give that wife of yours a poke in her hairy pudding.

Considine lowered his head when he heard this. You see the truth was that Hugh Considine was an extremely devout and holy man and because of this his fellow workers had established that taunts of a bawdier nature tended to be more effective than certain others they had attempted. Inititially their friend and colleague prayed for the strength to withstand these quite unnecessary provocations – and for a considerable period the various novenas and rosaries did, in fact, sustain him. But whether on account of the fact that he had been working too hard or maybe due to the quite extraordinary physical beauty of his spouse – her long wavy hair, into which she sometimes threaded rose petals, cascaded all along her back – it had arrived at the stage that it most definitely had begun to upset him. To the degree that he kept enquiring, having just arrived home:

– Them boys on the road. Do they be looking at you, Molly?

– Och sure, boys is boys, replied Molly – unfortunately.

Because that was not the response that her husband had anticipated.

In Irish folklore it is routinely asserted that access to the *Stray Sod Country* is gained by means of the unholy gate.

And that once you have reached it, you will find that you have been deceived and that you have now arrived in a place where the world can never be the same again. Your senses will have been overtaken by a heightened faculty of observation which can only result in the most unnamable terror of all – cosmic loneliness.

Hugh Considine now found himself on the other side of that unholy gate.

He sat rigidly at his kitchen table, staring straight ahead of him – like a somnambulist. He knew someone was trying to rob him of his reason.

He could have sworn that someone touched his elbow. Which was why he remained in a state of extraordinary agitation – and this was how affairs were set to continue.

Again the following day as he made his way along the *tar road*, he found himself the object of evasive scorn from his fellow labourers, who were remarking on the curiously hunted and furtive manner with which he now carried himself – as if expecting to be waylaid at any moment. There are few sensations more distressing than that of being constantly under surveillance. His face was accentuated by an unnatural pallor.

The air was soundless as Hugh Considine proceeded along the road. Through the boughs and sprays of the leafy elms no sigh or motion was audible. He stared at his colleagues but could identify no face that was familiar.

That same night in bed he overheard a soft tapping behind the wall, directly above his head. He stared at his wife – she was sleeping, and had heard nothing. The following night it came again – this time even softer. As he strode along the tar road the next day, he repeatedly applied his handkerchief to his forehead. Suddenly a soulless, unjoyous laugh broke out somewhere close by. Then he realised that it had issued from the lips of a fellow labourer, one who once upon a time would have qualified as an eminent friend and neighbour. But no longer – for, like the others, he had been transformed into a featureless, unreachable foreigner, strategically placed there for the purpose of deepening one's aloneness. The unholy gate had been firmly slammed shut. Hugh Considine cried aloud, trembling violently as he did so:

– *What are youse all looking at me for, boys? Why are youse saying these awful things? Why are youse telling these terrible lies?*

Even as he spoke the words, Hugh Considine knew that his entreaty was pointless. For all he knew they were no longer even *men*. The labouring man on the spade close by had reacted to his outburst by simply laughing – but with a smile one might find on the face of a changeling. As this thin smile extended and Hugh heard him taunt:

– Boys, but I love that hairy old pudding.

It was later that same evening when his wife Molly was leaning down to remove the griddle cake from the oven that Hugh Considine did his best to avoid the attractions of her fine shapely haunches – as he stood in the doorway of their cabin with his shovel, seeming grave. Looking ashen, in fact.

– What are you doing with that shovel, Hughie? his wife enquired, slapping her hands on her thighs as she approached him, before adding:

– Did you have a good day on the *tar road*, working?

– I did, replied her husband, smashing open her head with the iron implement, before helping himself to a hunk of griddle cake – looking down at her body as it lay there on the flagstones. There didn't appear to be any blood, he thought.

As I stood there watching, in the chimney-corner shadows.

15

The episode with the discredited Classics teacher James A. Reilly aside, Father Gus Hand had come to regard his time in Rathwilliam College as representing more or less the happiest period of his life. Especially those first few years before the disgraced teacher had gone and spoiled everything. He winced a little now as he contemplatively paced the grounds of the presbytery, for even the faintest memory of that awful affair sickened him. Imagine kissing a *twelve-year-old boy!* Whoever heard of such a thing?

In the end, however, justice had prevailed and the loathsome reprobate had received his just deserts. He had always had his suspicions about that fellow, he considered. I mean, he didn't even play football for heaven's sake. Something which the clergyman could not even begin to understand. What kind of example could that possibly be to give growing boys, he insisted. After all, every youth in adolescence needs to let off steam. *Mens sana in corpore sano.*

Of course, there could be no denying that the classics had their place. But Father Hand had always reserved a special preference for physical gamesmanship. Which was not all that surprising, really, when one considers that, as a student himself, he had acquired a reputation as a fearsome fullback.

– Like a great strong bull he is! his colleagues would remark whenever he appeared flexing his muscles on the field. If he could only watch that temper!

A fact which was indisputable, he agreed – for he knew that he'd always possessed something of a short fuse. But that was just because his standards were so high, in sport as much as any other area of life. In this regard, he tended to be particularly proud of his presidency of *Cullymore Soccer Club*. Under his stewardship the town club had blossomed in recent times – with every red farthing meticulously accounted for. He had taken it to new heights, all the boys in the *Cullymore gang* agreed – all his old staunch friends and comrades. The greater proportion of the club's income now came from the proceeds of the various little variety shows, plays and quizzes which the priest had taken upon himself to organise. But which would never have been a success without the loyalty and expertise of his colleagues. Yes, without the cooperation of such men as Patsy and Barney, the priest's Herculean efforts would have come to nothing. He found himself smiling as he wondered what a certain Mayo donkey might have made of that.

– Well, Father Peyton, any views on that then, have you?

After which fresh musings regarding the exploits of the so-called *Hollywood Priest* began entering his head, provoking a broad, triumphant grin. For he knew his band of brothers would always be on his side. Yes, Patsy and the lads would gladly have joined him in taking that Yankee smart alec down a peg or two. Yes, as he paced the lawn with his hands linked behind his back, Father Peyton right there and then seemed to appear in all his glory to Father Gus Hand – but this time with his customary arrogance and superiority mysteriously absent. *Why, unless I am mistaken, Peyton,* chuckled the parish priest to himself, *you appear somewhat downcast – like some pupil who has been caught in the act, in the throes perhaps of some minor transgression!*

He laughed as the Mayo idiot averted his eyes. Then tossed his head back with contempt.

– Why you're not even worth it – I couldn't even be bothered! snorted the parish priest of Cullymore.

Just before being distracted by a tug on his sleeve and looking down to see one of the *Scrawkey Dawes*, jumping up and down in a state of great excitement.

– *It's the devil again, Father – we're after seeing him up at the church!*

Fortunately, it was early days yet and the inevitable gossip had not yet begun circulating. It was simply a matter of time, of course – as the priest knew well. Soon it would be raging through the district like wildfire. His stomach turned as he stared at the red letters dribbling down the front of the sacristy door: FATHER HAND HAS TO DIE.

– I'll make him regret he did this! hissed the priest, clenching his fists – knowing full well that the hideous rubric could but be the work of one man. He resolved to make his way to Reilly's hovel at once.

The situation was now crystal clear – if the disgraced teacher did not give a firm commitment to mend his antisocial ways, then the parish priest would ensure that he was immediately arrested. From now on it would be a matter for the police, he fumed. Yes, Mr James A. Reilly was on notice from this point on. As he blundered onward towards the lake he felt quite happy. But just then, out of nowhere, he found himself wrongfooted by an unexpected sensation of extreme alarm.

– *You are not Father Hand,* he had distinctly heard a voice saying, *you are not Father Hand, did you hear me?*

He searched for his beads and, frozen to the spot, began stammering a prayer as best he could. Cold drops of dew were standing out on his forehead. He pulled himself together, pounding frantically on the hovel door. With his every move being watched by the keen-eyed fox, as it circled the tree stump to which it was lashed, snarling accusingly and grinding its teeth, pawing in the dirt. Finally the priest could stand it no longer.

– Stop looking at me like that, do you hear? Quit your gawking, fox!

But the animal persisted. As the crude door at last swung open.

– Reilly, are you in there! the priest bawled hoarsely, falling inside. I'll teach you to damage my property, you cur!

He stood in semi-darkness, in silence, catching his breath as his heart beat furiously. But for a *Primus* stove and a number of contemporary appurtenances, the clergyman might have blundered into a peasant domicile of a hundred years before. Stacked bales of yellowed newspapers stood in lurching, unwieldy towers, and above the black range hung a line of filthy clothes. A copy of *Horace's Odes* was lying open on the table, as a shaft of light fell on an upturned kettle, from which proceeded an orderly regiment of woodlice. Outside the infuriating animal persisted with its scratchings and whines, whittling away at his already frayed nerves. He was still afraid that he might hear the unfamiliar voice again – the one he had imagined, if indeed he had imagined it. Then out of nowhere he was alerted anew – by the sound of the television bursting into life, its black-and-white rays sweeping the walls like a searchlight. *Michael Miles* the compère descended some steps in a silky plaid suit.

– *Yes, it's Friday night and it's Take Your Pick!*

The studio audience began cheering and clapping and it was more than the clergyman could bear any longer. Quite exhausted, he lowered himself into the torn upholstery of the broken armchair. He could not steady his recalcitrant, quivering hand. The plump man's smarminess he began to loathe, grinning as he read from a pile of cards.

– *Jesus Christ!* cried the priest, aloud.

– *You are not Father Hand*, the whisper returned again, *what you are is a stranger*, as he flung himself forward and fiercely struck the television set – the ensuing darkness affording him some peace.

In the silence he trawled the deep pockets of his soutane, in an unsuccessful effort to retrieve his missal – he must have forgotten it. Tears of frustration prised their way to his cheeks. As he found his foot resting upon a solid metal object. Exploring its contours as a blind man might do, he realised that what he had come upon was actually, in fact, a rusted old nutcracker. A clever plan began forming in his mind.

– Now we'll see who's so smart, Mr Fox, he grinned, now, Mr Reynard, we shall see.

Luxuriating in his decision, he cradled the cold squat object in his lap, recalling a similar item he had discovered in the coach house many years ago in Rathwilliam. He had come upon it quite by chance one evening when making his daily rounds. It was funny, he thought, how your memory could be stimulated in this way by a simple object. For right there and then in the gloom of James Reilly's lake-shore hovel, Father Hand was back once again in the study hall of Rathwilliam College – on the 6th of March in the year 1949. When he and his boys had once more distinguished themselves before the entire school, with their performance of that year's annual pageant: *The Heroes of Old Rathwilliam*.

The tumultuous applause vividly returned to make him giddy, as a chorus of boyish exultation erupted.

– *Let's hear it for our hero, the one and only Father Hand!*

The very man now who emerged so proudly before them on the podium – with his big fists squared – as if he himself were some Titan of old.

– *My boys!* he cried – and their cheers lifted the roof.

But that was all long ago and here now in this musty hovel he found himself shaking violently, bellowing as he clutched the nutcracker.

– A warrior, you hear? Do you hear that, James Reilly? You think you can deface my sacristy door – do you, you profligate! Is that what you think? Because if you do, then, my friend, you have another think coming!

And he strode out the door like some colossus of ancient times.

When James A. Reilly returned from Enniskillen, where he'd been to fill a prescription, he found the door of his house broken in. Not only that but discovered that his property had been invaded. He was in the process of dealing with this realisation when he became aware of a most unexpected and unsettling silence that seemed to be hanging in the air. For which, as it transpired, there was a logical explanation. As he realised when he found his pet Funzel, prostrate by the stump with his head caved in, with the nutcracker lying beside him on the grass.

16

The morning after he'd perpetrated this deed, Father Hand woke up a moment just before the break of dawn – to find himself overwhelmed by guilt. Which had still not abated after he'd eaten his breakfast. Mrs Miniter was prattling on about the canonisation of Edel Quinn, a missionary to whom she had a special devotion.

– *We'll have to storm heaven, storm heaven and Our Lady. Yes, Father – that's what all of us will have to do. We owe that much, at least, to Edel.*

Ttththt! the priest was thinking. *Ttththt!* For the love of God doesn't she ever shut up!

– I'm off to read my holy office, he said then. That was a lovely breakfast, Una.

He wasn't feeling at all well, with the fox's little face returning again to plague him, as he paced the cinder path in the garden, doing his best to immerse himself in his holy office, dwelling on those happy days in Rathwilliam when somehow it had all made sense. Especially during that glorious week when the house exams were in full swing – *Intermediate Week*, as it was called, that lovely part of the year when the morning dew would lie low on the fields and the boys, between tests, would rest beneath the spreading laburnum.

Ah, *Intermediate Week*, how wonderful it was, he mused, until degenerates had to come along and ruin everything – them and their stupid accursed foxes! *Why did you make me do it, James Reilly? I hate you!*

These thoughts prevailed as he made his way briskly through the streets towards the church, hoping his heart would not start beating fast, doing whatever he could to distract himself. All in town was as it ought to be, ordinary life proceeding in the middle of yet another ordinary day. There were boys playing football and younger ones playing marbles – and the girls in a little ring reading comics and sewing. The post office was packed, and Barney Corr didn't have a minute – run off his feet as he chatted to all the housewives. Then along came the baker, in his van all the way from Balla, merrily whistling as he threw the doors open and drew out the steaming trays. O look, there's Happy Carroll, murmured the priest as he chipped a stone with his toe, and my old friend Mrs Markey, standing in the doorway, sweeping up her step.

– That's not a bad day now, she called. Will you be popping in for a drop of soup later, Father?

– I might, he replied, I very just might!

Already the dossers – Duxass, Winky and Jo'burg among them – were taking up their positions at the corner. Do you think you'd ever see the likes of those fellows at the missions? He had had to chastise them from the pulpit, for heaven's sake, a pack of Teddy boys, that's what they were

– nearly as irresponsible as that young Fonsey O'Neill who had gone to England, and for whom he had held such high hopes once upon a time. Ah well. At least young Manus Hoare was as devout as ever – maybe even more so. He had seen him in church a lot recently, and his presence at the retreat had, happily, been strong and constant.

A group of young girls were skipping outside the *Yankee Clipper*, chanting *Three six nine the goose drank wine the monkey chewed tobacco on the streetcar line*. Through an open window a gramophone was playing – as Golly Murray accompanied her son Boniface home from school. Before pausing in front of the drapery window to take a look in at the boys' clothes – especially the white shirt and tie that she had purchased for her son's *First Communion*. Which unfortunately the child couldn't make because he had caused too much disruption. He might make it next year, the nun had, apparently, told her. Ah what a pity – still, God is good and maybe he'll improve. Then along came Conleth Foley, setting out for the lake with his easel under his arm, looking very dashing in that spotted dicky bow of his. Not forgetting good old Dagwood, lighting up a cigarette as he emerged from the snooker hall in his white-spattered overcoat – heading home to look after his birds. An awful man for the pigeons – had his wife's heart broken with them – *Those damned things have the place destroyed on me, Father*, she had told him. But it was a highly competitive sport, as he knew – and there was no talking to him. Still, he was one of the decentest men in town, Dagwood Slowey – give you the last bit out of his mouth. And look, there goes Albert Craig the dentist, turning into Barney Corr's. The priest smiled for he could hear it all plainly as he watched the two men chatting through the window.

– Good man, Albert, and what can I get you? asked Barney with his customary smile.

– I'll have a pound of pork sausages and a small bit of suet. That ought to do me for today, if you please, Mr Corr.

– Coming right up, no sooner said than done!

Lord above, if it isn't Jude O'Hara, famed schoolteacher and star of *Oklahoma*, giving me a wave, thought Father Hand, as he swings his brass-topped ebony walking cane. Most likely going through the script of *Tenebrae* in his mind's eye.

– *You ask me to punish this man but I can find no wrong in him!*

Not forgetting the Fosters, yes, here they're coming now, mused the priest, with the pair of them holding hands like youngsters. Isn't that nice. And listen – what's that Bodley's singing? Why it's *Three Coins in the Fountain*, from the film of the same name.

And there's my counterpart talking to them – the one and only Dean Harry Gribbins, trotting along to the *Salvation Army* band hall. He was talking to me yesterday about organising a little recital in the square, maybe sometime after Easter. He wants the whole community to sing a song that will express all our feelings – *The Old Rugged Cross* is the hymn he has chosen. In memory of the *faithful departed* of Cullymore. Which will one day, but not for a long time yet, please God, include myself and Happy Carroll, the very man who's coming strolling with his thumbs tucked into the bib of his blue overalls and with his pencil tucked behind his ear. Is it any wonder, he thinks, they should call him Happy, for he's always grinning from ear to ear. And why not, for as Dean Gribbins says it's the greatest little community in the world. He's right about that. Look at them here as they go about their business, nodding to each other, exchanging their harmless little snippets of gossip – the glorious correspondence of everyday life. Thinking about bingo as they scrub their front steps, or memorable football matches as they fork garden dung, closing their eyes as they puff on the sweetest pipe smoke. With the steam-and-soda smell of washday lingering in the air, as if to freshen all their private dreams – the unrivalled achievements of champion pigeons, darts games won and darts games lost, the solid and unstinting optimism of a town that knows its name and knows its own people.

As the abattoir drayhorse munched oats in a nosebag, the golden crack of its urine resounding solidly against the pavement, Father Hand, smiling, gesturing across to Patsy the barber:

– Not a bad day now, Mr Murray, my good man!

– No indeed – she seems to be picking up, Father!

– Although I hear we might get a touch of rain later!

– Ah please God it'll keep off!

And the cleric passed on, so proud of his town he might have almost burst. Until, out of nowhere, he found his heart standing still in his chest. For who was loitering outside

Dagwood's snooker hall, waving – none other than his nemesis, *James A. Reilly*!

The parish priest just couldn't believe what he was seeing. Already the scoundrel was making his way across the street. To the clergyman's amazement he was whistling as though he hadn't a care in the world. Father Hand continued to be baffled. For, throughout the course of their conversation, the wretch's attitude remained stubbornly insouciant.

Pah! There can be no doubt whatsoever about it, the fellow is truly mad! he found himself thinking. He had probably forgotten all about the dead animal.

The teacher informed the clergyman that he was looking forward to the market day this coming Thursday.

– Glory be to God, exclaimed Father Hand excitedly, didn't I go and forget it was market, James! It went and completely slipped my mind!

– I daresay, Father, James Reilly continued, I daresay there'll be a right big crowd arriving. Would you say so yourself?

– I would indeed. Cullymore has one of the best fairs in the county. Everyone knows that.

Father Hand was considerably relieved by this quite unanticipated development. His adversary was conversing quite reasonably now. It was wonderful, really, the way things had turned out. That he could be having a normal conversation with James, he meant. It restored one's faith in the capacity and resourcefulness of human nature.

– Aye, these market days, James – they're great for the town, the priest continued, especially in hard times like these. They'll always bring their share of business.

– They will, agreed James, then out of nowhere adding, rather suddenly:

– And no doubt you're being kept busy yourself, Father! The clergyman smiled, declaring himself *up to his eyes*.

– With the forthcoming production, which you may have heard of, he explained, at Easter. Our next little effort in the dramatic sphere – entitled *Tenebrae*. As a matter of fact, I'm on my way down this very minute to have a chat with some of the principals.

– The *principals?* queried James.

– Yes. The principal actors, I mean, of course, James. Barney, Patsy, Happy Carroll and all the lads. Ah, *Tenebrae* – it's going to be the show to end them all. I can feel it in my bones.

– *Ex tenebris lux*, said James with a smile. *Out of darkness cometh light.* Well, I hope so for I could certainly be doing with some of that – *light*, I mean!

– Yes indeed! the priest interrupted enthusiastically. From the agony in the garden to His final redemption with His father in Paradise.

– It's wonderful, Father. It really and truly is. But then, of course, it comes as no surprise – after all, back in good old Rathwilliam College, your shows were regarded as the stuff of legend.

– Och I dunno, replied the priest – contriving a rather unconvincing show of humility, I wouldn't say that.

– *The Lad of Old Ireland*, continued James, *Who Fears to Speak of '98*? There was no one could touch you as a producer. You were always renowned for the sheer spectacle of your pageants.

– Yes, replied the clergyman, yes, James, I suppose in a way I was.

– Then there was, of course, the one that not so many tend to know about. The lesser-known one.

– Oh? said the priest, and which one would that be, James?

– That would be *Funzel's Murder*, or *The Killing of a Little Innocent Fox*, as it is also known.

James indicated that he was on the point of continuing the discussion when Father Hand looked abruptly at his watch, explaining that he was already late for his meeting with his actors. And that, much as he was enjoying their conversation, he really had better be getting along. James indicated that of course he understood.

– You're a busy man, Father Hand, and don't I know it. You have better things to do than stand talking to me.

He cupped his hand and called after the priest as he hoisted his cassock and hastened down the street:

– You're an honour to the town of Cullymore, Father. But don't worry, for very soon you'll be getting your reward – a bullet in your callous fucking face.

17

At the tender age of eighteen years there are very few on this earth who would actually consider making the audacious claim that they perceive themselves to have, in fact, inherited the very planet itself – but that, right at this very moment, was what Fonsey O'Neill felt like doing. Knowing in his heart, of course, that such good fortune did not occur by accident and that there were those without whom his life would never have been altered in the spectacular way it had in recent times. And amongst that small and select group no one was more important than his old friend, the former Latin teacher, James A. Reilly. Who had never actually *taught* him, in fact – but still, he owed the man an enormous debt. And it was one that he intended to discharge – something he had been wanting to do since his early teens, when he had begun visiting the ramshackle hovel by the shores of the lake. Of course he knew about the man's reputation – what adolescent boy didn't? But the former teacher had never so much as laid a finger on him. And now, after his year and a half away, he would at last be seeing his old friend again.

It was hard to believe that it was actually happening, thought Alphonsus, as he stood there on the deck of the

B & I ferry – that he was making his way back to his home-town of Cullymore. Almost eighteen whole months since he had first gone to England. Yes, forsaken his humble red-brick terraced home, with his father's words still ringing in his ears:

– You'd be better off beyond. Much better chance of fitting in over there.

Not that he blamed his father – for he knew he had never quite recovered from his wife's early death – of tuberculosis.

It was a source of great pain, not to have known his mother longer – but this did not prevent him from indulging in a moment of the sweetest satisfaction when it occurred to him just how proud she might possibly have been of her son. For there were very few youths of his age, not from the sleepy little town of Cullymore, at any rate, who would have managed to last that length of time in England. Not only that – but who among them would have been able to say, like him, that they had arrived home in glory, brandishing a wallet bulging with hard-earned notes. Alphonsus knew in his heart that his father had never really expected him to succeed. Most likely he had spent the eighteen months awaiting the sound of his timid knock on the door. One which confirmed his unvoiced fears – that his son was cut from the same cloth as himself – that he was docile and deferential, obsequious almost to the point of embarrassment.

Well, just how wrong could old *Pops* be, he thought, as he drank in the bracing sea air.

Wrong, like the rest of them, and those were the facts. For they could say what they liked but the irrefutable truth was that Fonsey O'Neill had gone and *done* it – had lasted the course against all the odds. His breast swelled with excitement as he recalled such terms for the description of emotions from the time he had spent as a young teenage boy, serving before Father Hand's altar. Whether the old fellow was square or not, he had always, like a lot of people, been fond of his parish priest. And was looking forward to renewing their acquaintance. Especially now that he was so much more mature and enlightened. For he himself would have been the very first to admit that he had been more than a little emotional in his youth. Indeed, it was Father Hand himself who had described him as a *deeply sensitive and obliging lad. Possibly the best of all my servers.*

Sure he had been sensitive, he mused, leaning over the railing, watching the smoke of his *Woodbine* curling – maybe, at times, to an alarming degree. He had been far too acutely aware of the world and its imperfections, entertaining philosophies which espoused the virtues of virginal self-sacrifice. There were times in his younger days when he had found himself worshipping dutifully in the church – praying, above all, that his soul would be rendered immune – throughout all his trials, continue to be uncontaminated.

All of which seemed so infantile now – the ludicrously inflated expectations of an inexperienced boy.

But they also seemed quite touching in their way – having passed on, faded into history.

Fonsey ran his fingers through his oiled hair – smiling wryly as he gave a little involuntary shiver. It had been inevitable, he thought, that all of those boyhood experiences would one day die – it couldn't have been otherwise. Certainly not after he'd met Verity Foster – a girl of his own age with whom – there could be no other way of putting it – he had become *besotted*. As she made her way to the Protestant *Collegiate School* in her plaid skirt and braided black blazer, they had got chatting – for almost half an hour, he remembered.

He had wept that evening for he knew what had happened. The longing which had seized him in his kitchen – it had become all-consuming. It was frightening too. But there was something quite luxurious about its power, which made him want to be devastated by it. In its sheer intensity this was a feeling vastly superior to any swooning of the soul he'd formerly experienced.

Verity's hair was as bog cotton bleached in the sun. Her hands were pale and her blue eyes glittered.

He began to follow her regularly after that, but could not summon up the courage to address her. He carried her school photograph everywhere he went. *Angel* was the word he had written above her head and, in the nights when his father sobbed, lonely in the kitchen, Fonsey O'Neill strove not to feel superior to all others in the town – with the new grace and ardour that was pouring into his heart.

She wore white socks and read books in the café. One of the books was *Nancy Drew*. Every night he kissed its covers. And withdrew a number of similar titles from the library. Twice a year the *Collegiate School* held a hop in the Cullymore tennis club. Trepidatiously he had approached her and asked her to dance. She was wearing perfume. Yes, she said. *Russ Conway* was playing, fluid octaves swirling, expert melodic fingers sweeping wildly up and down the keyboard.

– Do you like *Russ Conway?* he asked her as he placed his arms around her waist.

– No I don't, replied Verity Foster, to tell you the truth I prefer *Billy Fury*.

It was hard to believe, Fonsey found himself thinking, that it was almost three years ago now. And here he was, against all the odds magnificently redeemed, making his way back to his good old hometown. Boy, he reflected, with a beaming smile, what stories he had for Verity Foster. She would hardly be able to keep her hands off him – just as soon as she heard of all the places that he'd been. Of course there was no point in being arrogant about it – no, the best thing to do was to keep your powder dry. Ever so subtly just slip in little pieces of information, insert them casually into the conversation.

Just then he overheard a sudden bout of coughing behind him and looked around to see a large, heavy-set man, bristled as a boar, leaning over the side of the boat.

– Going back then, son, he heard him say, back to the old sod like myself – what's your name?

– O'Neill, he replied, they call me O'Neill.

The bristled boar sighed, releasing a long low whistle.

– There's a song that I know about you, my good man. *Teddy O'Neill*, ah boys, but there's a tune.

Closing his eyes as he burst into song:

– *Not even the sun through my casement shines cheery*
Since I lost my darling love Teddy O'Neill!

The big man swaggeringly puffed his chest, took a long drag of his cigarette as the remainder of the melody drifted out across the foaming water, as Fonsey grinned and considered just how exact and wholly appropriate it was. That a complete and utter stranger, a man he'd just met, could acquaint him of the fact that there was a song he knew about someone called *Teddy*.

For that was how he saw himself now, Fonsey *Teddy* O'Neill – as the Teddy boy who'd decided it was time to return, triumphant – yes, fully grown, a proper man. With the schoolboy that he'd once been having died somewhere between Skegness and Cullymore. His name for ever now was Teddy O'Neill, fearful of nothing and more than capable of taking on the world. Coming back to claim what was his – to ask Verity Foster to be his bride. He smiled as he thought of her lovely face again – just as the big man's boar-hand slapped him.

– Let's go below and have ourselves a drink!

– Rightsville! laughed Teddy – in exactly the same accent *Billy Fury* had used. The night they had met in the *Nimbus Club* in Soho.

– Two large whiskies apiece! bellowed the boar, as down the hatch the amber liquid flowed effortlessly and Teddy didn't even bother listening to the old boy, who like all of that generation was kinda OK but at the end of the day square. No, he wasn't at all interested in what the bristled boar was saying, or the glass that was trembling in his hand:

– Do you think, son, we'll recognise it – will there be a place in the old sod for you and me, or will it have turned old, a strange country where we'll never find a home, lost like that poor old mutt tumbling out there in space?

No, he had more to think about than old ramblings the like of that – now that, at last, Teddy O'Neill was a man.

18

I suppose you could say that it was really more of an impromptu gathering than a party. It was Ralph Foster, who had made the suggestion, quite unexpectedly.

– Let's go down to the *Foresters*, he had said.

Which was something, ordinarily, the Fosters would never have done – or Blossom or Dean Harry Gribbins, either. Not in a million years, to be honest.

But, on this occasion, Blossom Foster had professed herself delighted.

– It's a special event, she agreed, reaching up to the hatstand for her mink stole, I mean, why wouldn't I be delighted. After all, I knew that Austin and Verity were fond of one another. But I had absolutely no idea that things were quite so far advanced.

It was for this reason that Blossom had made it her business to take her future son-in-law's hand and to whisper affectionately into his ear:

– I'm absolutely over the moon for you both. I really and truly am.

For his part, Austin Fry was seen to grin from ear to ear, clasping Verity's soft hand with pride in his own.

Thus it ought to come as no surprise that the little party or impromptu gathering turned out such a success. Especially when they made it their business to call by in the *Vauxhall Saloon* in order to add Albert Craig to their number. And who, in spite of his customary taciturn nature, almost immediately assimilated the sense of near-euphoria that was palpably evident as they motored towards the exclusively Protestant club.

The announcement had come as such a wonderful surprise, they repeated many times to the dentist, professing themselves absolutely over the moon. They had had a good laugh then about having arrived just in time to catch the dentist practising his tuba in the front room.

– *Douglas Bader* in a big brass band! laughed Bodley, shaking his briar out the open window, as Blossom shook her head, saying:

– Dear dear! Practising away in the sitting room, he was!

Albert, like Bodley, was an enthusiastic member of the Salvation Army Band and could be heard most nights, refining his talents. But right at this moment he had declared, when he saw them arrive, he was delighted to be provided with the opportunity for some respite, as he rushed out to get his trilby and sheepskin.

– It's just the ticket right at this very moment, he announced, pushing up his black-framed spectacles, a few halves in the *Foresters*. I've been beavering away at this bloody thing for hours.

It was great that Albert had agreed to come, the various participants would find themselves agreeing later, whenever they looked back on the *Foresters* party.

106

For he really had contributed a lot to the proceedings.

– I never really believed that Albert could be so hilarious, Blossom became fond of saying, he really was a scream that night. Her eyes misting over as she dwelt on her fond memories of that very special occasion.

– What a comedian. I really never knew! she remarked to her husband, who nodded affectionately behind his *Times*.

For he, more than anyone, was acquainted with his mischievousness.

– *That's my name. I don't know why but there it is!*

He loved to imitate the comedian *Harry Worth* – a routine which he had begun at the monthly dances over which he presided in the *Masonic Hall*.

– Albert Hoppity's world-famous hops! the teenagers all called them.

He had even sung some tunes that night – when prevailed on by none other than Verity. Somewhat reluctantly, he had consented to pipe a few bars of the Rosemary Clooney favourite – *This Old House*.

Which Verity loved, she told the dentist as she clapped.

Something which of course Teddy O'Neill knew nothing about. Nor would he. No, he was destined never to hear a single thing about it or the *Foresters* gathering – or even to suspect it had ever taken place.

Indeed had he been informed of its occurrence in the days after his arrival home on the B & I ferry most likely he would have obstinately refused to believe it.

For the simple reason that impromptu gatherings in the town's public houses by inhabitants of the Protestant persuasion – even in the *Foresters* with its particular history and Empire Loyalist associations – would have been so rare as to be credibly dismissed, and not just by the likes of Teddy O'Neill, as belonging to the realms of self-indulgent fantasy.

But, oblivious as Teddy might continue to remain of the announcement of Verity Foster's forthcoming engagement to the young civil servant, also a Protestant, Austin Fry – the simple facts were was that it was already a *fait accompli*. Like it or not, the betrothal was effected. It was a fact of life. Whether he might choose to accept it or not. Yes, every bit as real as their impromptu little gathering that unexpected February night in the *Foresters*.

What fun they had had, as Blossom became fond of remarking, even years later. Adding giddily:

– What they must have thought of us at all at all!

– I have to play my Tuborg! Albert kept repeating, with his black thick-framed glasses hanging down over his nose, as he launched once more into his *Harry Worth* impression:

– *That's my name. I don't know why but there it is!*

But it had been Ralph their police officer son, Ralph their eldest and only boy, who, without a doubt, had struck the most amusing tone of the evening. With his hilarious tales of James A. Reilly, the unfortunate vagrant who lived by the lake.

– I couldn't believe my eyes, Mother, he told Blossom. I was just taking the bike out for a spin and there he was again – calm as you like, with that ancient old disaster of a gun beneath his arm.

– You can't be serious! remarked Austin Fry, who wished to impress his future in-laws with a profound display of civic responsibility. You mean he doesn't have a licence?

– O it's primitive, Austin, God only knows where he came upon it. One look was all it took to establish that it's not going to do much damage now. I don't think to be honest he has a bad bone in his body – he's certainly not going to use it on anyone. To be perfectly honest, I feel sorry for the fellow. I find him a most intelligent chap and I really would like to do something for him.

– Still, the law's the law, insisted Austin Fry sternly, and we can't have people going around willy-nilly. With guns, I mean. Not in this day and age.

Blossom Foster enjoyed a renewed ripple of pride, approving wholeheartedly of the young man's highly developed sense of orthodoxy. She did not even consider objecting as Austin placed his hand over Verity's.

– You'll never guess what he told me, Mother, Ralph went on.

– Please tell me, Ralph, pleaded Blossom, I find your stories so amusing.

– *I've got to go home to play my Tuborg!* interrupted Albert – slapping his thighs as he erupted in a bout of shrill laughter, nodding his head in approval at his own joke.

Ralph coughed lightly, then proceeded.

– Looks up at me there as we're talking away and, without so much as flinching, announces:

– I saw him standing where you were last night, Ralph. He came to tell me that I had been chosen.

– Who did he mean? What was it he saw?

– He couldn't bring himself to say, he told me. Just kept repeating that he had been selected. The truth is going to come out in the end, he kept saying. When at last we arrive in the *Stray Sod Country*. So get yourself ready, Sergeant Foster.

Verity kissed Austin's hand and pressed it to her cheek.

– This is exciting, said his sister, do please continue, Ralph.

– I've never heard anything like this in my life, exclaimed Austin rather sourly, it really is – well, it's quite insane.

– Cullymore town is a funny wee place, laughed Bodley, you'll find that, son, as time goes on.

Ralph leaned over to his mother and continued.

– In the *Stray Sod Country*, that's what he kept saying.

– The *Stray Sod Country*?

– Together but alone. Strangers in town, strangers in our skins. That's what he kept repeating over and over.

– The *Stray Sod Country*, if you don't mind, sniggered Austin Fry as he looked at Verity.

– I'm afraid you'll have to get used to them, son – these Catholics and their extraordinary superstitions.

– However, if that's not enough, what do you think he revealed to me then? That I'm to be murdered myself, apparently! In front of my wife and children if you don't mind!

– *What a madman!* interjected Austin Fry.

But Blossom Foster had already lost interest in the poor unfortunate fellow who lived by the lake – for she was too busy looking at her future son-in-law and Verity. Who were lovingly gazing into one another's eyes. Blossom reflected how gratified she was by the scene, thinking to herself how fortunate they had been that her beautiful daughter had at last seen sense – and had forgotten about that *oddity*, that strange pale misfit who came from the terraces but who, thankfully, a year and a half ago, had upped and vanished to England. What was his name, that rather uninspiring, slope-shouldered youth?

– *O'Neill!* she remembered, yes, that was it, Alphonsus O'Neill! I am just so pleased that we no longer argue the way we used to do, that she no longer sees fit to mention him in my company – and at last has found herself a decent Protestant boy.

19

— You're the fucking living spit of your man, *whatyoucallhim Tommy Steele*, the old boy on the B & I ferry had kept repeating to Alphonsus, hacking hoarsely behind a thick cloud of smoke. And although Fonsey wouldn't actually have been a fan of the cheeky-looking Bermondsey singer, it had to be admitted that the man's description hadn't altogether displeased him.

Which was the reason he was now smiling as he sat in a corner booth of the *Cullymore Café* where Mrs Markey was going about her business, wiping her hands on her apron as she made her way past a poster of none other than the Bermondsey Boy himself, crudely Sellotaped to the wall above the jukebox. Teddy had spent many of the happy and maybe not so happy hours of his youth and early adolescence right here in this very café, always attended to graciously by Ellen Markey – she was a long-standing friend of his deceased mother's. He knew that she liked him for the same reason that everyone warmed to *Tommy Steele* – it was that disarming grin and his impish quiff, just like *Tommy's*. But the English singer could never be his hero. Old bristle-neck on the boat – he had got it completely wrong, thought Teddy, fingering the silver identity bracelet on which he'd had the letters *BF* engraved.

– *Billy Fury*, he murmured softly, I know how much you love him, Verity.

Teddy was laughing now – chuckling to himself as he swilled his coffee, reflecting on the old boy's innocence in such matters. And how far he himself had come since leaving town. Why, once upon a time, he would have run a mile if anyone had suggested he put *Brylcreem* in his hair. Not to mention brazenly sport a bracelet in honour of *Billy Fury*. Whose style of dress he also imitated proudly, with his Cuban-heeled boots and bum-freezer jacket.

Such ambitions on the part of a Cullymore youth would have readily been dismissed not only as impertinent but laughable – once upon a time. But not now, thought Teddy. Musing how likely it was that his mates in Butlin's of Skegness would have been shocked by the revelation that the person now known to himself as *Teddy* had, not all that long ago, once been considered an extremely devout and wholesome Catholic boy. Almost to a fault, indeed – as some of his neighbours had been known to observe. Although, of course, they would have been more than aware of the reasons for it – what with his deceased mother having been one of the holiest women in the town – not once in her life missing morning Mass. Before being struck down with tuberculosis at the age of forty-seven, when Alphonsus had been just eight years old.

It had been cold in the terraced house after that, he remembered. He knew that his father was broken-hearted and desperately lonely. He didn't take to the drink or anything like other bereft fathers might have done. But after her death he appeared to become more or less incapable. He would sit for hours on a Saturday doing the pools. But he never won anything – a fact which he would lament unreasonably, and for extraordinarily protracted periods – staring aggrievedly into space, as though the whole world had resolved to set itself against him. Very few words were ever exchanged between father and son. It could be at times like they'd somehow slipped back in time, as though the house had eerily been submerged beneath an iceberg. And there was nothing they seemed capable of doing about it. It was during this period that he gave himself to prayer and contemplation and began to think that, perhaps, as his teacher had so often suggested, he might, in fact, be amenable to a religious vocation – destined ultimately to become a priest. Knowing he had decided to follow such a path would have made his mother immensely happy, he knew. With the result that, for long hours, he would retire to his room in an attitude of rapture, on the verge of swooning, as he knelt there before so many sacred pictures, with hands parted and eyes raised. Surrounded by his mother's holy books, her beads entwined around his youthful fingers. The idea of self-sacrifice had then held a parlous attraction for him, with his person exuding an aura of the clearest certitude. In his banishment of sinful longings he had begun to perceive himself as the proud possessor of a soul unblemished. No touch of sin would be permitted to linger on his lips.

But that all seemed so long ago now and a new set of commandments attracted his attention. He sat there

smoking in his corner booth. Flexing the winkle-picker toes
of the boots he had purchased in Dean Street in Soho. He
shoved the butt of his cigarette into his pocket and rose to
his feet.

Sinking his hands deep in the pockets of his jeans as he
breasted the air of main street, he thought just how great
it was to be home. Just how fucking great it actually was.
Although it wasn't going to be without difficulties, he
reminded himself. And it wasn't going to be easy for Verity
either – at least not at first. To take in all the changes, everything that had happened since the two of them had last been
together. The thing that worried him most was – where in
God's name was he going to start? There was just so much
to tell her, you see. But the very fact that he was older, so
much more mature and, of course, streetwise – that would
make it all so much easier. It was all well over a year and
a half ago now since he'd seen her. Maybe what was most
amazing was that Verity Foster had ever been interested in
him at all – ever been in the slightest bit bothered about
him. How could she not have been embarrassed by his silly,
inexperienced attitudes – and all that praying he'd done as
a kid!

Jesus, he thought, scooping his metal comb from his
pocket.

It didn't matter, he told himself – all of that was over
now. No, if his eyes dimmed now and his heart was full of
love it was not because of any saint or Sacred Heart. But
because of Verity Foster and her alone, he thought, raking
the comb's teeth through his oily hair – that *goddamn*

lovely lady to whom he was going to tell everything about Skegness, maybe even mention the night that *Tommy Steele* had played in the ballroom. And how he hadn't even bothered to go. Because *Billy Fury* was more his bag. *Billy*, in whose honour he had purchased a certain item.

– *Look!* he thought of himself declaring – lifting up his wrist to *show some silver*.

– *You know what those letters BF stand for, honey?*

As he swept her up in his arms and kissed her, a man at last after all this time. In the streets of a town that now fitted him like a glove, because he had tamed it and it did what he said.

– *Cullymore, I'm home!* he cried out and gave a whistle, seeing Verity Foster looking up in adoration.

20

– Rockall, Hebrides, south-west gale 8 to storm 10, backing southerly, severe gale 9 to violent storm 11. Rain, then squally showers. Moderate, becoming poor.

The sea can be cruel and the sea can be cold but sometimes the sea can be snug and scrumshy: snug as the snuggliest, loveliest glove. Especially if you're fortunate enough to be tucked up in your bed, right in under a nice warm fluffy counterpane, with cotton sheets covering you like a great big tent, far from the thrashing crashing pounding ocean.

Which now accurately described the situation of Patsy Murray the barber and his wife Geraldine as they luxuriated in the soothing tones of the announcer, who might well have been a sagacious and avuncular divinity, surveying affairs from the loftiest of peaks – not entirely unlike myself, I suppose.

– You're listening to the BBC.

Golly tugged the bedclothes up to her neck. The time was now 00.52, as the shipping forecast concluded:

– Atlantic low 991, expected 130 miles west of Rockall, 1,011 by 01.00 tomorrow. Area forecasts for the next 24 hours – Viking variable 3 or 4.

Golly loved the names, and always had – it was as though at last you had attained the longed-for harbour.

– Cromarty, Forth, Tyne, Dogger 2 or 3, veering south-east 4 or 5. Occasionally rough in Cromarty and Dogger at first. Rain later. Moderate or good.

What gratified me most was that she felt so secure, under the care of this kindly deity, one who had her individual welfare at heart. It was the most beautiful sensation, she thought. Just as she realised that her husband was addressing her. Yes, her spouse was enquiring if she wouldn't mind *just a little* adjusting her position. In order that he might manoeuvre the bolster for added comfort. She readily complied and the large bulky pillow was duly adjusted. Patsy smiled and returned to his Littlewoods pools coupon – chewing on the end of his pencil, doing his best to calculate the First Division Football League results.

Without thinking, he frowned and asked his wife did she think that Newcastle would succeed in holding Chelsea to a draw this coming Saturday. Golly smiled, turning a page of her *Woman's Way*. As the generous, mellifluous tones of the wireless receded, she experienced the slightest twinge of neuralgia in her cheek.

– But I don't know anything about football, she said.

Patsy Murray found himself laughing heartily.

– But of course you don't. I got carried away there. I don't know what I was thinking, Golly.

The throbbing pain had already begun to pass, she thought. But the fact was – it hadn't. As she pressed her palm to her cheek, a wave of despondency followed the growing realisation that the neuralgia was not, in fact, waning at all. Her mouth now also felt dry and she began to fear that, like the previous night, she might not be able to get to sleep. She wished she had not read the magazine article – for it was still bothering her. In spite of herself she turned back the page. Its title was *Rome: Three Coins in the Fountain*.

She bit her lip as she read once more: *The eternal city of Rome holds untold riches for the casual tourist and traveller. Once you have visited you will never be the same.*

It was there that the author and her lover had met, by all accounts – there, by the side of the world-famous *Trevi Fountain*. It was here she had been united with the man of her dreams.

Because the article had reminded her of Blossom Foster and Hope Fairleigh-Warburton, Golly's nails were making indentations on the margins. She wished they were not – but those were the facts, that was what her nails were doing. She could hear them whispering softly outside the hotel, and even though she was imagining it it seemed so real. Thank heaven no one could read your mind, she mused regretfully – as the voices drifted into the sealed secret chamber of her soul.

– Poor Geraldine, Blossom was saying, briskly dabbing her cheeks with her compact, did you see the way her eyes lit up? She rarely gets out of the house, poor thing – what with her little boy, the handicapped fellow Boniface. It was good of us, I think, to invite her to our fashion show, Hope.

– Well, what use is our faith if it does not prompt us to do good works, agreed Hope.

Blossom Foster crinkled up her nose and she chuckled heartily through a cloud of compact powder.

– Even if she did go and marry a Catholic!

– Tee hee! laughed Hope – covering her face like a giddy little schoolgirl.

All of a sudden Golly was seized by an impulse to switch off the wireless. Its dreary monotony was becoming infuriating, she told herself. But, in the end, she resisted the temptation. Coughing instead and patting her chest.

– Oh bother, she moaned, as her husband asked:

– What did you say there, dear? I thought I heard you saying something just now.

Patsy had reached the Second Division League tables, with the question uppermost in his mind being: would *Leyton Orient* trump *Huddersfield* this coming Saturday?

But he didn't ask Golly this time – remembering how exasperating she found such questions.

– You and your pools, she responded irksomely. Give me a headache, some of the things you say.

His knee jerked abruptly as his wife moaned again – a smaller cry this time.

– Are you all right, Golly?, he enquired tenderly.

– Yes, pet, she replied – doing her best not to stiffen. Trying to display no hint of anxiety. The BBC pips which had made the world seem so colossal, and yet so paradoxically comforting and manageable because you were all tucked up in bed listening to them – they were gone. Vanished as though they had never been there, and along with them the illusory sense of ease which they had facilitated. Once more the shockingly inhospitable maw of the cosmos yawned. Far across the town, a dog had begun to bark. She knew that dog. It belonged to the schoolteacher, Jude O'Hara. It barked three times more – then all returned to silence. While goose pimples bred on Golly Murray's skin and she averted her eyes from a twinkling patch of stars. Because they made her want to cry, in fact. Placing her magazine on the locker beside the bed, she found herself thrusting her fist against her teeth as a profane but sadly familiar strange thought assailed her.

– *Set fire to me, Patsy,* she heard herself whisper.

I was amused as I watched her – poor little thing, she seemed so *vulnerable.* So susceptible, really, to any suggestion I might have in mind. *Sail Away* was playing on the wireless now, in a universe which, to her, seemed to care only for the majesty of its own creation.

– Goodnight, said Patsy Murray to his wife.

– Goodnight, she replied, bracing herself for a restive sleep, during which she might sense there was someone in the room. A thought which she would never be able to mention to anyone else. They might lock you up. As I stood there – motionless and solitary, sighing by the window.

21

Golly had been especially ill at ease on account of what had happened with Boniface earlier on that day. She had tried stiffening her resolve – but somehow the thoughts – they had kept on coming. Maybe if she hadn't had the misfortune to meet Blossom Foster – she felt sure that was what had started it all. That was the reason she had been impatient with her son.

– And I know I didn't imagine the way she was looking at me. I just know it. *I don't care what anyone says!* she told herself.

For she knew the ways of Blossom Foster well, her raised eyebrows and her subtly slighting smiles. The critical tone of her voice, the way she looked askance at what you had on. She could tell by the brusqueness of the older woman's manner that the fashion show to which she had taken the trouble to invite her might as well have never happened. Her suspicions had been correct.

– I'm really looking forward to meeting all the girls in Dublin – Hope's friends, I mean. One of the buyers from *Switzer's* will be there. We're going to discuss the success of the fashion show, and of course perhaps plan another for next year. I'd really love to invite you, Geraldine, but, as I say, it's all been arranged by Hope and her sister. Anyway, it might be inconvenient for you.

– But I didn't say I wanted to go. I don't mind if I'm invited or not.

– Of course you don't, dear. It's just a little gathering in Hope's house, that's all. Nothing special. Only I've to be in Dublin with Bodley on business. I probably wouldn't even bother going myself. How's Patsy?

– He's very well. He's fine, thanks.

– And business is good?

– Yes. You know Patsy. He keeps things ticking over.

– *Twenty years in business and never once drew blood.* I always thought that was very funny, Geraldine.

– Yes, Blossom. It is.

– I was wondering, would you both maybe come by one evening for a spot of bridge? Do you think your husband might be interested?

– No. Patsy doesn't like bridge.

– O. Never mind. You can come yourself – have you someone to look after the little fellow? I'm sure you have.

– Yes. But why are you asking me that?

– What, dear? I'm only . . .

– That isn't a problem. *It isn't a problem!*

– Honestly! Goodness me, Geraldine, you don't have to *shout* – I heard you, dear!

Then she beamed and took her hand.

– Please will you ask him? It really would be so lovely to have you both!

Then she went off. Calling back, as usual:

– Tattybye! See you soon!

Was it any wonder she was in bad humour, she asked herself. It was just a pity that it hadn't passed when she heard Boniface coming in from school.

– Babbie! Babbie! Ip's me, Bonnie! he had called.

Little Bonnie arriving home with his schoolbag. He was eight years old now and had just gone into third class. He was very bright too, or so she had been told – at any rate for a boy afflicted with *Down's syndrome*. Which, for a lot of mothers, could make things difficult – as she had been reminded, with indecent enthusiasm, by a nurse in the labour ward only minutes after he was born. But of course not for someone like you, Golly, she remembered Blossom Foster insisting. No, all of us mothers have certain resources, her fellow townswoman had sensitively announced. And had smiled when she had said it. But of course she had, thought Golly. After all, Blossom likes smiling. One night she had dreamt that they met again on the street. And she saw Blossom leaning into the pram to tickle his chin – smiling.

– Who's a good little *Catholic* baby? she had heard her say. Who's my good little handicapped fellow?

And Golly had awakened beside her husband, unable to bring herself to tell him about the dream, as she released a small perplexed peal into the night.

She had found herself listening with affection as Boniface skidded across the lino of the shop. Before bursting into the kitchen with a yelp – tossing his schoolbag into the corner as always, calling out:

– Babbie! Babbie! Babbie oo dere!

He wasn't capable of pronouncing *Mammy* properly. It was a pity about his speech – of course it was, as Blossom had remarked on a number of occasions.

– But I'm sure you have the wherewithal to deal with that too, Golly, she had observed. In spite of herself Golly hated it when Boniface did that – called her *Babbie*. It embarrassed her in front of all the other mothers. She wondered had Blossom Foster ever harboured feelings of embarrassment. No – of course she hadn't. And even if she ever had, she could always go off to Italy to forget them.

– We simply can't make up our minds, Golly love, she remembered her saying, we're such sillies, Bodley and I. One minute it's the Alps and the next we're back to the eternal city! So, tell me this, dearie – have yourself and Patsy decided on Bundoran yet?

After dinner, Boniface Murray had eaten his rice.

– Do you like that, Bonnie? his mother asked as she stood over him. Beaming, bright-eyed, from ear to ear, tweaking his little apple cheeks before folding her arms proudly and looking down at him. Her lovely little apple-cheeked boy. He said that he did, he liked it very much, as he spooned great dollops of the dessert down into him. He loved *Ambrosia* out of the tin. She sighed as she watched him, ladling away there with his spoon. Then it was time for his game with the shooter. She assisted him in setting up the cereal box as a target. He liked to do it every day. She stood the *Kellogg's Cornflakes* carton on the table.

– *Whee!* he cried as the pea hit the target, ecstatically clapping his hands as he squealed:

– *Whee-hooey! Fuck!*

Golly's voice had been a model of restraint.

– Please stop saying that, be a good boy now, won't you?

Because she knew the other boys would make fun of him whenever they heard him swearing.

– *Fuck! Fuck! Whee-hooey!* he yelped again.

As the pea went *pop* and down went the target – her son clattering across the floor to retrieve it.

– *Fuck! Whee-hooey! Me-pea!*

– Boniface, now listen. There's a good boy. Boniface, love – do you know you're so good, his mother smiled.

But Boniface, unfortunately, was much too preoccupied with his target practice to listen. And as a result it had seemed like an eternity had passed before Golly found herself standing over her son clutching a silver dinner fork in her hand – seeming to stand outside herself as she heard her voice say:

– It isn't me, Boniface. Someone else is making me do this.

She shivered again and looked down at the utensil. Then she heard:

– *We might have another fashion show next year. Maybe you can come to that one. If you can get a babysitter for . . .*

There were tears in her eyes.

Then, to her horror, she realised what she'd actually done – shoved the prongs of the fork into the boy's arm.

Her boy's astonished face was now the colour of the rice he had been eating. As the sheer enormity of what had just occurred – of the act which his mother had just now perpetrated – began to seep into his slow-witted brain. He looked down towards his arm where she had punctured the soft rubbery flesh with the prongs. It was only a small wound, barely visible really, and if you wanted to, you could have convinced yourself it wasn't really there.

But Boniface Murray didn't feel like doing that – and the more he inspected the red marks the more consumed by recrimination and sorrow did he become. He began to sob convulsively and shiver. Before racing upstairs – beside himself with fear and disappointment.

Set fire to me, Patsy, will you do that for me? thought Golly Murray as she lay there inert beneath the moonlight that night. With the BBC pips long faded away. While her husband snored peacefully, completely oblivious of the pleas of his guilty wife – happily burning there, ever so grateful she was being properly punished for what she had done. As, somewhere beyond the towers of roiling smoke where her cries of remorse continued to go unremarked, she heard a familiar voice calling out:

– *Bodley!*

As two packed suitcases were placed in the *Vauxhall Saloon*, and Blossom Foster was heard crying out, enquiring of her husband had he remembered to bring the coins for the *Trevi Fountain*.

22

Twice a month Una Miniter the priest's housekeeper arranged her appointment in *Monique's Hairdressing*.

Where, once inside, she would invariably find herself treated to the full and undiluted attentions of none other than the proprietress herself. *Monique's* was a very busy salon indeed. Why the constant chatter that proceeded therein might have been likened to a hive of bees buzzing at the very height of summer, fragrant as a grove when the May flowers are in their brightest bloom.

– Monique, the owner's mother had once confided in Una, had always been full of ideas as a child. But to think that one day she would actually open her own business!

– I have to say that the thought never once occurred to me, she told Una. To be honest, I thought they were just whimsy – the daydreams of an ordinary growing girl.

Monique's, however, proved anything but whimsical – as a matter of fact had become so successful that notice of seven days was now deemed necessary in order to secure an appointment. Even someone like Blossom Foster could not afford to take one for granted. Which was just as it should be, the elegant lady herself suggested to Una Miniter, as the assistant attending to Blossom's hair hummed a popular tune by *Tommy Steele*.

– It's only right and proper that, no matter who one is, continued Blossom, there is no such thing as preferential treatment. It is only fair that each individual is treated equally. Even if my husband and I are going to Italy next week – that ought to make no difference.

– I wish I could say I was going there, Blossom, or anywhere like it, sighed Una, for no particular reason settling her downturned palms on her thighs in perfect symmetry.

– O I don't know, mused Blossom, there's an awful lot of organising to be done when it comes to foreign holidays. If it was Bundoran or somewhere local like that it would be different. But it isn't, is it – it's Italy.

Monique passed by in her blue nylon smock and complimented her assistant on the job she was doing. The assistant paused for a moment, hand on hip, giving herself to contemplation with her chin propped on the cradle of her thumb and index finger, before triumphantly declaring:

– Well, honest to goodness, do you hear me, Mrs Foster! I wasn't sure for a minute who it was you reminded me of – but of course now it's clear – who else could it be, only *Grace Kelly* herself!

– We're travelling via London, went on Blossom, we don't normally but we have relatives in Hampstead and it really would be nice to see them.

She moved just a little in the blue padded chair.

– *Yes! I'm coming!* called Monique abruptly, tapping Blossom on the shoulder and excusing herself for *just the teensiest wee second.*

– Make sure and give this woman the kind of treatment
we might reserve for the Queen!

– Indeed and I will, you can be sure now, Monique –
after all, it's not often she comes in here, the royal Princess
of Monaco herself!

– Ha ha! laughed Monique, see you in a jiff!

Was it any wonder, Blossom pondered privately, what with
the way Monique's salon was going, that Ruby's, the rival
hairdresser's across the street, was rumoured to be in a very
bad way indeed.

– Before Monique opened up, she whispered to Una,
Ruby was making a mint, do you know. But now that's not
the way it is at all.

Her face darkened as she continued:

– Now if you go in there, Una, do you know what I'm
going to tell you – you'd be lucky if you found two or three
in it.

– Maybe it's because Monique gets the younger crowd,
Blossom? ventured the priest's housekeeper.

– Well, maybe but of course, between you and me, the
truth is that she actually provides a much better service.
And all these things that Ruby has been saying about her
won't change that.

Mrs Miniter was puzzled.

– Things? she quizzed. What kind of things?

– Well, that all the Catholics have started coming in here.
That they're going out of their way to come to Monique.
That they're making it their business to come and support

their own kind. That's what Ruby's seen saying, Mrs Miniter. That they've stopped coming to her on account of her being a Protestant.

– That's simply not true! insisted Mrs Miniter, rising stiffly in her chair. I don't know how Ruby Johnson can even think of saying such a thing!

– Yes, they never darken the door of my salon now, she says, and it's due to the fact Monique is a Catholic too – one of them. But I have one question to ask you, Una – what difference should that make? I mean – ask yourself – what religion am I? What faith does Mrs Blossom Foster practise? Yes, of course I'm a Methodist – I mean, everyone knows that. But does that influence – and more to the point, should it – any decision I might make regarding my hair? It most certainly does not, Una. There's the answer to your question. For, as you well know, the reason I come here is that one will always go, and is entitled to do so, where one will find the better service. And Miss Ruby Johnson, I'm afraid, will simply have to get used to that fact. I mean business is business. My husband, as you know, is a bank manager of much reputation and standing. And that's the first thing he'll tell you, Una. There is no such thing as loyalty in the world of commerce. So no matter what Ruby, God love her, might think – I'm afraid she'll simply have to learn.

– *Now!* chirped the assistant, good-humouredly returning, humming and bustling as she arrived up to Blossom's chair, with her elegantly manicured hands sunk deep in the pockets of her shiny smock.

– And how is Prince Rainier doing, if I may ask, Princess Grace of the Enniskillen Road?

– Well honestly, sweetheart, you really are a tease! But do you *really* think I look a little like her?

– The dead spit, laughed the assistant, the absolute image!

– Even if I am a Protestant – ha ha!

– But sure no one minds about that in here!

– Of course they don't – in Cullymore *we're all the same! This is a great little community, so it is!*

As they all, almost in ecstasy, joined in with the refrain:

– *In Cullymore we are all the same! This is a great little community, so it is!*

Which even the dourest of individuals would have to find amusing – almost as amusing as the agony of the Son of God himself, an event which was proceeding simultaneously in the band hall, with Barney Corr defending him vehemently, bawling in his robes as the *Tenebrae* rehearsals continued.

– No, no, no, project your voice! shouted the director, irksomely jabbing his cane.

– For Christ's sake, Jude, I am projecting!

– Try it like this: *You come before me and ask me to convict him – but I can find no wrong in him!*

– Naw, but maybe I can find a good bit wrong with someone else! Someone who thinks they're great just because they once acted in *Oklahoma!*

– Ah for heaven's sake, Barney, don't be childish!

– You and the *Imitation of Christ!* What do I care?

– Here, boys! pleaded Dagwood Slowey, temporarily laying down his spear.

132

23

– Listen to me! Will you pay attention?

Happy Carroll made a face and joined the rest of the cast, throwing Barney Corr a filthy look as he did so.

They hadn't been getting on since the start of the scene – in fact the butcher had accused him of not being able to act.

– If you're not going to learn your lines then there isn't any point in you coming along at all, he had snapped.

Patsy Murray had intervened and suggested that maybe *Tenebrae* wasn't worth all this.

– We have to remember that at the end of the day it's only a play, he insisted.

– That's right, called Jude O'Hara, so why don't we try it one more time from the top.

Conleth Foley was in charge of narration, sitting along the wall with his leather folder on his knee. He set the scene beautifully, with the Apostles and Jesus arriving into the moonlit *Garden of Olives*.

– What the fuck are you looking at, Corr! bawled Happy all of a sudden, flushing furiously in the face.

– I can't bloody well work like this! responded the irate butcher, tossing his pages to the floor.

Just as the door swung open and in breezed the parish priest:

– Boys, but am I lucky to have a group of men as dedicated as youse. All I know is, all I can say, is that I have been involved in dramatic productions for a long time, but I never met actors of this calibre. Youse have me like a youngster I'm so excited about this coming Easter!

Father Hand sat down and swung his right leg across his left.

– Very well! he instructed, carry on! Don't mind me!

Jude O'Hara looked at Happy and the butcher.

– Once again then, lads, right from the beginning. That was great – youse are all doing terrific! Are you ready, Conleth?

Conleth Foley flipped a page and cleared his throat, settling the folder on his lap.

– *Above the Garden of Olives, the moon was shining in a dark brooding sky . . . !*

– *Would youse not wait one hour with me?* demanded Patsy Murray, parting his hands in pained imprecation.

The remainder of the rehearsal went off without a hitch. There was a faint glimmer of tears in the priest's eyes.

– *Old Rathwilliam* was nothing to this, he informed them proudly when the scene had concluded, not *The Heroes of Old Rathwilliam*, not *The Lad of Old Ireland*. I'm speechless, Jude – keep up the good work!

Then he told them he had business down at the soccer club and went off, as proud as Punch.

– That just shows you what we can do, beamed Patsy.

– Yes, if people said what they were supposed to say, sulked Happy.

– What the fuck do you mean by that? growled the butcher, his irateness returning with a vengeance.

– Just because you have *two* parts doesn't mean you can make things up and act like you're the star of the show!

– I didn't make anything up! What are you talking about, Carroll, you fool?

– For the love of Christ! snapped Jude – who never swore – how are we ever going to get this done?

– Please, pleaded Patsy, as Conleth shook his head in exasperation.

– Look, suggested Jude, why don't we leave this scene for now and give the crucifixion of Jesus a go. What do you say, men?

– It's all the same to me, said Happy, shrugging his shoulders.

Barney the butcher ascended the stage, clearing his throat as the new scene commenced.

– You ask me to find this man guilty. Well, I am sorry to have to tell youse, I can find nothing wrong with him.

– *No, no, no!* snapped Jude O'Hara, waving his arms in the air again. Happy is right – you're putting in lines of your own again, Barney. What do you mean *I'm sorry to have to tell youse?* That's not in the script!

– To hell with you and your script! bellowed the butcher, throwing off his robe and clambering back down the steps.

– Ah for God's sake, lads – if we don't stop this carry-on the whole bloody thing is going to be a disaster!

– I think the best thing we can do at this present moment is *take five*, suggested the director, as Patsy and Conleth nodded their assent.

By the time Father Hand had returned from the *Soccer Club*, Una Miniter was already in the kitchen, preparing his tea as usual. Everything was as it ought to have been, with the main evening bulletin about to begin.

– *Here is the news, read by Kenneth Kendall.*

In spite of certain tensions at the *Tenebrae* rehearsals, of which Jude O'Hara had only just acquainted him, Father Hand felt reasonably comfortable and relaxed, sitting there in his fireside chair. But he turned alarmingly pale when out of nowhere he heard an ear-splitting cry – exactly like the one Mrs Markey had released that day in the café. He flung himself from his chair and raced into the parlour. To find himself swearing – reproaching himself bitterly as he did so.

– *You fucking cunt, James Reilly!* he wept, *you despicable rascal, to make me do this. You rotten, low-down, no-good scoundrel!*

For, instinctively, he knew, as always, just who was the architect of this *latest affront*. With every single fibre of his being he knew who was responsible. For spoiling the peace of his evening again. He felt *so* vengeful. How ironic, he found himself thinking, that only minutes before, while making his away along the cinder path towards the presbytery, he had been reminiscing fondly on those lovely early years in Rathwilliam College – to the extent of actually humming the school anthem to himself. His spirits having been lifted by the sheer commitment of Jude O'Hara, and, in spite of their minor disagreements, the dedication of all the members of the town *Drama Guild*, and all the members of the Cullymore band of brothers – the old *gang*, which included Barney and good old Happy Carroll, not to mention Patsy Murray and Conleth Foley – one of the finest artists in the county. Yes, in spite of these tiny differences of opinion, which were par for the course in the world of amateur drama, in general they had been making terrific progress and the priest had no doubt whatsoever that their performance of *Tenebrae* was going to be a massive success. As he found himself considering just what *Bing Crosby* might happen to think of that. But he didn't have to because, in actual fact, he knew!

– *It kicks Father Peyton conclusively into a cocked hat!* he heard Bing say, and laughed as he thought of what the Mayo mule would have to say about that.

But how galling it was that, in spite of all this coming glory, he was standing there now, humiliated in the privacy of his own home, being cruelly taunted by his arch-nemesis.

The priest retched violently.

– *Loathsome dog! For that's all you are!*

He became so light-headed that he actually had to grip the ledge of the window.

– *You ought to be in jail, James Reilly!*

Which of course was the truth – for what he had done on the poor innocent Jerome Brolly. Of course, the Junior 3 student had, unquestionably, been good-looking. But that, irrespective of how much it had overwhelmed the weak and dissolute James Reilly, meant nothing at all to Father Hand. No, it would be a long time before the Senior Dean of Discipline at Rathwilliam College would begin spending his valuable time dreaming about boys dressed like film stars, floating around in silver-white gowns with their hair pinned back, flapping their silly black eyelashes at people. The truth being that Father Hand had never much liked Jerome Brolly. Back in those days in 1940, during the war. When the impertinent student had walked around like he owned the place. O it had been a really good trick, what Master Brolly had done, Father Hand recalled. A very good trick indeed, my man. You see, Jerome he had been thinking he was all the big smart fellow in Rathwilliam. All the big clever Dicky from Dublin, what with Daddy being a barrister and everything. Which was why he could look at you – even at a senior dean – in that smart-alec way of his. Even though he was only sixteen years of age. With an expression that seemed to say:

– Excuse me, country bumpkin priest – would you ever be so kind as to get out of my way?

Ah but he hadn't been such a clever Dicky whenever the Dean had succeeded at last in cornering him. O yes, Brolly the smarmy cheek-giver had slipped up there, and finally received what he had richly deserved.

What did you think of that, Jerome Mr Brolly? thought the priest. Not very much, I am sure I can safely say!

Father Hand steadied himself against the table as he stood there trembling in the parlour, wiping the perspiration off his forehead with his sleeve. He hadn't really wanted to recollect the incident at all, but it kept coming back, as though someone or something was encouraging it. And with uncanny clarity. It might have happened just yesterday, he thought. There had been all sorts of rumours after Brolly had visited Father Hand's study. But the only time the priest had found himself genuinely concerned had been when the boy's parents arrived down from Dublin. Thankfully on that occasion the President of the college had shown his true colours – triumphantly supporting Father Hand to the hilt.

– He must have sustained the injuries in a fall, he told the parents. Or on the football field, perhaps.

And that was enough for Jerome Brolly's father – an old Rathwilliam student himself, and a former county footballer in his day. After that, Father Hand was immensely relieved. There would be no more cheek out of the insubordinate Brolly. Who, in collusion with James A. Reilly, had brought opprobrium upon the college. There had always been something about that particular student which Father Hand had *never* warmed to – with his saint-like expression but in behind it just the faintest flicker of mockery. Which he recalled one night from a disturbing dream. When he had awakened to find none other than Jerome Brolly himself – standing in a recess by the bookcase, with a small vaporous cloud, of all things, hovering directly in front of his mouth.

– *Please*, Father Hand heard himself whisper, *please, Jerome or Dorothy – whatever you call yourself – please have mercy on me, a poor priest!*

In the monstrousness of the darkness, thrusting the bedsheet into his mouth.

It was rumoured – by sullen, malcontent souls, the cleric decided – that, after being summoned to the Dean's office that particular night, Jerome Brolly was never the same again. As far as Father Hand was concerned, however, he would gladly and justifiably repeat the punishment.

As he stood there in the parlour viewing the scene before him in his mind's eye.

– *They have no right to criticise me!* he cried out shrilly. *I was Dean of Discipline – and insubordination of that order simply could not be tolerated!*

He smashed his fist into the centre of his palm.

– Damn him! he snapped. Damn the cheeky little bastard to hell!

Then he realised once more exactly where he was and looked up to see Mrs Miniter staring at him aghast. What she had just heard had shocked her to the core. Perhaps even more than the sight which had only just recently compelled her to release the ear-splitting cry he had heard – for the desk's open drawer contained a dead rat.

– Father! she pleaded, please show some restraint! Don't let him make you do the like of that! Don't, I implore you, permit him to inveigle you into doing the devil's work – I just heard you cursing, God help me, Father Hand! It's not right!

But the priest no longer cared.

– James fucking Reilly has gone and done it now! he snapped. Do you hear me, Una! He has definitely gone and done it now! This is definitely *it*, for sure!

He roughly pushed his stricken, astonished house-keeper out of the way and found himself out in the open air, hastening, flush-faced, in the direction of the *Stray Sod Lake*. Where he knew his brazen quarry would already be congratulating himself on his triumph.

– James A. Reilly, you schemer! he bellowed, grinding his teeth as he barrelled on with undaunted purpose. Trying not to think of his housekeeper – vomiting violently in the aftermath of the horrid discovery, plunging her face into her hands – screeching, with her shaking finger pointing in the direction of the open drawer.

– There's a *duh-duh-duh*-dead rat inside there, Father!

Not only that but swarming with maggots.

– You've really topped yourself this time, Reilly! bawled the priest as he braced himself outside the hovel door, squaring his fists in anticipation of his adversary's appearance.

But of James A.Reilly there turned out to be not a sign. Even the leaves on the tree were motionlesss. As the priest cried out:

– Come out here! Come out where I can see you, scoundrel!

The derelict shack was, in fact, entirely empty. But of course it was. It was hardly going to be that easy for the priest. No, one required a little more drama than that. Which was why I arranged it – the little episode which saw a hirsute vulpine snout appearing dramatically from behind some nearby bushes – causing poor Father Hand to cry out pitiably. Because the momentary vision, it really had looked the dead spit of the unfortunate *Funzel*, whose head he had decimated with a rudimentary metal implement.

Entirely defeated, the parish priest set off for home, with his forehead covered in a cold clammy dew. He went into the cleaned-up parlour and poured himself a stiff whisky. Catching a glimpse of his reflection in the mirror above the fireplace, he noticed that his complexion was distressingly pale.

– I wonder should I arrange for a rest cure, he thought, maybe after the performance of *Tenebrae*. Yes, that's what I'll do. Have myself a little time away . . .

As he swigged the whisky, all choked up. Before, to his deep disappointment, he heard the familiar whisper again, clear as a bell.

– Soon you will be with me – in *the Stray Sod Country*.

24

Thankfully, some hours later, the parish priest's apprehensions had diminished significantly, with a healthy rose-red hue returning to his cheeks as he snoozed away in his study, and I conveniently availed of the opportunity to persuade the slumbering post-prandial prelate back to those sweet and innocent times that he treasured most of all – those years of glory when he had ministered so proudly to his boys in Rathwilliam.

Yes, slumped there in his chesterfield, once again he was back in that wartime year of 1940, eighteen years earlier, when a single light burned in the servants' quarters and he made his way across the hushed quadrangle. It amused me to observe that, even in dreams, Father Hand remembered the forbidding intimation he had experienced that night – the feeling that he might, in fact, be the very last man alive on earth. And that the amber rhombus cast across the square was the sole indication of life now remaining in a world entirely consumed by darkness. Such were the thoughts proceeding through his mind as he opened the door of the junior corridor and found himself pacing the echoing hollow building. It seemed so unnatural being alone in Rathwilliam – with the house, unusually, being entirely deserted – all the boys having departed for a match in Armagh.

The docks of London, he had just heard on the wireless, were reported to be ablaze, with bomber aircraft droning menacingly all through the night. Why, thought Father Hand, when the world was in such turmoil, did he persist in permitting these nagging irritations to undermine him so much? He resolved at once, finally, to dismiss them from his mind. And, furthermore, to dwell no longer on the behaviour and attitude of the student known as *Jerome Brolly*.

That the fellow was insubordinate was regrettable, certainly – but not, until recently, to any degree greater than any of the other students. Or so he had assumed. But there had been a marked change in his behaviour since the disgraceful incident with the now dismissed master, James Aloysius Reilly – who, in broad daylight, had actually interfered with him – in Junior 3 class. He lowered his head and rubbed his chin. His chest was tense and he was finding it increasingly difficult to breathe. How could that be? Sometimes, quite recently, he had begun to even wonder if his thoughts were *his own* at all. But all of this, he concluded, was so much nonsense. Then, somewhat relieved by his display of certitude, he found himself returning to his subject once more. Perhaps it was understandable, he considered, that Jerome Brolly might be a little bit snooty – after all, he did come from a wealthy and well-connected Dublin family.

It was a miracle, even, that they had consented to commit their progeny to an ordinary, somewhat undistinguished and parochial minor seminary such as Rathwilliam. Surely Clongowes Wood or one one of the more celebrated Dublin colleges must have beckoned? It did not matter; all that mattered was Brolly's refusal to respect the college rules – cocking a snook at authority whenever he felt the opportunity presented itself. And, of course, what with this recent development, he now had been presented with a glorious opportunity to do just that – thanks to James Aloysius Reilly who, by his actions, had thoroughly compromised the dignity of the college's authority – of Father Hand, of course, and also his staff. Every time he saw Jerome Brolly now, that was the inference he drew from his omnipresent smirk.

– *I was interfered with*, he heard Brolly say, *in front of everybody. What that, in fact, means is that I can now do as I please.*

Another night the priest had had his dream again. The one in which Brolly appeared – attired in a gown of white and brilliant silver, bewilderingly with his hair pinned back. Why, thought the senior dean giddily, he looked for all the world like some kind of *film star*.

– Have you seen any of my pictures, the priest heard him enquire, perhaps you have. I'm *Dorothy McGuire*. And I know that you like me – even if you let on you don't. You all like me – I can see it in your eyes, you big fibbers! Especially you, Senior Dean. You're the biggest fibber of all. You're not as different as you pretend from *Master Reilly*. Well – *are you?*

He had awakened in his bedroom, quivering from head to toe. But that had been a long time ago.

– *That was a long time ago!* he repeated, clenching both of his meaty fists.

As the firelight before him wavered and flickered, as though in a kind of eerie ballet. There in the presbytery, in his Chesterfield chair.

It was inevitable, he remembered, that in the end things should have come to a head. They had been standing in the quadrangle on that afternoon in wartime, on a day in 1940, just before the students were due to go off to the match. Dean Hand had snapped his fingers as he called the student over.

– I see you're wearing a new tie today, Mr Brolly, he began.

And was rewarded yet again with that supercilious, predictable sneer. Which seemed to contain the following sentiments:

– *That is correct, Father Hand – yes, I am. But I'm sure, however, that being from the depths of the country you really wouldn't be familiar with items to be purchased in the finer tailors' of Dublin city.*

– Stand up straight when I am talking to you, do you hear! the Dean had snapped harshly.

Sluggishly, reluctantly, Master Brolly had complied. Now, however, it was Father Hand's turn to smirk.

– There's a very fancy pattern on it, isn't there, Jerome? There's a very fancy pattern on your tie, isn't there?

He had actually smirked himself when he had said it. Master Brolly, however, didn't appear in the least fazed.

– Yes, Father. It's *fleur-de-lis*, he explained condescendingly.

At this, the Dean's eyebrows immediately were raised. A number of the boys close by were laughing openly. But not, however, at Master Brolly.

– Well, *fleur-de-lis*, continued the Dean, that's very nice for you. I'm glad to hear it. But I must say it reminds me of something else – something you might see on a woman's scarf at Mass. What would you have to say to that now?

– Yes, Father. If you say so. If that's what it reminds you of. After all, you're the Senior Dean.

He found himself growing cold – scales of resentment forming on his skin as he stood there towering over the boy, with Jerome Brolly preparing to make his departure. He was so furious that at any moment he was afraid he might curse. His nails were hurting his palm and he could feel the veins throbbing in the back of his neck. He turned and made his way back to class.

– *Come on, fleur-de-lis!* he heard one of Brolly's pals chuckling.

Subtle insubordination – how effective it could be, thought Father Hand. Knowing that, right now, there was nothing he could do. If only there was *something*, he kept on thinking. If only fortune could smile on him, some way help him out . . .

Then he mightn't feel so sickly, so aggrieved, wouldn't be cheated by self-loathing and suppressed rage. But good fortune at that point chose not to intervene.

*   *   *

147

And now here he was, on that dark evening, with the boys all having departed to the match and the college completely emptied, in that wartime blackness of the year 1940, standing in the centre of a grubby tiled corridor with the vastness of the quadrangles sweeping far beyond the windows with it seeming as though there wasn't another soul abroad in the world. He heaved a sigh and interlaced his fingers at the base of his stiffened spine. Before finally taking the decision he had been resentfully mulling over and climbing the stairs in the general direction of the junior dormitory – more specifically to the private cubicle which belonged to Jerome Brolly. And Dean Hand prayed, oh how he prayed, as his heart continued to beat furiously – imploring his Saviour that he might find what he hoped for, hidden out of sight underneath the impertinent pup's bed.

It was well after ten now and the students had all returned. Dean Hand had arranged for Jerome Brolly to be summoned to his quarters immediately after night prayer had concluded. The priest, ever so gently, closed the door of his study behind the boy and smiled at him. Once inside, Jerome Brolly was his usual smug, entirely self-possessed self. However, this was a state of affairs which was not destined to obtain for very much longer.

– I'm sorry to have to call you here Jerome, at this late hour, explained the priest, before adding:

– The game, I hope, was an unqualified success.

– Yes, Father. It was.

– It was good to see the team win, wasn't it? It's always great when Rathwilliam wins.

– Yes, Father.

– Yes it is. I'm glad we agree on that, Jerome.

Father Hand had never felt so good, so flushed with possibility. It was glorious to watch.

A lock of foppish brown hair fell down in front of Jerome Brolly's face. The boy was tall yet slight, with long tapered fingers. So sure of himself, in spite of his pronounced effeminacy, thought the priest – which was something which tended to further enrage him.

– I'm sure you're wondering why I've asked you to come here to my study tonight, Jerome.

– Yes, Father. As a matter of fact I am.

– *Yes, Father, as a matter of fact I am*, mimicked the priest, as he went on:

– But of course you are. That's to be expected, and of course I shall happily tell you.

The boy nodded and placed his hands behind his back, watching as the Senior Dean opened his desk, with no show of triumph at all producing the glossy magazine out from the drawer. This particular periodical supplied the reason that Jerome Brolly was to offer no protest whenever his parents were eventually summoned to Rathwilliam College. His face had turned the shade of parchment when it was produced – in contrast to its lurid, garish cover. Which depicted the figure of a pouting female model, her curvaceous form clad in black lacy lingerie, with the title *GIRLIE GLAMOUR* arched above her wavy golden head. Poor Jerome was crying as Father Hand stood glaring at him. Already the youth could have been in the *Stray Sod Country*, with the unholy gate closed firmly behind him. Adrift and aghast in surroundings once so familiar, the warm and well-lit confines of a priest's study – a priest with whom he had once got along. But who now was rolling up his sleeves with a sense of purpose that was fierce and intent.

They had scarcely been in the room fifteen minutes and already Jerome Brolly was sobbing like a girl. As Dean Hand jabbed him once more in the chest – thrusting repeatedly with the knuckle of his index finger.

– Smirk at me now then, *Mr Fleur-de-lis!*

– Please, choked the boy, whose forelock now was dark and moist. The magazine had been contemptuously discarded, lying forgotten on the desk.

– Get on your knees, said the priest to Jerome Brolly. Who complied without hesitation.

– *Apologise!* demanded Father Hand, with fury blazing in his eyes.

– *I apuh . . . puh-pologise*, stammered the boy.

As his custodian mock-applauded with a pantomime enthusiasm. Before requesting that Jerome Brolly stand upright once more.

– Not quite the dandy now, are we, Jerome? he snickered.

There was mucus and saliva intermingling on the boy's lips – as he fiddled pathetically with his fingers.

– *Nuh-nuh-no, Father Hand.*

– *Nuh-nuh-no, Father Hand,* laughed the Senior Dean, tossing his head back, before sinking his balled fist directly into the pit of the boy's abdomen. Somehow I don't think you'll be bringing magazines into Rathwilliam ever again, will you?

– No, Father, I won't, said the boy as Father Hand violently struck him across the face.

– No, Father, you won't, he laughed, as he jerked his thumb – in the direction of his study door.

– *Get out, Brolly!* he hissed contemptuously. *And don't come back!*

Just at that moment noticing that on the cover of the newspaper lying beside the disgusting magazine which he had thrown on his desk, there was a largish photo of an aeroplane suspended over the blacked-out buildings of London – a Luftwaffe bomber. Flying high above the tracers, droning steadily on through the night.

Much later on, in the small hours of the morning, Father Hand awoke, and discovered that he was crying. It was then that he saw her – his beloved mother, now quite alive. As she crossed the room and came over to comfort him, mopping his brow as she had done so many times, long ago in the past. Stroking his forehead and reassuring him that, no matter what happened, irrespective of whatever terrors or uncertainties might arrive to plague him, she would always be there by his side. Because he had made her proud when he became a priest. The proudest woman in the whole town he had made her. And nobody, not the devil, or James Reilly, or even this boyish insubordinate cur Brolly, would ever come between them and their love.

– *Mammy!* the priest choked, biting his knuckle – as she waved to him from across the room before vanishing into the clear light of dawn.

25

– I wish a frigging atom bomb would fall on that hall, preferably when the whole lot of us are in it!

Patsy Murray felt like giving the whole thing up, he said.

– Don't talk to me about *Tenebrae!* he continued.

Conleth Foley stroked his chin gravely as the two men made their way towards the *Yankee Clipper* after rehearsals.

– What's the use of putting on a play if everyone in it doesn't pull their weight?

– He's a most exasperating man, I grant you that, sighed the artist.

The source of the agitation once again was Happy Carroll – who had already missed three rehearsals, with his ludicrous excuses completely pulling the wool over Jude's eyes.

– I swear to God you just can't believe that man's oath, sighed Patsy as he pushed the pub door open, he'd lie through his teeth to get his way.

The latest, apparently, was that the carpenter had been spreading rumours regarding the parish priest – he'd encountered Father Hand having a *mad fit* in the street, he claimed.

– Right there in front of Mrs Markey's, he had told

everyone, with spittle on his mouth, I swear to God – looking like he'd just seen a ghost.

– Maybe it was the saucy rogue, someone suggested, who's to say His Nibs wasn't behind it?

But by this stage everyone had had more than their share of talk about supernatural forces – particularly now that it had long since been established that Mrs Markey's scream had turned out to have a perfectly rational explanation. Her new *Hotpoint* mixer had simply malfunctioned. That was all there was to it. And it only embarrassed them, discussing that now. Which was why when Happy Carroll arrived into the pub and started the same talk all over again that Patsy Murray decided he couldn't take it any more.

– Ah for Christ's sake, Happy! he had snapped irascibly, you and your fucking blather about Devils. Quit these tired old rumours, will you? They're stupid!

– Well, stupid or not, the carpenter obstinately continued, I know what I seen and there was definitely something wrong with Father Hand. I mean, people don't stand in the middle of the street shaking and talking to themselves unless there is something amiss. Stiff as a fucking board, he was!

– *Shut up!* interrupted the barman, we've had more than our share of that old hearsay and superstition – cut it out now, once and for all!

But Happy Carroll made it clear he was not to be swayed.

– Youse can say what youse like but I know what I seen. Just then Barney Corr arrived in and tackled the carpenter head on about rehearsals.

– If I was Jude O'Hara I'd have kicked you out of the show long ago! he grumbled.

– Aye, well, you're not. You're just a bloody butcher – one who sold me a dud chop not two days ago, if memory serves me right.

– O by Christ, Carroll, but you are one smart-alec cheeky bastard. I'd just as soon have it out with you right here!

– Think you're great because you're playing Pontius Pilate. You weren't so great last Wednesday when he had to ask you to do it four times.

– That's true, maybe I couldn't – but at least I was *there*. Not like you this past couple of weeks – do you think you're Marlon Brando or something?

– Ah go to hell, you big fat tub!

– Here, come on now! intervened Conleth Foley. There's no need for that. Let me get the two of youse a drink!

But Happy had already returned to the unpopular subject of Father Hand's purported *fit*.

– Yes. If I didn't know I'd say he was definitely possessed, he portentously repeated.

– That is definitely the last fucking straw! roared the butcher, at his wits' end. If someone doesn't make this fellow shut up, I'll drag him out to the street and kick some sense into him myself! We're all in here for a quiet drink, and nothing more!

– You can't blame a man for telling the truth, countered Happy.

– You wouldn't know the truth if it hit you with a hammer – and well everybody in this town knows it, Happy Carroll!

The carpenter returned an infuriating smile. As Barney Corr clenched his fists in his pocket.

What is most amusing about that particular incident is that, for once in his humble self-serving life, Happy Carroll had actually been telling the truth. The parish priest had, in fact, experienced something approaching a seizure – and in broad daylight, in the street, as the carpenter had insisted. I had arranged for his departed mother to whisper softly into his ear:

– *Where is Augustus, my lovely Augustus? I am lying on my deathbed and my beloved son is not here to hold my hand.*

He had been choking like a child, in fact, trembling helplessly as he thought of her, and how he had missed her death in the hospital – just by a whisker, something which he had regretted all of his life. Poor thing – in its quiet devastation, the incident wreaked as much havoc as had the bombers long ago in 1940 over London. But then, I suppose, isn't that always the way – poor Father Hand, just about making it home to the presbytery, exhausted by emotion and irresolution, standing there dumbstruck as though on the very shores of eternity itself.

The men had all gathered in the soccer field for the evening match – among them Patsy, Conleth, Jude O'Hara, Dagwood Slowey and Happy Carroll. The referee's whistle had only just announced the commencement of the second half when they all looked up to see Father Hand making his way across the turf in his flapping soutane. And, contrary to what Happy Carroll had been saying, looking not at all like someone who had experienced any kind of debilitating inner crisis.

– Ah would you look at him there – breezing along and not a bother on him, laughed Patsy, didn't I know damned well!

– I hope you're listening to that now, Happy! laughed Jude O'Hara, rocking back and forth on his heels, puffing away merrily on his curling briar.

– Ah would youse ever fuck off! chirped Happy.

Everyone was in great humour now.

Then Conleth Foley jabbed the air excitedly, cupping his hand over his mouth as he called:

– Leather it into the square there, lads! Bury it, do you hear me? Boys, but that young lad's playing a fucking stormer! Oops, didn't see you there, Father Hand!

– Don't mind me! laughed the clergyman, arriving up, rubbing his hands as he joined the men enthusiastically. He had to concur with the consensus, he declared, adding that he had always felt young McCormack had it in him.

– Would you look at him there! yelped the priest suddenly, as the young fellow struck the ball vehemently with the toe of his boot, sending it just a fraction wide.

– *Wow!* cried Patsy Murray, shaking his head in exasperation, if that had gone in . . . !

– We were home and dry, we'd have been absolutely home and dry! sighed Happy Carroll.

There was no talk at all now about the supernatural. All that nonsense had, thankfully, been forgotten. Which pleased me no end, I really have to say. Convenient.

– This could be dangerous! shrieked Patsy Murray agonisingly – covering his face with his hands as he did so.

– Sweet Mother of Jesus! groaned Dagwood Slowey. And dangerous indeed it was seen to prove – but just for a few brief moments.

As the small knot of supporters heaved a collective sigh of relief. Patsy Murray tugged the collar of his donkey jacket. Just as out of nowhere they heard a familiar cry – and saw Barney Corr coming running across the turf – looking like he was on the verge of a cardiac arrest.

– *Stop the game! Stop the game, do youse hear me!* he bawled.

– For the love of Christ will youse stop the fucking game! he pleaded, grabbing the clergyman roughly by the arm.

– Don't youse understand? I've just heard! *Duncan Edwards* is going to die!

The young Manchester United player was worshipped in the town. He had been lying in a hospital bed ever since the Munich crash.

The mood in the pub that evening was so bleak that it reminded Jude O'Hara of '47, he claimed, the year which had seen the worst winter ever recorded, when the farmers had lost all their crops, when the country had finally gone bankrupt, it was avowed. It was difficult to believe just what was happening – grown men openly sobbing. It had been bad enough, they choked, to lose seven players.

But now, to have it confirmed that *Duncan Edwards* had, in fact, now joined all the others. What had happened was simply unthinkable.

– He was just twenty-one, murmured Patsy, choking.

– Just twenty-one, echoed Conleth Foley, sipping his stout, staring dazedly out the frosted window.

– All gone, choked Happy Carroll, *Colman, Taylor, Byrne* . . . and now young *Duncan*.

Such was the depth of the community's grief that no one had even noticed James Reilly coming in – sitting alone over by the window. Or overheard what he'd casually remarked to the bleary-eyed drunk beside him, releasing the words as though rationing them out – in what seemed a narcotic haze.

– I used to be called Master Reilly, you know. But not any longer. I'm not in charge of my own mind any more. Someone else has taken on that responsibility. But I've been given a special assignment. That of murdering Father Hand.

– That's good. I'm glad to hear that, mumbled the drunk, sluggishly fingering a pattern of coins on to the table. I'll make sure and come and visit you in the nuthouse.

James A. Reilly didn't bother to reply. As he stared straight ahead of him, meticulously preparing the events of the following day. All of which had come to him in a dream – which, initially, had featured not the murder of a mere dog. But that, in fact, of Blanaid Miniter, the niece of its owner. *Precious little lamb*, I had whispered in James's ear as he had tossed and turned that night in the loneliness of his hovel.

– Goodnight, said James, drifting vaguely out the door.

– *Umph!* replied the drunk.

There wasn't so much as a sound in the bar.

26

The dog's death was a dry run, really – a kind of rehearsal, to prepare James for Father Hand. It had always been Mrs Miniter's custom to take *Toby* for a walk in the mornings – to go as far as her brother's where, as always, her sweet niece Blanaid, aged ten, would be waiting to swamp the little Jack Russell in affection. The young girl simply loved to see them coming, and to bring them out the back to her lovely apple orchard. This was where it had been decided to do the deed. Mused James A. Reilly as he oiled the casing of his civil-war *Lee Enfield* – the so-called antique that had belonged to his father.

– You'd be proud of me, Daddy, he found himself smiling – laughing giddily, in the routine ecstatic manner of the psychiatrically troubled. It was really the death of Funzel which had finished him off in this regard – discovering the poor animal as he had that day – upon his return from Enniskillen. Thus did our quaint little melodrama effectively begin, our miniature earth-shaking *Sarajevo* entitled perhaps *The Lonely Death of Toby*. But before we go into the details of that, let us return to the presbytery and the redoubtable Mrs Miniter herself – who, having recovered somewhat from the disovery of the maggoty rat, was admitting two men who declared that they wished to see her employer on some business – with quite an interesting proposal, as it turned out.

– Do you know what, Mrs Miniter, I still have that awful throbbing in my head, the parish priest had been saying when the doorbell rang.

To which his housekeeper, rather curtly, had replied:

– Well, Father, I'm sorry, but I have absolutely no sympathy for you. Didn't I tell you two or three spoonfuls of *Veno's* was enough? That's a very strong cough mixture, you know.

– I know it is, Una, agreed the priest, it certainly is – for I was up half the night – wasn't myself at all. But I think the fever might be clearing at last.

As he repaired to the parlour to meet his two visitors. Hoping the effect of the *Veno's* would soon wear off. He had not wanted to think about *Peyton*. A wave of crimson flooded his cheeks, induced by a combination of shame and deep resentment. That familiar *chuckle* – that unctuous *sneer*. What was *Mr Showbiz* talking about now, he found himself wondering, in that stupid, put-on American accent of his. Why, announcing that none other than *Pat Boone* was coming to play in *Madison Square Garden*.

– Obviously, Father Hand, he heard the Mayo donkey bragging, if *Mr Boone* does agree to appear then what we shall be looking at is an increase of massive proportions in demand. The only thing that would worry me then would be – is *Madison Square Garden* capable of holding all our potential punters?

Then Father Hand remembered that in actual fact he was standing with his friends in the presbytery parlour, with the schoolteacher Jude O'Hara and the artist Conleth Foley looking over at him fondly.

It was 3 p.m. on the parlour clock. Father Hand nodded as Jude O'Hara smiled.

– Very well, Father, the schoolteacher said, that's more or less it. A commemorative *Duncan Edwards* service is what we have in mind – a special Mass to pay our respects to one of football's true legends.

Father Hand proclaimed himself delighted by their proposal. The grogginess had passed. He briskly paced the floor of the room.

– Whatever money we make, we can send it over to the *Manchester United Supporters' Association*. They, in turn, will pass it on to the unfortunate dependants. Lord, when I think of it, those poor young lives – now all lost!

– The most dreadful tragedy in football history. I can't get their young faces out of my mind.

Conleth Foley snapped the clip of his leather briefcase shut, releasing a small moan as Jude O'Hara sighed and wrung his hands:

– Liam Whelan, his poor life cut short – Tommy Taylor – God rest him.

– And not forgetting Roger Byrne.

Father Hand nodded balefully as he reached in the deep folds of his soutane, producing his rosary as he began, automatically, to ply the beads. Already both visitors had fallen instinctively to their knees. The priest was doing his best not to think about those who were doing their best to blight his life – not only James Reilly but Patrick Peyton as well.

– *Thou O Lord wilt open my lips!* he intoned, as his visitors responded eagerly:

– *And my tongue shall announce thy praise!*

– The *Flower of Manchester* we shall call our memorial! declared the priest, punching the air in a moment of quite extraordinary *Veno's*-fuelled enthusiasm.

Conleth Foley's enormous banner appeared the following week, proudly strung across the main street of the town: DUNCAN EDWARDS: THE FLOWER OF MANCHESTER.

Which, as it happened, was first admired by Happy Carroll, in the early hours of Sunday morning, on his way to a scheduled assignation in the car park behind the cinema. Knowing, of course, that if this tryst with the authorities were ever to be revealed, his reputation and, more than likely, his life would be forfeit.

– I understand you have information for us, said the policeman, emerging out of the shadows, regarding an impending raid on a certain police barracks.

Happy Carroll was agitated, for he appreciated perfectly the gravity of what he was doing. But he couldn't help it. He needed the money, he had lost a lot lately on the dogs. And, anyway, he persuaded himself, Manus Hoare and those idiots would probably never get around to bombing anywhere. After all, they were just kids, he thought. So he took his payment and scuttled off home – admiring as he went past the *Flower of Manchester* banner, rippling a little in the gentle breeze.

27

It had been Barney Corr's idea to order the mock-coffin, which Happy had knocked up in no time at all and Una Miniter had asked the nuns to decorate it with black crêpe. It looked winningly appropriate and solemn, resting on trestles in the church centre aisle.

The building was filled to capacity for the service. *Poor Duncan Edwards* was all you could hear as the congregation respectfully lowered their heads. Father Hand appeared before the altar, ascending the steps as he parted his hands, assuming his customary position in the pulpit. The silence became total as he patiently cleared his throat.

– There were forty-four people on that aeroplane. Twenty-three of them perished. Out of those individuals, out of that dreadful number, seven, we thought, had been players with Manchester United, a team much loved in this little town we call Cullymore. But now, regrettably, and it breaks my heart to have to utter these words today, we are forced to add to that heartbreaking roll-call the name of another deceased – that, my dear people, of *Duncan Edwards* – the *Flower of Manchester*.

The parish priest thumbed a tear from his eye. It seemed an age before he was capable of continuing. A child in the front row began to sniffle helplessly.

– Since 1952, ladies and gentlemen, *Duncan Edwards* made no less than one hundred and seventy-five appearances for Manchester United. Between the years 1955 and '57 he won no less than eighteen caps for his country.

Standing by the coffin in their black armbands, Patsy Murray and all the *old gang* didn't so much as move a muscle, staring straight ahead. The hoarse echo reverberated in the vaulted vastness, echoing with fragile majesty.

– It must be emphasised here today, my dear people, the priest went on, that these men will never truly, never *really* die. For all of them are martyrs for Manchester United and also for a game that they loved. He lowered his head.

– Yes, all of these men – all eight of them now including *Duncan*, born in Dudley on October the 1st 1936, and who, throughout his short life, professed his pride at being an ambassador for his hometown wherever his football career took him – are martyrs of a true and special kind. Busby's Babes – Cullymore deeply loved them, thought of them as their own. So now I would ask you to join me in a final decade of the rosary as the soul of *Duncan Edwards* makes its final ascent towards heaven, to play for ever in the Old Trafford of the sky.

He nodded at Jude O'Hara and the director of the forthcoming Easter play inhaled deeply.

– *Duncan Edwards!* he called out, dangerously close to weeping.

– If you please, said the priest, making a fluid conductor's gesture. As his flock replied in unison, in tones cracked with grief but nonetheless powerful:

– *Duncan Edwards!* they responded.

As the litany then proceeded.

– *Roger Byrne!* read Jude, gripping the sides of the lectern tightly.

– *Roger Byrne!*

– *Geoff Bent!*

– *Geoff Bent!* they boomed.

Jude's eyes glittered sadly as the memorials, at last, concluded.

In the aftermath of the service Father Hand felt himself prouder than on any occasion he could remember throughout the course of his adult life. Even the altar boys noticed his good humour, nudging each other as they watched him go past. With not so much as a single thought about Father Patrick Peyton on his mind.

– That great big clodhopping Mayo fool! he chuckled to himself. Who's going to be worried about the likes of him, the ridiculous little Mayo ass.

Why, as he heartily rubbed his massive hands together, he professed himself delighted that, solely by his efforts and achievements, he had routed the braggart wholeheartedly from his mind. Which was how it seemed at the time. As clear and uncomplicated as his housekeeper announcing she was bringing her little dog *Toby* for a walk. I mean who in their right mind would want to murder a poor old Jack Russell? But then everyone, of course, was not in their right mind.

28

Golly Murray was making her way home from the dentist and was in considerable pain, so Blossom Foster's voice was just about the last thing she wanted to hear. But there it was. Her heart began sinking.

– Yoo hoo, sweetie! Yoo hoo – it's me!, Golly heard.

Already Blossom was crossing the street, accompanied by her companion, Hope Fairleigh-Warburton.

– What a wonderful banner! Doesn't it look magnificent, Mrs Murray? *Duncan Edwards* – the *Flower of Manchester!* Well done, Father Hand! A very good organiser – isn't he? All the same it's sad, in the circumstances – isn't it? That dreadful plane crash! My goodness me!

– Yes, replied Golly, it really was the most appalling tragedy, Blossom. Quite shocking, but one must accept it, I suppose. Imploring privately that the violent shudder which she had just experienced, stimulated by a deep embarrassment at her own reactions, had gone unnoticed. In the normal course of events, as she well knew, she would never have behaved in such a stiff and unnecessarily formal manner. But she realised now that she was, in fact, blushing fiercely, thinking of how ludicrous her choice of words actually was. *Appalling* was one of them, and *one* was another

– how unconvincing they sounded emanating from her lips. But what was even worse was the fact that she had been using them in the hope of impressing Blossom Foster and her swanky colleague.

– I really and truly do think it's admirable, organising a service such as that, smiled Blossom, continuing:

– I'd have gone along myself, of course, if I could. Protestant or Catholic – it makes no difference when it's something like this. But I was unavoidably detained, I'm afraid. But Golly dearest, now that I have you – Hope was just saying how she couldn't get over the fashion show. And she's only just got some good news herself!

Hope Fairleigh-Warburton explained that she had recently been appointed to the position of senior fashion buyer with a select London department store.

– *Harvey Nichols*, but of course you know it, continued Blossom eagerly.

Golly said that no she didn't, looking away.

As Blossom went on:

– There is simply no one she doesn't know.

– In the world of fashion anyway – ha ha, explained Hope good-humouredly.

– Why that's really wonderful! Golly found herself suddenly ejaculating, once again stung by her quite un-necessary display of eagerness. She had even, she was shocked to realise, begun to imitate Blossom's mannerisms.

– We're having a little cake sale, said Blossom.

– Is it for a cause? Golly found herself enquiring, shrilly.

– Yes, confirmed Blossom, it's for the Sally Army. Indeed it was the *Salvation Army* ladies who suggested it in the first place.

There was a deep throbbing pain at the back of Golly's throat. As Blossom coughed and politely suggested:

– But I'm sure that wouldn't matter much – or would it?

– In what way? asked Golly uncertainly.

– You wouldn't mind that, yourself and Patsy – it being for the Sally Army, I mean. As it isn't a Catholic organisation. Would it really matter? Of course it wouldn't! If a person wants to leave their own faith and accept the decrees of the Catholic religion, then that entirely is their own business, and ought to be. But maybe you'd be too busy with your son?

– With my *son*? replied Golly – quite taken aback.

– Yes. Little Boniface, I mean. He's adorable, Hope. What age is he now, seven? Or is it eight?

– Eight, stammered Golly, he was eight last birthday.

– But that of course is not for me to say. Maybe you *would* have the time to get involved. And it really would be great if you could. I'm sure in another way it would be useful to you – if Boniface was proving, in whatever way, to be *difficult*.

– *He's not difficult!* snapped Golly. *He isn't difficult!*

– No, I know he's not difficult, interjected Blossom hastily, but what with you being married to Patsy – what's this they call it, this *Ne temere* decree – where the children by law have got to be brought up Catholic, would that in any way tend to make things complicated? From Patsy's point

170

of view, of course. For *we* most certainly wouldn't mind. As I say – we'd be glad of the help! What do you think, dear? Do you think I'm making too much of it perhaps? Do you think you might like to take part in some way? *Hmmph?*

Golly could feel those brown eyes piercing sharp as needles. But, summoning whatever meagre resources remained at her disposal, she decided she could not permit this state of affairs to proceed any further.

– Why on earth would anyone stop me taking part in a cake sale if that was what I wanted to do? How on earth could I let such a thing happen? Please tell me, Blossom!

Blossom gently placed her suede-gloved hand on Golly's forearm, visibly experiencing a small tremor of pleasure.

– Listen to you, Golly – *raising your voice in public!* Not that I mind, of course, Mrs Murray – you're just showing your enthusiasm, that's all!

– Stop calling me Mrs Murray – my name is Geraldine! Stop calling me Mrs Murray!

– Why of course, Golly – I didn't know you minded! Yes, Geraldine – by all means, of course.

Somewhat sullenly, Golly found herself capitulating. She felt that her adversary had trumped her again. Which she had – her cheeks once again were burning painfully.

– It really will be the greatest little event. Oops! Little bit of a spot on your glove there, I see! Here – let me! Hope darling . . .

Hope Fairleigh-Warburton produced a handkerchief, vigorously rubbing the back of Golly's hand.

– There we are – now clean once more! Spotless, yes, Blossom?

– Clean gloves, the hallmark of a lady!

Golly's lips were taut and dry – she looked away as Blossom gripped her hand. Leaning in forward so that both their cheeks were almost touching.

– So what's the verdict – what does Geraldine think? Do you think you might be able to come along? After all, you did so well to make it to our last little outing! And you looked so nice – didn't she look well, Hope?

– I've said it once and I say it again. She looked ever so splendid at our little show.

– Why she might have been *Audrey Hepburn* herself! beamed Blossom.

Golly gasped.

– *Audrey Hepburn*? she heard herself choke, returning repeatedly to the spot which Hope had cleaned. It felt like a wound.

– Yes! chirped Blossom, *Audrey Hepburn* in *Roman Holiday!*

– I'd like to come, replied Golly, realising that she had again dropped her eyes, but you're right. There's always Boniface to consider.

Blossom nodded and plied her elegant seed-pearl bracelet. As she sighed:

– I understand, yes. Yes, but of course I do. Well, if you do decide to come, Hope and I will be delighted to have you. I'll send you an invite just as soon as they are printed, dear! But promise me, Mrs Murray – you genuinely will try?

– Yes, choked Golly, I promise that I'll do my best.

– You do that, dear. O, I'm so excited myself – I really am. You must think me such a silly – do you, Golly?

Golly replied that no she didn't. Without warning, suddenly asking:

– Do you still want me to help sew some dresses?

Blossom looked at Hope but Hope turned away.

– No, explained Blossom, we haven't really had the orders we expected, I'm afraid.

Then she gathered up her handbag and, with something of a luxurious shiver, said:

– Well, we must be going – hopefully now, you'll be in a position to come along. And help us swell the coffers of our glorious protestant Sally Army! Protestant, do you hear me – I'm such a kidder!

Golly's eyes were salty and stinging, as Blossom took her companion's arm.

– *Ta ra!* called Hope Fairleigh-Warburton, turning to blow a farewell kiss.

There were a few men talking and smoking by the lamp post and for the briefest of moments Golly became convinced they were talking about her. Perplexingly, the lips of one of them somehow seemed to form the word *Golliwog*.

She decided they could see that her face was still burning crimson – they had probably even noticed her obsessively rubbing at her glove. As the pain in the back of her neck began to worsen – her resentment so fierce now she could scarcely contain it.

Audrey Hepburn! she swallowed, perspiring, as she thought of Blossom, bafflingly attired in a figure-hugging

173

black jersey and with brass hoop earrings dangling from her ears. But with her head stock-still as she lay across the steering wheel, a tendril of blood trickling from her ear. Golly could not believe she had just thought such a thing, but the fact was – she had.

She had.

29

It was getting on towards 1 a.m. on the night of the fabulously successful *Flower of Manchester Memorial* and now, preparing himself for a well-earned rest, Father Hand was pleased that his earlier good humour showed no sign of abating. He had never been in such good form, he thought – positively exhilarated, in fact, pulling on his striped pyjama bottoms, knotting the waist cord and fastening up the loose-fitting cotton jacket. Not even bothering to look at what the scoundrel James Reilly had gone and left on the parlour table this time. A cartridge clip for a .303, if you don't mind. Along with a stupid note which the priest had torn up immediately: *THE TIME IS APPROACHING, FATHER HAND, GET READY.*

– He's an even bigger simpleton than I took him for, laughed the priest, but the hopeless fool will have a long wait if he thinks the like of that will intimidate me!

All attempts at reconciliation were now at an end – there would be no further pretence. But what continued to infuriate the priest was the fact that he had not yet been taken into custody. What was the civic guard playing at, for heaven's sake?

– So be it, if that's the way he wants it, the clergyman decided, smiling to himself as his head touched the pillow, resolving to visit the police station in the morning. With any luck, that ought to conclude the matter once and for all. As sleep finally came to him, he released a snort of absolute glee.

– Ha ha, he laughed – as if someone of my reputation is going to be cowed by a fool who lives in a filthy hovel! Someone like me who showed Father Peyton where to go! No, you've done your damnedest, James A. Reilly – and it has all come to nothing. My Manchester martyrs have seen to that. So bye bye James Reilly – and that clodhopping mule from County Mayo too!

30

There was a sheepskin hanging over the back of the chair as Ralph Foster smoothed back a strand of his girlfriend's hair.

– *Entering you is the only heaven I know, or want to know,* he said, gazing longingly into Imelda Hoare's eyes.

The first time she had heard him speaking in that way, Imelda had feared she might die of embarrassment. Never in a million years had she ever heard such sentiments – certainly not addressed to her.

But over time she had become accustomed to the policeman's spontaneous romantic utterances – learned to even expect them. She was mad, absolutely mad about Ralph Foster. Or *mental* as the girls in the office would often say when talking about fellas.

She had never encountered anyone like him in her life. And it wasn't just because he was the owner of a bike – a gleaming silver MV 350 cc, which as he had told her was the same machine that *John Surtees* rode. Not that it mattered to her – for she didn't even know who *John Surtees* was, or that he had finished second to *McIntyre* in the 1957 Isle of Man TT races. And neither was it because he was a Protestant, from a well-to-do Methodist family who lived in *Dunroamin* on the Enniskillen Road. If there could be said to be one overriding reason, she often thought when dreaming of his face, it was because he hadn't so much as a single trace of shame in his make-up. Which was something which made her feel privileged – free and, at times, almost exultant. For the simple reason that all her life she had been surrounded by shame – suffocated by it. There appeared to be people around every corner who were waiting for you to arrive in order that they might present you with valid, persuasive reasons as to why you ought to be ashamed of yourself. Of your clothes and your body and your family and your religion.

Imelda, just like the returned emigrant Fonsey *Teddy* O'Neill, had been born and reared in a humble two-up, two-down terraced house. But she wasn't ashamed of it. Even if all her life she'd been listening to stories as to why she ought to be. Sometimes, on her lunch break, she would drift into a daydream and make a decision that what she wanted to do most was rename, once and for all, the little town where she had been born. It wouldn't be called Cullymore any longer, she decided – *Town of Shame* was what it would be rechristened.

Once, when they were in bed, she had informed Sergeant Ralph Foster of her private, mischievous proposal – and how he had laughed.

– Boy, do I love you, girl from *Town of Shame*! he had chortled.

It wasn't anyone's fault, of course. That Cullymore was drenched in self-reproach and humiliation. No, of course it wasn't. It wasn't as if her mother and father woke up every single morning God sent and availed of the opportunity to announce to themselves:

– Today we will make sure to remind our children of the lowly station which it has been their misfortune to inherit in life and to remind them that they should never forget as they grow into their late-teenage and early-adult years that they must, in every way open to them, demonstrate their innate self-loathing – plodding about with their heads hung low, apprehending their person as if afflicted by a faintly offensive aroma.

Nonetheless, that was how they perceived themselves – in common with a great many people from the town of Cullymore.

A place to which she now only rarely returned. Not tending to bother since her father had passed away and her ailing mother been removed to the county home. Having, regrettably, in recent times, begun to *dote*.

It had had a bad effect on Imelda's younger brother, Manus – and she was often, later, to associate this development with the beginnings of a certain personal waywardness. And his tendency of late to associate with what she thought of as a *bad crowd*.

Manus, now being the sole resident of the family home, would often try and persuade her to come back to the old place. But she would never consent, preferring the anonymity and social life of the city.

Imelda Hoare dearly hoped that Ralph Foster would one day become her husband. She loved his warm soft body and big arms – but not those alone. She admired the aura of self-assurance and authority which he exuded. And his wisdom too – which seemed in excess of what might reasonably have been expected from a man of his years. For Ralph Foster was as yet only twenty-five. He felt so sturdy, so self-contained. As if, already, he had seen it all.

Even when she confided in him her anxieties as regards the recent behaviour of her nineteen-year-old brother, he had displayed a degree of sympathy which had left her speechless. After all, as she well knew, being a member of the *Royal Ulster Constabulary*, the much-despised Northern Ireland police force, he would have been perfectly entitled to exhibit resentment – to even show bitterness towards Manus and his dangerous, would-be political cronies, as he described them. He knew only too well that Imelda had long since suspected her brother of being associated with members of the *Irish Republican Army*.

Who, once again, and only recently, had pledged to renew their efforts to smash the illegal frontier that divided their country – once and for all putting an end to British interference in Irish affairs.

– After Mammy went into the home, she said to Ralph, laying her head on his shoulder and shivering a little, he started running around with ne'er-do-wells. There are times when it gives me the willies even thinking about what he might be getting up to.

There were times too when she'd look up at Ralph and kiss his face.

– *Enter me*, she'd say – to her own astonishment – as his oak-like arm slid around her waist.

– *Enter me, Ralph.*

Words she never dreamed would ever pass her lips.

She could barely hear him as he dimmed the light – but felt the comforting squeeze of his hands on her lower back.

– He'll grow out of it, honey, she heard him say, make no mistake about that. Sooner or later, as always happens, he will lose interest. This *Operation Harvest* is just a lot of hot air – the *IRA* simply don't have the manpower. As a matter of fact, I don't even think they have the will. It'll all blow over in a couple of weeks.

– I hope so, Ralph. Ralph, will you always love me? He didn't even have to bother to make a reply. She knew he would. She was secure in that. And it made her happier than she'd even been before in her life.

Imelda worked in the Dublin civil service, employed as a copy typist in the *Department of Education*. Before moving into her somewhat dingy flat, located in the Dolphin's Barn area to the south of the city, she had resided in a girls' hostel run by the *St Louis* nuns. As she had told Ralph, she loathed them profoundly – calling them *bitches, the devil's witches.*

– Bitches, Ralph, she said, witches who have horns.

– Dear me, laughed Ralph, you're getting as bad as my own dad now, becoming a little bigot. When my old man and Albert Craig, when the two of those old rascals get together, they're liable to come out with statements the same as that. They have this thing about Catholics – but I only laugh. O a right pair of old-fashioned bigots they are, especially whenever they have a drink. Don't, now, be getting as bad as them!

Imelda stiffened but smiled as she pinched his cheek.

– It's nothing to do with bigotry, Ralph – how can I help it if those dried-up old biddies have nothing to do but interfere in people's business. Inventing more reasons for us all to feel shame.

– I wonder what they'd say if they saw the two of us here, honeybun.

– O I know what they'd do and I know the reasons why. Mad for it, Ralph, mad for it, so they are – and that's what has them the way they are! Kiss me, Foster – kiss me hard! I want them to hear me squealing when you're doing it!

– Here I come, sister – it's time for you to get ready!

– Glory be to God, have them Protestants got no shame?

– It's Sergeant Ralph Foster coming in to land!

Ralph Foster visited the flat without fail every fortnight and his MV motorcycle attracted a great deal of attention as it stood there, gleaming away – stately and imposing in the driveway of the crumbling Georgian mansion. As indeed did the framed photograph which stood in a position of prominence on her mantelpiece – showing fair-haired Ralph for all the world like some gauleiter in leather, proudly elevating his TT trophy in black shiny gauntlets.

Sometimes, when sitting at her typewriter, or clutching her morning cuppa in her hand, the enormity of the word which she had lately begun to enjoy so much simply uttering would, once again, begin to form on her lips and she would experience a tremor of illicit delight. As she wondered did any of her work colleagues ever privately whisper to themselves the word *enter*.

It was hard to believe that, once upon a time, and not so very long ago, she would have been revolted by such a thought – by ever daring to give voice to such a blasphemy. Not now, however. Those days belonged to a vanished time – the days of shame that had all but disappeared. In these new days Ralph Foster could *enter* her any time he wanted. Whatever he so wished, Ralph Foster could do that, smiled Imelda Hoare. He could do what he liked. He could take her to the *Charcoal Grill* above the *Carlton Cinema*, for example. For a meal, or to the pictures, or maybe, if she asked him, to the teatime dances. Or, who knew, perhaps a stroll in the evening by the canal. Would she like to go to *Jammet's* restaurant? he had recently asked her. But isn't that expensive, Ralph, she had gasped. As his blue and twinkling Protestant eyes had shimmered, as he took her hand, folding it effortlessly and neatly into his own.

– That doesn't matter, not a whit, my dear lady. Not for my special copper-haired queen. Why just the other night, she thought, what had he done – he had gone and surprised her completely again. By buying her a present of a nightdress, of all things. Now what man in Cullymore would ever have had the courage to go do something like that? Every one of the boys would have keeled over and died of shame rather than dream of doing such a thing. And yet now here he was – Ralph Foster, ever so sensitively slipping his hand underneath that very same nightie, before magically and powerfully sliding his body inside hers. Banishing as he did so whatever might have remained of the Cullymore shame – its last vestiges dissipating as they moaned. And, writhing underneath him, Imelda saw the sky above Dublin City change colour – turning rose, in fact. Flush, the colour of roses, she saw it change to, pressing her tongue firmly into Ralph Foster's ear. As he pushed back a hair strand and whispered the words she loved – with a glow of love radiating from his countenance:

– *Entering you – it's like entering heaven.*

– *I want you to enter me and stay there for ever.*

31

It was a pity, Golly Murray had always thought, that her son Boniface hadn't been allowed to make his *First Communion* just because he had thrown a tantrum in front of all the others. As a result of which he had to be kept back and sent down to the senior infants where everyone else was much younger than him. When Golly explained to the sister concerned that she had already gone to the expense of buying him an expensive new white shirt and tie, she found herself informed that nothing could be done. That those were the rules, and like anyone else she would have to abide by the school's regulations.

One of the activities which the infants particularly liked was playing with *marla* – the Gaelic name for plasticine. There was a special corner where all the plasticine was kept in a box. This was called the *marla box*. Or, in the Gaelic language: AN BOSCA MARLA. Sister Dominicus had printed the title with marker – on a white piece of rectangular card.

Each day at two o' clock the children were allowed to play with the *marla*. In the comfortable surroundings of their spick and span infants' classroom. Which Sister Dominicus insisted on keeping spotlessly clean. There were lots of lovely pictures on the walls. There was *The Postman* – or

Fear An Phoist, as he was called in Irish. Most of the infants could manage the Gaelic pronunciation but unfortunately it presented enormous difficulties for Boniface. He really could not seem to get his tongue around it. Just kept fluffing and stuttering until finally Sister Dominicus decided she had no choice but to give up. Not that the boy was severely handicapped or anything – she wouldn't say that. He was just a bit slower than any of the others. Which was what she had told his mother.

– It's good for him to spend time with the infants, she had explained, away from the rougher boys in third class. It does him good – and you can see that he likes it. He especially loves getting to play with his *marla*.

On the wall opposite *The Postman, The Farmer – An Feirmeoir* – stood proud and red-cheeked beside his trusty plough. And, right there beside him, the most important person of all – *The Priest*. Or *An Sagart*.

When the nun had asked poor Boniface to pronounce it one day, he had gone and made a show of himself trying to say it. With saliva clotting his mouth as he went all red. Lots of the infants had laughed.

– I'm afraid he has a few problems with the Irish, Sister Dominicus had quietly informed his mother. Before adding:

– But the *marla*, yes – he definitely loves that.

Yes, *marla* was one thing Boniface Murray loved. He really and truly loved being allowed to play with *marla*. There were so many things you could make with it, you see. There were people first of all. O what fun he had making those people. Rolling up little coloured balls to make their roundy heads.

And when that was done some more *marla* to make their bodies. After that it was legs and arms and feet and hands – pink and blue and green and red. But like most of his classmates, Boniface didn't stop there. It wasn't simply his intention to fashion just ordinary old *marla people*. Anybody could do that. No, there were lots of things you could make with this gloriously pliable modelling dough. Birds' nests, for instance. There were times when Boniface actually considered that he might like making those more than anything – even more than *marla people*.

What he really liked to make to go along with the nests was a little stacked pyramid of birds' eggs. And then *marla cows*. With a little fence around the herd as they all stood proudly leaning across the bars. Gazing fondly up at their creator – Boniface Murray, the eight-year-old son of Patsy and Golly – or *Golliwog* as some of her neighbours rather unkindly called her. On account of her blonde corkscrew hair, of course.

One day Boniface made a basket just like his mother's. It was an ordinary shopping basket the very same as the one she carried up the street. And, having just finished it, he found himself having a magnificent brainwave. Yes, Boniface Murray found himself struck by a really and truly brilliant idea. He would put them all into one basket – his great big pile of different-coloured eggs. It was a great idea – the best idea ever, he thought. Or so it had seemed.

But now it didn't appear that way at all. No, sadly it didn't seem like that – because all the eggs were ruined – smashed into a pulp. Yes, all of them were completely beyond recognition.

More than anything he had experienced in his short life of eight years, this development greatly upset Boniface Murray. Mainly because he had enjoyed the experience so much. Making all the plasticine eggs first of all, and then pretending to go up the town shopping with the basket. And now this had happened.

See what it looks like now, he thought. It looks like a pile of rubbish, that's what.

In his simple-minded way the boy struggled to understand.

As he stood there, bewildered, in the middle of the kitchen, playing with his fingers – aimlessly wiping them on the flowery curtain. In the process casting hostile glances in the direction of his mother. Who was standing there facing him, ramrod-stiff. Obviously still feeling immense shame over what she had just done. Already a number of faltering attempts at mitigation had been summarily rejected.

Golly was at a loss as to know what to do. Beneath her son's nose there were a number of different-sized bubbles of mucus – throbbing with an independent life of their own. One of them, thought Golly, seemed bigger than the others. Almost the size of one of the eggs, in fact. Of the little purple one she was holding in her hand. Which was resting there in front of her, in the hollow of her right hand – just about the size of the average marrowfat pea.

The effects of Golly's dentist's anaesthetic were only beginning to wear off, and she found herself in an extremely vulnerable state. The last thing she wanted was to think about Blossom Foster – or Hope Fairleigh-Warburton who had cleaned a spot off her glove. But still she kept thinking about them.

– *The hallmark of a lady, I always say!*

She pressed her hand against her flushed, swollen cheek. It was still very painful. She hoped Albert Craig had not made a mess of it. Maybe if he hadn't spent so much time jabbering, she thought, gossiping away about James A. Reilly – with the latest news being that the tramp had, apparently, broken into the presbytery and left a note.

– But, of course, the dentist had continued, he's far too cute to go leaving any evidence. Not so much as a finger-print, I'm told. Father Hand is like a weasel. Apparently along with the note he left a cartridge clip. And although I shouldn't say it, Golly – do you know what was written on the bit of paper, Mrs Murray?

– No, she had replied – although she really didn't care – all she wanted was to get away. The dentist paused before switching off the drill.

– *The time is approaching, Father Hand.* That's what it said. Now did you ever hear the like of that? What is Cullymore coming to at all, Mrs Murray? As much as to say the priest is going to die!

Why did she have to meet them again, Blossom and Hope – on her way home from the dentist's, for heaven's sake – when the difficulties with Boniface were still fresh in her mind. He had been playing up again in singing class – had developed, as he often did, a fixation with one of the tunes. Which, as Sister Dominicus, in no uncertain terms, had informed her, he had persisted in singing all the way through Catechism class. The tune in question, the good sister had explained, was *The Clapping Song*.

– This type of thing tends to affect discipline, you see, the nun explained, as sympathetically as she could, I mean what I am saying is if I allow him to sing away, just let him ramble on with it any old time he chooses, then the others, being infants, are bound to do the same. What I'm saying is, little Boniface must learn that, the very same as the others in the class, he must keep quiet when he is told. That is, if he is to be allowed to continue coming down to us in infants.

And now here she was, back standing in her kitchen, cupping a tiny ball of plasticine in her hand. Cowed in a corner with a stupid piece of *marla*, having lost the trust of her now wary and suspicious son. As he stood there, trembling, staring out into the empty street, fiddling nervously with the floral curtain. Why couldn't he have behaved just like the others?

– *Why!* she demanded tearfully. If only he hadn't taken a fancy to the stupid song. That ridiculous *Clapping Song* of all things.

– *Twee dick nine goose dwank wine monkey chew bacco on stweetcar line!* he had kept singing, according to Sister Dominicus – clapping his hands and laughing, in spite of her repeated pleas not to do so.

In the end it was perhaps inevitable that Golly would find herself demanding of her son:

— Why can't you even make the plasticine eggs properly? Why do they always have to be so stupid and shapeless? Will you for the love of Christ stop making a show of me once and for all, Bonnie!

Those were the words which had tumbled from Golly's lips – just before the unfortunate catastrophe. Before, worn out with emotion, the exhausted woman had swept the plasticine basket out of her son's hand, and with a ferocity set about destroying all of its contents. The extent of her own furious passions had utterly bewildered Golly Murray. And it was an incident which was destined to haunt her for the rest of her days and would contribute considerably to the development of a condition her doctor later classified as *clinical anxiety*.

But all of that was yet to come – as she stood there staring at her quite heartbroken and confused child. Wondering as she did so what it might be like – to be like *Laika* out there in space, snug in a bucket out amongst the stars. With the years going by until the inevitable happened, that everyone who'd ever known you would eventually stop even mentioning your name, retaining only the faintest memories of how you had once seemed – of your eyes, your face, the sound of your voice. Would you be free then, she wondered, glassily staring at the *marla-pea* reposing in her hand – for all the world like a tiny little planet.

32

Teddy O'Neill, having been absent from his hometown for over a year and a half, obviously could not have been aware of the touching, heart-warming inscription which had been carved on a certain gatepost one afternoon when two young people happened to be taking a walk in the country. No, Teddy was to know nothing of the rubric *Austin loves Verity* which had been fastidiously whittled into the wood by a respectable and ambitious young gentleman whose acquaintance the returned eighteen-year-old had yet to make – *Austin Fry*, in other words, the fiancé of Verity Foster – who was employed as a clerk in the Northern Ireland Office and was engaged to be married within one year to his attractive and beloved lady. He had just completed the carved dedication with a flourish before turning to beam:

– You're the picture of *Eva Marie Saint*, Verity, I swear you might as well be her twin! he told her, beaming, folding the penknife and replacing it in his pocket. And it was an assertion that would have been difficult to refute, for it did most definitely appear as if the star and current toast of Hollywood, the leading lady from *On the Waterfront*, no less, was indeed walking the byroads of the Cullymore countryside – smiling at her boyfriend in her raised sunglasses, bemusedly turning a dog daisy in her hand. Yes, that was exactly what Verity Foster was doing, sweet, smart Verity, diligent student of Queen's University who looked every inch the double of the gorgeous star. She even knew who had written the script, something which Austin hadn't a clue about.

– *Budd Schulberg*, she informed her boyfriend as they strolled hand in hand along a line of beech trees. Austin had been impressed but also a little embarrassed – persuading himself that she knew it only because it had probably come up on her course in Belfast – where, of course, she was now studying arts.

– You have it all with you, he laughed as he squeezed her hand, before posing, to his own amazement, the question:

– Would you mind very much if I kissed you, Verity?

– Of course not, silly. You can kiss me all you like.

There could be no mistaking Austin Fry's shyness – he had not been with many girlfriends before – as he lowered his head, then lifted it again to kiss her on the lips. With his features assuming something of a pained expression, which Verity, in fact, found not at all unattractive, laying her hands on the lapels of his jacket, and with her happy eyes twinkling as she whispered:

– You're the loveliest fellow! Do you know that, Austin?

– Now our names are on that gatepost for ever, he told her – considering himself one of the luckiest men in the world. Ever since his good fortune in meeting Verity Foster.

*   *   *

What Teddy O'Neill, the former barman and trainee redcoat in *Butlin's of Skegness*, who knew absolutely nothing about two names entwined on a wooden gatepost, would like to do now more than anything, he told himself, as he waited by the *Stray Sod Lake* for his old friend and mentor James A. Reilly, was to head off into town with him and have a good few drinks – tell him all about his experiences across the water. But he had been waiting for an hour and there was still no sign. He decided to take another look. He pushed open the door of the corrugated-iron hovel and sat there reading an ancient newspaper from one of the bales. ALLIED PUSH CONTINUES, he read. He would have liked to watch some telly, but it was one with a slot so you needed to have coins – and he hadn't any. He looked all around him in the earthy, musty hovel and wondered how anyone could live in such conditions – much less someone he knew and respected, such as James, the once deeply-respected teacher from Rathwilliam. There were classical volumes scattered all about – *Horace* and *Livy* seemed to be there in abundance – and assorted periodicals of all kinds. The small television was the only concession to modern living – a present, he knew, from a still-loyal sister. The rest of his family had long since abandoned him, Teddy was aware. It was common knowledge. To keep himself busy he decided to light a fire – shoving wood in the grate as it blew out great gusts of choking, acrid smoke.

But he didn't mind – all he cared about was seeing James again. Or *Dorothy McGuire*, as Manus and some of the boys unkindly called him. What would make a man do the like of that – kiss a student, he wondered – but then, of course, as James had explained at length, around that time he hadn't been *himself* at all. With his mother unwell – dying, in fact, in the county hospital. There had been recurrent rumours, however, to the effect that he had gone *off his head* long before the much talked-about event in the classroom. Had actually been seen wearing lipstick at the pictures one night – at a showing of *The Spiral Staircase*.

Teddy was really enjoying the fire now – basking luxuriously in its warm orange glow. It wouldn't be long now before James arrived home – from Enniskillen or wherever he was. Boy, it was going to be great. They would have themselves the father and mother of a chat. A great old chat and some yarns about old times – and all the experiences from Skegness and London.

He smiled as he leaned back, cradling his arms behind his head before lighting up a *Woodie* and lifting up a book he found lying close to hand. It was a collection of the odes of the Roman poet *Horace*, opening on to a page with a sentence underlined. Teddy remembered it instantly – James was always quoting it.

Odi profanum vulgus et arceo – I shun and keep removed the uninitiate crowd. I require silence. I am the Muses' priest and sing for virgins and boys songs never heard before.

He knew well what Manus and the boys would have to say about that – not that it bothered him. He had met plenty of *funny boys* over in England, he reflected – and in fact it had made him feel kind of worldly – cosmopolitan. A little bit above, perhaps, some of his colleagues. Old-fashioned fellows like Manus Hoare, for example – who tended towards the unimaginative and, to Teddy's questing mind, grimly orthodox. An ungiving creed which self-righteously convicted James A. Reilly of his crimes – and declared that he ought to be kicked out of town. For, as far as Manus was concerned, there was nothing more to James's condition but that of being a *completely mental whore*.

It had been no more than he deserved to get dismissed from *Rathwilliam College*, pronounced Manus, Imelda Hoare's brother. Casually adding that it wouldn't cost him a thought to go out this minute and give the fellow what he richly deserved – a damned good thumping. It was Teddy, in fact, who had succeeded in dissuading Manus. Insisting that he had been visiting the man for months and that, in all the time he had known him, he had never once approached him – not in *that* way. But Manus had remained sullen and resentful.

– *Tabharfaidh me cic ins na magairli do*, he would say, that's what he needs.

A good kick in the balls would soon sort him out was how this particular piece of Gaelic translated.

– That's what he deserves, Fonsey – nothing more and nothing less, *Dorothy McGuire* – disgraceful scut.

Through various letters, after he had gone to England, Teddy had learnt how Manus had become involved with a certain kind of people, members of the *Irish Republican Army* by all accounts, which had recently been activated in the area. Teddy had already mentioned it but Manus had completely dismissed his objections.

– What would you know? You've been in England too long. You don't understand. There's trouble coming in this country, Fonsey. And I intend to play my part. It's up to the younger men like you and me now – our generation will once and for all finish it.

He'd gone on for ages then talking about James Connolly – the 1916 revolutionary leader who'd been executed while strapped to a chair. But, whether he knew it or not, Manus Hoare had been wasting his time – for Teddy hadn't been listening to a word he said. Because he'd been too busy thinking about the Mass which they had just attended with Father Hand. Being a different man now, and having met so many people in London – men like Hubert Considine and all his friends, some of whom were avowed atheists and saw no shame at all in saying so – he would have preferred not to bother going anywhere near the stupid church at all. But his father would have been shocked or hurt or both so he decided, for the sake of peace and harmony, to comply with what was expected of him in a small town such as Cullymore. It wasn't that difficult for him, anyway, just to trot along with Manus Hoare – who, of course, as was routine with committed Republican types, was a devout churchgoer and devotee of the Virgin Mary – and, in the process, share with the lads some of his adventures in London and Skegness. Manus, in turn, revealed some of his own more recent activities – ever since becoming involved.

– I go to the training camp, it's in this place down in Wicklow – men from all over the country go there. We're learning Irish and we sing Irish songs. We're going to mount an attack on a police barracks. But don't you ever breathe a word of that, Fonsey. It's important.

Much of it went over Teddy's head. What he did find very amusing, he told himself, however, was this extraordinary new-found espousal of religion. Why, scarcely over a year before, Manus had displayed no more interest in the subject than Teddy himself. Now he was given to making absurd and unnecessary declarations of faith – with the same unswerving conviction he seemed to display in everything.

– I just know it was Reilly who turned you into a pagan, Fonsey O'Neill. I remember you going to Mass and you were holier than anyone else. You were as religious as anybody in the town. And now look at you.

Teddy couldn't deny it. What Manus said was a simple statement of fact. His father had often even boasted of his son's singularity in this regard.

– He's not like some of these other lads that you see. He even locks himself away – reading from prayer books and holy magazines, for hours.

And it was true. As a matter of fact, so true that, in a way, he would often wander about the town in a dream. That's what Verity used to find so amusing – whenever they took their strolls by the lake.

– It's essential to my well-being, being a regular communicant, he had actually, quite seriously, remarked to her on one occasion.

– I must attend to my prayers and meditations.

In an attitude of mesmerised rapture he would present his Protestant girlfriend with a flower – a primrose, perhaps, or one of the cowslips that blossomed along the *Stray Sod* shore.

There could be no doubt at all that it was this preoccupied, self-absorbed attitude which had led to Teddy's being bullied at school. In the rough-and-tumble atmosphere of an establishment which catered for over two hundred brash country fellows, his attention to what he considered his *good offices* was roundly derided. And this was where James Reilly had stepped in. Teddy had begun visiting him – dropping by to see him any chance he got. Until, gradually, James Reilly had become the boy's trusted friend and confidant.

– They just don't appreciate your sensitive nature, pay them no attention and they'll soon lose interest. Scorn the uninitiate crowd, despise them and soon you'll see. I was a teacher long enough myself to know what they are like.

Which, in fact, was what had actually happened. His coarse detractors – aware of the shadow of protection which the Classics master had pledged – they soon migrated to pastures new. But Teddy never forgot the kindness, and the attention James had paid when he had no one to turn to.

And here he was, a grown man now, thought Teddy, as he stretched himself out beneath the smoke-stained low ceiling with its single light bulb and creosoted rafters, with the warm glow of the hearth providing the cosiest coat of comfort which he now tugged tightly and wrapped around him, pondering casually just how it might have come to this – how James Aloysius Reilly, a once respected, indeed much admired academic, had permitted himself to descend into such a state – residing in what Manus had described as a *Godforsaken pit.*

Not that it mattered to Teddy what Manus said – not about James. For, in a curious kind of way, the former teacher had always seemed a kind of outsider to Teddy, a sort of Bohemian figure whose breadth of learning had already placed him outside the fold, and which entitled him to look down on the likes of Manus Hoare and his relatively unlettered associates. Which was the way that Teddy himself had begun to see them – looking down derisively on their somewhat backward opinions, especially now with his *year and a half* behind him. Some of his pals held views he'd have expected from someone such as the old-fashioned Father Hand, perhaps. In other words someone who had never been outside Ireland in his life. He remembered the same Father Hand taking advantage of his position in order to disparage the name of James A. Reilly. Had recently been present in the congregation when the priest had encouraged his parishioners to treat the teacher as they might an outcast.

– As far as I'm concerned, we have already given the fellow far too many chances. But not this time – it has gone too far. I *know* it was him who broke into the presbytery. Not only that but left a threatening note. The police insist I must have more proof. But I know it was him – I know it was Reilly, who has already brought more than his share of disgrace upon our town! Well, I won't allow it to happen, do you hear? I will cast him out as an agent of perfidy! For that's what he is, do you hear me – the very accomplice of evil itself . . .

Although he had been actually present at the service, standing alongside Manus Hoare, the significance of that statement had been completely lost on Teddy O'Neill, for he did not credit such primitive fantasies – considering the possibility, indeed, that if the clergyman were to come out with such things in England he might well be viewed as something of an eccentric himself. But there was another reason too that he had paid little attention – that reason being the fact that he happened to be at the time entertaining a certain little indulgent fancy of his own. One that went by the name of *Foster – Verity Foster*, to be precise. Whose face he found himself now dwelling on once more – as he lay back in the glow of the firelight, with his hands cradled behind his head. Until three soft taps interrupted his thoughts – ever so discreetly. Who could that possibly be? he wondered.

— *James!* he cried out, leaping dramatically to his feet. Throwing the door open, only to discover nothing but the faintest stirring of the leaves. Which, put plainly, quite amazed him – for he had definitely heard the sound of tapping.

Somewhat shaken by this occurrence, the youth drifted down to the water's edge – he thought perhaps James was hiding – and that it had been him who'd knocked on the door, perhaps. But he found no trace of his old friend. He began experiencing an uncomfortable prescience of ill. And could not seem to rout these new misgivings.

– *I hope I'm not going to end up like my old pal Hubert!* he cried.

He remembered Hubert's stories about the *Stray Sod Country*. But did his best to dismiss such thoughts. Emphasising how illogical the whole thing sounded. It had been Hubert Considine who had first acquainted him of the very existence of such superstitions.

– A lot of silly old folk-tale nonsense, really, his mentor had insisted – albeit somewhat unconvincingly.

Hubert had been the first he had ever heard using the word *depression*.

– That's where it came from, if you ask me. There's no such thing as the *Stray Sod*, Alphie – or any place called the *Stray Sod Country*. It's just a way they discovered, I guess, of explaining things. Frightening emotions. Things like depression, or extreme loneliness. Sometimes in life, when a crisis comes along, you can find yourself overwhelmed by what were once quite manageable surroundings – familiar and comforting. Then you find that the faces you once knew are, ever so slowly, growing different, becoming strange. And you begin to wonder did you *ever* belong – the familiar has turned, and become unfamiliar. And you know that you're alone – there's no one can help you.

Though he had always liked Hubert very much, it unsettled Teddy whenever he heard him talk like that. He wished he wouldn't. It was Hubert who'd set him up in London – who had pulled some strings in order to get him the job in Skegness. Hubert Considine had been genuinely street-wise, in a way that Teddy could only dream of becoming. But for Hubert he would probably still be pacing the streets of London, grimly clutching his *Evening Mail* in search of work and accommodation.

It had been great to be able to share his rooms in Hackney, for there wasn't a spot in the city he didn't know. It was Hubert who had brought him to the *Colony Rooms* first, and after that to the famous *Nimbus* nightclub, also in Soho.

Hubert Considine was an accountant and was employed by a Holborn insurance agency. How he got away with his behaviour Teddy would never know. But he suspected it was because he was simply efficient and really good at his job. Or was at least whenever he decided to show his face. Sometimes he would lie in his bed for days – whenever the *black dog* took him, as he explained.

Then he would lie there, heavily medicated, often as not inebriated with whisky.

– I'm sorry, he would say, with his hand falling limp.

Whenever he was like that, the conversation could tend towards the illogical and disjointed.

Once, Teddy recalled, as he sat there now by the leaden lake, with his skin puffy and pale from the tablets, Hubert had looked at him and, with no trace of identifiable feeling, had murmured:

– I think I've arrived in the *Stray Sod Country*, young O'Neill.

– *But you said there was no such thing!* Teddy, in his innocence, had vehemently remonstrated.

203

Hubert had often spoken of a strain within the Considine family. Of a close relative on his father's side, with a name similar to his own. Who had arrived home to his cabin one day, to split his spouse's head open with a shovel. He'd showed Teddy a drawing – he looked like Hubert's twin.

It was a story that Teddy did not like to hear. The hairs on his neck rose erect when he heard it. But Hubert would persist in that curiously indifferent voice – as though it belonged to someone else, not him.

– Maybe to the *Fetch*, he had once suggested.

But Teddy didn't know who the *Fetch* was – and, in any case, had already had more than his share of superstitions.

– Maybe that's who'll escort me to the *Stray Sod Country*, lead me towards that anonymous shore, sighed Hubert – with a tear shining in his eye.

As he waited for James by the lake's still waters, such were the thoughts which absorbed young Teddy O'Neill, and try as he might he could not dismiss them – fidgeting agitatedly. He was thinking about the night they had gone to the *Nimbus* – one of those times when there wasn't a trace of the *black dog* about Hubert. Boy, was there anyone to beat him whenever his old pal was like that? There was only one answer to that and it was *no*. There simply was no one in London who could match Hubert when he was untroubled, as far from the *Stray Sod Country* as you could get. Teddy felt proud – simply to have known him.

Because, unlike so many of his countrymen, not only was Hubert not ashamed to say he was from the little, unremarkable town of Cullymore but could actually, whenever he wanted to, positively enthral people with his extraordinary tales from the countryside of Ireland – people who included colleagues such as ordinary English working folk, not to mention any number of Caribbeans and Asians. Everyone he knew and laboured with, in fact. Delighting them with stories of *characters* – numbering among them the redoubtable Father Hand.

– I swear to God, my friends, he really does think he's Mr Showbiz come to Cullymore. He genuinely thinks he's the *Larry Parnes* of Ireland. Why, if you were to give him half a chance he'd be over here in a flash scouring the *Two I's* and all the other West End hangouts. He'd have *Marty Wilde* and *Billy Fury* flown over on his private jet! To do the rock-a-hula and say the rosary in Cullymore! Yes, in our little town we got the king of skiffle and rock and roll, right, young Alphie?

At nights himself and Teddy would laugh themselves sick about *Father Hand* and all his antics – not to mention all the other characters who lived in the town – *Dagwood* from the snooker hall, *Patsy* the barber, *Barney Corr* and all the rest – each one more colourful than the next.

– Not forgetting *Jude O'Hara*, star of *Oklahoma* and the town's answer to Cecil B. De Mille!

But all of this was nothing compared to the recent establishment of the *Blue Army of Our Lady*, a militant branch of the *Legion of Mary*, which Father Hand had founded as a response to the disturbing upsurge in violence along the border – during the course of which a number of customs huts had been burned. But of which the *Virgin Mary* already had the measure.

– *They think, these young bucks,* Hubert would continue in a note-perfect imitation of the effervescent priest, *they think that they can convert England and make her see the error of her ways. Make her see sense by loosing off a couple of popguns, planting bombs under bridges and torching huts. No, no, no and ten times no, I say! For the conversion of pagan England will only come about when we light our lamp of persuasion – when Cullymore town becomes as a beacon upon the border! A beacon that will burn brighter than any other throughout this decade of the glorious 1950s! With no assistance whatsoever from Frank Sinatra or Lucille Ball!*

– Lucille Ball? someone would choke unexpectedly, bewildered, leading Hubert then into the story of Patrick Peyton, and the continuing rivalry that existed between the two men.

– *Solely in Father Hand's befuddled head,* of course! Hubert then would laugh uproariously.

Lying back in the keel of the small wooden dinghy, Teddy did his best not to think about the knocks that he'd heard on the hovel door – three soft, gentle and discreet taps. The light had already begun to fail. There was a waterhen hooting and a blue moon had begun to form – hanging, it seemed, with almost perfect balance and stillness between the velvet tips of two tall bullrushes. Conferring on the scene the aspect of some dimly remembered childhood fairy tale. As a result, as Teddy's eyes began to close, he experienced the most comforting sensation of well-being. He made a pillow for his head, succumbing to the patient and vivid procession of images, a treasure trove from childhood's memory – during the course of which he saw himself once more on the grassy slopes of the railway cuttings, visible from the lake, in the centre of which his small vessel now reposed. He was sure that James would be along at any moment.

As his mind recast the world, just as it had done in those youthful days of yore when Teddy O'Neill, at his kitchen table, would apply himself diligently to his scholarly labours – constructing a place of inner peace, entirely from the elements provided by his colouring book.

A world just like this one, thought Teddy as he stretched again in the little bobbing craft, a small pink trail of cloud drifting languorously past the treetops.

He dispensed with the remains of his cigarette, thinking that, of all the times he had spent with Hubert, the period he most valued was the very first weekend he had come to visit him in Skegness. There had been lots of *skirt*, as Hubert called it, in the camp – girls employed as barmaids and skivvies. There had been a North of England *doll* that Teddy'd liked. But, try as he might, he could not seem to give her what she wanted.

– I know you like me, but how *much* do you like me? she had repeatedly asked him.

As they lay there, smoking, in the small hours in the quiet of the chalet. In the end she took up with some fellow – from Tyneside, same as herself.

He would often see them around the place afterwards, maybe jiving together in the ballroom, or having a lager perhaps in the bar. He was glad about that – for now he could think properly about the person he really:

– *Loved*, was the word he now whispered to himself. For now he could think about Verity without guilt. Verity Foster, the girl he had never stopped loving.

In a matter of a few short months to become an adult – a *proper* adult, Teddy thought. Having become more mature – slower to anger, much more reasoned. Something for which he was now immensely grateful. For having become so much more aware of his own potential, dispensed with the inadequacies which before he had accepted as his lot, he no longer thought he wasn't good enough for the likes of Verity Foster. And had once again started carrying her picture in his wallet. No longer worrying about any troubles they might have had – that was all in the past, there were no obstacles now. No obstacle which could not be overcome, that is. He felt really terrific about himself these days, he reflected – because of the way that things had turned out.

Three weeks after parting from the North of England doll, he had made an irrevocable decision. The only one he could possibly make. After a year had elapsed he would return home and ask Verity Foster would she agree to become engaged. Which he was absolutely now convinced she would. After all – Alphonsus O'Neill, he was a completely different man.

He lay there there imagining her face when he at last approached her. The moment he had dreamed of which would soon be at hand.

– I was thinking, Verity, that maybe you and me, we should get hitched.

He promised himself that he would display no small hint, not even the slightest *sign* of arrogance. So what if he'd been to England? he told himself, blowing a curl of smoke as he grinned, so effing *what*?

And did it really make all that much difference that he'd been to the *Nimbus* and met *Billy Fury*?

Nope.

And the hell with it, big deal if he'd been to the *Two I's*. It did not matter – all that mattered was her and him. But he shivered again as he thought of the soft gentle taps on the door – and wished they hadn't happened. The way they made him feel – it was just like on that Sunday afternoon when Hubert Considine had failed to appear in Skegness. Sending not so much as a note or a letter. He shivered uncomfortably as he recalled it now. In the height of that summer he remembered himself as he stood there, trembling – just like now. The cold at that time – quite inexplicably it had been *unbearable*. He could have sworn he had heard someone whispering his name from a corner of the room. But it had just been the drink – that and an overactive imagination, he decided.

He didn't want, in any case, to dwell on those days. They were history, all of them. He reached in his pocket and took out his wallet, pressing the photo of Verity to his cheek. Then – his heart leaped – he heard his name being called from the shore. It was James Reilly – waving his arms wildly.

– Hello there, old friend! *Mirabile visu – Alphonsus O'Neill!*

James A. fried some sausages on the *Primus*. Then the two of them sat down to watch telly. This was a great old turn-up for the books, thought Teddy, spearing his banger.

– We're just in time for *Take Your* Pick, laughed James, with his narrow shoulders heaving as he added:

– I never miss it, young O'Neill. It takes my mind off things, you see. Here he is now – yes, it's *Take Your Pick* with your host Michael Miles!

The ample compère descended the steps, smiling broadly in his shiny plaid suit. James Reilly grinned and produced two battered tin mugs. Then, without warning, the TV screen went blank. James Reilly erupted, furiously flinging the mugs away. Teddy O'Neill was alarmed – more than alarmed. For he had never seen James like this before.

– *Now do you see what's gone and fucking happened!* he bawled hoarsely, in tears. Now what the fuck are we supposed to do? Where are you, you bastard you, Michael Miles! Are you listening, Alphonsus – give me a shilling! A shilling, quick, or Miles – he's gone for ever!

Teddy shook his head.

– I don't have one, Master Reilly – not with me, I mean.

His friend's face twisted up in rage, to such an extent that Teddy became extremely wary. There was something terrifyingly unpredictable about this behaviour.

– O but, Miles, you are the stupid bastard! Now I've no option but to fix it myself!

Reilly fell to his knees and disappeared in behind the set, stabbing dangerously at the back with a screwdriver. Then, without warning, the picture reappeared.

– I'm sure you're wondering how I did that! announced James – beaming as he rose to his feet.

– How *did* you do it? asked Teddy, aghast.

– O I didn't do it. It wasn't me – it was *him*!

– Who? asked Teddy, entirely perplexed.

– Him – who else? My minder and protector.

– Who's this protector? What's his name?

James A. Reilly burst into laughter, tossing away the screwdriver, trembling palely.

– *Nobodaddy*, the *Fetch* – hell, son, I don't know. Call him what you like but whatever you do don't call him early in the morning, ha ha –!

He laughed for a bit then all of a sudden retched – wringing his hands as he sat by the fire.

– I think when it's all over that I'd be as well to take my life.

– When all what's over? asked Teddy – seriously concerned.

– After I've murdered Father Hand, I mean.

Michael Miles was gone, in his place was a uniformed band. Assembling their instruments as they began to play.

– *The Old Rugged Cross*, said James, raising the teapot dazedly, I've always loved that one, it reminds me of a time when the world made sense, hopelessly missing the tin mug as he wept copiously.

33

Albert Craig closed the door of his dentist's surgery gently, checking it twice with a firm press of his shoulder. Then off he went, *hop skipperty hop*, suggesting no one so much as the subject of the film *Reach for the Sky*, the famous air ace *Douglas Bader*. With whom he liked to compare himself, and with whom he shared many admirable qualities – but undaunted courage was not one of them, and no matter what he might like others to think, the truth was, unlike the World War II pilot, he had not, in fact, been deprived of his leg at thirty thousand feet but by a two-foot-high dry-stone wall outside Balla village.

So there he goes now, limping along, making his way home with a fresh cache of LPs tucked underneath his arm – the titles of which include *Bing Crosby Home on the Range*, *Underneath the Arches with Flanagan and Allen*, as well as others recorded by *Glenn Miller*, and *Flanders and Swann*.

As he drags his contumacious limb along, there seems something distinctly regretful about the dentist today – his humour clearly not as buoyant as normally would have been the case at this time of day. And the reason for this malaise was that he had just been informed that a certain dissatisfaction now existed with regard to his practice of holding certain monthly dances of his – these *soirées* as he called them, in the *Masonic Hall.*

Yes, by all accounts, according to Dean Gribbins, the little teenage gatherings which the dentist had been organising over the past few years were now the subject of some controversy. The hall committee had devoted a great deal of their recent meeting to the topic, apparently. As a result of which, Dean Gribbins had murmured, twiddling his thumbs regretfully, it had been decided that they had no option but to request that now, finally, they come to an end.

– *Much to our regret, Albert,* the minister had half whispered, *but I'm sure you understand.*

The truth was that Albert Craig was flummoxed – but, more important than that, deeply angry. For the decision seemed both high-handed and unnecessary. And he made these feelings clear in no uncertain terms.

– This is an outrage, Dean Gribbins, he had protested, and I resent the implicit slur on my character.

Which was why the latter had paid him a second visit – late at night, under cover of darkness. For he now had a few essential, if unpalatable, things to say. There had been certain *rumours*, he curtly informed the clearly shaken dentist. Regarding certain *inappropriate behaviour*, shall we say. Behaviour which was never to be fully explained, however. For the simple reason that the rueful Dean could not bring himself to say the words.

What had happened was this – a number of conversations had been accidentally overheard by some responsible members of the public. Conversations which included details to which adolescent girls ought not to have been privy. Which initially had surprised Dean Gribbins, for he had attended the *soirées* himself and found nothing untoward in them. In fact, he had considered them quite fun, and a great little outlet for Albert – who was, of course, getting on in years. They gave him an interest, being a bachelor man. He had always liked Albert and this was why he felt so ashamed, having to be the bearer of such insidious tidings. How he used to laugh when the dentist would put on one of his funny voices, making all the youngsters shriek with laughter. Sometimes it was *Harry Worth*, another time it might be cartoons. But now this.

It was Jenny Cartwright who had been overheard giggling – chatting with one of her friends, confiding in her that it was possible to *earn sixpence* just by kissing the dentist on the cheek. Mrs Cartwright's subsequent investigations had led to her becoming very concerned indeed. By all accounts, Jenny had been beaten. This was what led to Dean Gribbins' second visit. Which had been hard for him, given his long-standing relationship with Albert Craig. He had fully intended to ask the dentist:

– Did you ever chat *inappropriately* to young Jenny Cartwright?

But, at the very last minute, his courage had failed him. So he had been forced to seek refuge in the wavering shadows of innuendo.

In any case, the decision had been made. From now on the so-called *soirées* were to be suspended. His night-time visit effectively ended the Dean's relationship with the dentist, removed any lingering possibility of friendship continuing between the two men. Indeed the dentist, after he had left, decided in his fury to do some *suspending* of his own, as he put it. As a result of which, he was never to be seen in the Methodist church again.

Which was a great pity, as Bodley Foster had remarked in passing, what with Dean Gribbins and himself having been such great friends over the years. What was strange, the bank manager had added, was that, in spite of all his tomfoolery and humorous antics, usually after one or two *Tuborgs*, he had never actually heard the dentist swear. But now he seemed like a man possessed, as if someone or something had taken him over, directing his motivations and actions, willy-nilly. Profanity became almost a way of life, and he lost no opportunity to denounce the minister, in terms so obnoxious heretofore they would have been unimaginable. It amused me also, I really have to say – the sheer degree of wounded belligerence that the old dentist managed to muster. What of his inbred Protestant restraint, I wondered, where on earth had that disappeared to?

– I know what the filthy-minded fucker was thinking! he fulminated, but I'll see the bastard in court, so help me. Making such suggestions about a respectable man. One who has served this community well! However, don't worry, for he'll not be seeing me at his services again. I'll not bid the bastard so much as the time of day. Me that has neither chick nor child, the only bit of amusement I get outside of the *Foresters* being the innocent little dances I took it upon myself to organise. All good clean fun it was, the liars – with none of this rock and roll to be had. Or 'pop'. Decent, good-living, innocent music – but yet they find an excuse to condemn me! May youse rot in hell, Dean Gribbins and your slander-spreading committee of cunts!

It was sad for Albert, there could be no doubt about that. For what it meant in effect was that now he became a figure of fun, fated to die a lonely bachelor's death. Having allowed his suspicions to get the better of him – convinced that everyone in the *Foresters* was on the Dean's side – he was never to go to the club again. Bodley Foster attempted to call but somehow the dentist was always busy.

– I hope that they're proud, making up lies about an old man, he moaned alone over his *Tuborgs* at night, nothing better to do than gossip about their neighbours. I never so much as laid a hand on any of them wee girls – and never would. Ah well, sure I'll have plenty of time to listen to *Flanagan and Allen* on my own.

Bodley Foster also had some discussions with the clergyman, but none of these came to anything. In fact, Dean Gribbins, by this time, had begun to display an antipathy almost the equal of the dentist's. Demonstrating an intemperateness quite uncharacteristic of the man.

– You have no idea what he said to me that night, Bodley. I tried everything I could. Whether he likes it or not there has been serious talk. Information has come into my possession regarding his behaviour with a number of *other* girls. In any case, whatever his protestations, the committee and I have made our decision and that is that it's no longer considered appropriate. The *Masonic Hall* is closed – off limits to Albert Craig and his dances – and *that's it!*

It is of course possible – indeed very likely – that, had Dean Gribbins or any member of his committee become acquainted with the soft, harrowing moans which now routinely began escaping the elderly dentist's lips as he lay beneath the unlaundered sheets of his bed, they might well have paused and reconsidered their decision. If they had been capable, that is, of observing the old man's eyes as they followed the moon gliding soundlessly across the roofs of the town, recalling all the pleasure those *little soirées*, as he described them, had given him.

No doubt it would have been different if Albert Craig had been fortunate enough to have a wife – but he didn't. He didn't have a wife. All he'd had were his monthly dances – so that was that.

Which, I suppose, was why he proved so vulnerable, so suggestible. When one night, not so very long before his death, I entered his room for the purposes of observing him. And he apprehended me, entirely, in the guise of *Jenny Cartwright* – complete with brunette pigtails and bottle-green blazer. At first he'd just heard what he took to be an unremarkable noise – the creaking of the skirting, he took it to be. And had stiffened sharply beneath the covers – but not necessarily frightened. In fact so low in spirit that he allowed himself to hope that he might lay eyes on something precious – which would give him purpose, even elevate his soul. But as I emerged from my place of confinement, twirling my pigtails and treating him to an impish little smile, whispering *Give me sixpence* as I made my way across the floor, he realised that was not the case. As the tip of my tongue touched my wet lips I bent down to whisper in his ear:

– Give me sixpence, will you, Albert? That's all it costs. That's the price of entry to the *Stray Sod Country*. And it's a real good price – for you know you can stay there for ever, don't you? Sixpence into your unassailable new home. Come along, Albert, there's a good boy.

Like many of his associates, Teddy O'Neill had been to one or two of Albert's *soirées* – just for the laugh. Because they were mainly for youngsters, held between six and eight o'clock in the evening. But Teddy and the boys had found them hilarious – and Verity too, she had always been amused by them. How could you fail to be otherwise, to do anything but laugh as the old fellow with the big spectacles put yet another out-of-date record on the turntable, and launched into his impression of some old clapped-out music-hall comedians. On one occasion he had dressed up as a pantomime dame and all the young girls had started chuckling hysterically – Jenny Cartwright had actually joined him onstage, tugging his ringlets as she jumped up and down. Then he had asked all the kids up onstage and they had all had a ball, holding hands singing *On Mother Kelly's Doorstep*.

With, just as the finale reached its conclusion, the dentist flamboyantly whipping off his wig and, pushing his massive black spectacles on to his nose, returning to his all-time favourite, *Harry Worth* – kicking his leg at right angles, squealing:

– *That's my name. I don't know why but there it is!* with tears of joy streaming down his face.

As Verity had pointed out, the dentist might have been a teenager again.

Albert Craig lingered on until his death in the 1970s, with Jenny Cartwright appearing again at his bedside. Just before he departed this earth.

– *You know I'll never leave you, don't you,* she whispered, *and where you're going, I'm coming with you.*

As he looked at her – terrified, just as the rattle surged in his throat. *Deeply regretted by all who knew him, Albert Craig, b. 1898, RIP 1975.*

But that was all still in the future of course and right now, Teddy O'Neill had more on his mind than disappointed, deluded, crippled dentists. For the simple reason that he had not so much as slept a wink ever since he'd been out to James Reilly's hovel. He now wished he had never bothered going near the place.

– Gives me the willies, so it does, he whispered – even *thinking* about it.

But he was no stranger to such fears, whether he chose to admit it or not. He remembered as a kid going cold when he heard the window rattle.

– *It's only the sash cord*, he'd repeat to himself. Never finding it convincing. That was exactly how he felt now – glancing furtively in the direction of the window, or listening for three soft taps on the door. Taps, of course, never destined to come. I mean why on earth would one be predictable?

34

O hi there, Billy Fury, how are you doing, how are things? Well, stone me, ladies, can you believe it, look who it is, if it ain't my old pal Teddy O'Neill. Hi there, Teddy boy. Great to see ya, mah ole friend. You're looking good. You gonna be plucking a few tunes tonight? What's that you say – I doggone sure am, or my name ain't Billy Fury!

As he made his way across the town square, Teddy was grinning from ear to ear, hitting a stone a mighty kick and flipping his chewing gum to the other side of his mouth. He stood outside the *Masonic Hall*, where a proper dance was just about to begin – not some silly kids' party presided over by some limping loony with a stack of out-of-date records. No, what was coming was *real gone good*. And an up-to-date jive was exactly what Teddy O'Neill wanted to enjoy – for this good-time rock-and-roller had lost any remainder of that dumb old shyness – nope, all trace of that had well and truly been consigned to the past. He'd already been over in the *Clipper* and had a few jars – a couple of pale ales, in fact – same as he used to drink in London.

– I guess I gotta say that you sure are cutting an impressively handsome figure, Alphonsus *Teddy* O'Neill sir, he heard himself muse in a pleasurable fog of alcohol, enjoying the sound of his American twang.

He'd had five bottles altogether and was feeling pretty merry – striking another pose as he reached in his top pocket for his comb. Yes, he grinned, it's hard to believe that it could happen in a small Irish town but believe it or believe it not, ladies and gentlemen, there is absolutely no doubt about it. Nope, there can be no doubt at all about the fact that the latest sensation to hit the pop scene in this *real gone* year is the one and only Alphonsus O'Neill.

– *Rock-a-hula, baby o' mine!* he sang, flipping the comb and angling his knee, shaking it the same way he had seen *Billy Fury* do, curling his lip at the corner *à la Elvis*. He was still a tiny bit nervous, of course – he wasn't going to pretend that he wasn't – in spite of all the famous people he had met in the *Colony Rooms*, the *Nimbus* and everywhere else. But the reason for that was simple – it was because a certain special person was going to be inside that hall. Not just a special person but the woman he loved, for heaven's sake. Even the sound of her name could make him feel jittery.

– *Verity*, he whispered, *Verity Foster*.

Pushing the door of the dance hall open, out of nowhere he found himself, however briefly, experiencing the most extraordinary sensation of unease and he wanted to clear off out of there. But he'd had more than his share of such feelings in his time. And he wasn't about to let them bother him. Not now. Not tonight. Not in such familiar surroundings.

– *Shut up, Teddy!* he reproached himself. How about you give it a rest. For it's a load of bull – that's all it is!

He meant the *Stray Sod Country*, of course. Which was the story people long ago had used, as Hubert had – to explain why something you knew well could suddenly turn around and completely confound you.

– *A load of bull*, he repeated. Indeed.

Returning then to his *Billy Fury* accent:

– *Yup*, he began, how you doing there, Verity Foster? *Great tuh see yuh, gal – I'm home at last!*

He sank his hands in his pockets, sidling along the perimeter of the sprung maple floor, whistling a few bars of *Billy Fury's* latest hit. That is to say, one which he hadn't quite recorded, at least not just yet – a smoochy number entitled *Tonight They Met and Fell in Love Again*.

Teddy snapped his fingers and performed a little surreptitious dance.

– Just what is she going to think, *Billy Fury?* he asked himself, jigging, that purty babe who calls herself Verity Foster? Just what is that sweet little honey gonna think? That is what I would *laaak* to know!

A question, of course, to which he already knew the answer. Just as he knew some other important things – among them the fact that, for a certain little Protestant gal, there were gonna be a few surprises right here in the *Masonic Hall* tonight. Chief among them the complete disappearance of a once familiar pair of downcast eyes – not to mention a hopelessly hangdog expression! Yes, all those old dreary glimpses would be gone, those nervous edgy sidelong glances which seemed to say please don't bother looking over at me – don't look at me, I'm Alphonsus, I'm rubbish. No, that old predictably pathetic behaviour – it was gone now, vanished for ever – and that was the way it was going to stay. How wonderful it was going to be, thought Teddy – just witnessing Verity's reaction.

He gave some thought to what she might be wearing. Then he found himself thinking again about her smile. Her great big beaming generous smile. With her lovely fair hair tied up with a ribbon. His heart leaping when, all of a sudden, he thought he saw her standing right there across the hall. But no, he was mistaken: there wasn't any sign of his girlfriend yet. But any minute now she'd come striding through the door.

He rehearsed his stories about the *Nimbus* and the *Colony* again – and all the other clubs he had visited, with Hubert.

– There were times, you know, when me and Hubert, we'd drink the whole day long. Can you believe that, Verity? And as if that wasn't bad enough, when the pubs threw us out, then it'd be off to the *Two I's* to see *Billy*. Yeah, *Billy Fury*. What – you don't believe me? You don't believe that I met him?

– *You didn't!* he heard her gasp once more in amazement.

– Of course I didn't, doll – I'm only *gassing*, babe.

Except that he wasn't *gassing* to anyone, because it was true – as Verity Foster would soon realise.

He shook his head and smiled again, flicking his tongue against the back of his teeth as he rocked there back and forth on his heels. After he'd told her about *Billy*, he would firmly take her hand and lead her defiantly across the floor. Before asking the question which was consuming him inside – did she think it might be possible for the two of them to *get back on?*

Knowing for sure that whenever she heard about who he had met and just what he had been up to in this past year and a half what the answer was likely to be.

– *There is absolutely nothing that I would love better in the world, Alphonsus.*

So was it any wonder then that, when his old pal Manus and his sister Imelda arrived in, doing their best to attract his attention from across the floor, he would approach them grinning, with his head held high.

– Imelda's down for the weekend from Dublin, Manus told him.

– How's the civil service treating you? asked Teddy.

– I'm doing the best, she told him, not bad at all. And you, Mr Fonsey O'Neill, how are you doing since I seen you last? It's been an age!

– I been doing good, he replied, things have been neat, I got to say, Imelda.

Manus tossed his head back, laughing scornfully.

– Do you hear him, *neat* – talking like that and him hardly away a year.

– Eighteen months, Manus, one whole year and a half, old buddy.

– Old buddy! American-style talk now, if you don't mind!

– So do you like it in Dublin, Imelda? asked Teddy, casting furtive glances around the hall.

– I like it OK. But I'll bet it's not a patch on London. The city that never sleeps – isn't that what they call it?

– That's what they call it, Imelda! And one thing I got to say – it sure is true. Why it makes this place look so square you wouldn't believe. I mean, compare this place with the goddamn *Nimbus!*

– The *Nimbus?* quizzed Imelda, searching for her cigarettes.

– Och don't mind him, scoffed Manus, giving Teddy a playful shove, all he's doing is looking for notice. That's what you're doing, O'Neill – trying to show off, and don't deny it!

– Come on, little brother, said Imelda then, flipping open the packet of cigarettes and taking his arm, we're going off to get ourselves a lemonade.

Teddy gazed after them. He knew that Imelda was going with Ralph Foster the policeman. And he knew that her brother Manus was aware of it too – and didn't approve. As regards anyone involved with the security forces on the border, Manus availed of every opportunity to make his views clear. He unequivocally didn't approve – there was no room for debate.

But that was of little interest now to Teddy O'Neill – seating himself on a crude wooden bench positioned beneath a faded poster: ALL STAR BINGO OF 1956 – as he dispensed with any other considerations outside those which had immediate relevance for Verity and himself – and that included the precarious state of affairs on the frontier. The only conflict that interested him was the remote possibility

227

that someone still might try to come between himself and his girlfriend. He imagined himself squeezing Verity's hand as they waltzed.

– How's about the two of us go and live over there? We could go to the *Nimbus* every Saturday night. You reckon on that, babe?

He knew she wouldn't even be bothered to answer – her uplifted eyes would give him all the information he needed.

Then he looked over and saw his neighbour – Mrs Murray, the barber's wife. She was handing out sandwiches behind a row of big silver kettles. Smiling, he noticed, as she was joined by Mrs Foster – the bank manager's wife, and Verity's mother.

Mrs Foster, as usual, was in charge of everything – fussing away behind the refreshments counter. It was regrettable, Teddy sighed, that Verity's mother didn't like him very much. Golly Murray was different – it was a pity she wasn't more like her. She was kind and thoughtful – everyone in the town agreed on that. In spite of all the trouble she had with her handicapped son *Boniface*. Who, even now, was up to his tricks. Standing beside his mother wolfing down four or five sandwiches simultaneously – with jam and cheese plastered across his face.

– *Bonnie, please! Will you put those down!* Teddy heard Golly shrieking as she grabbed them, her son completely ignoring her as she did so, in fact reaching across to avail of some more.

Teddy fancied a bitter lemon, he mused. He went over eventually when Blossom had left her position.

– *O hello!* said Golly. If it isn't Alphonsus – and what can I do for you this evening, young man?

– A bitter lemon, if you please, Mrs Murray.

– Very well, she beamed, reaching down to the bottom shelf.

– So how is Patsy these days, Mrs Murray? I must pop in and get myself a *Tony Curtis*!

– O Patsy's doing the best but like them all he's up to his eyes with this play of Father Hand's. *Tenebrae*, it's called. They're all full of it. But, by all accounts it's going extremely well. They have very high hopes.

– I'm sure it'll be very successful, replied Teddy – keeping a vigilant eye on the door. His heart practically stopping the moment he saw Verity Foster come breezing in.

The same heart was beating furiously now as he watched her smiling with some of her friends, a gold chain twinkling on her neck, and her freshly washed hair sweeping out behind her. She was dressed in a wide-skirted floral frock and pink sweater. One of the things he had always loved most about her was that, in spite of her inheritance – she was a Protestant after all, with her father a highly respected bank manager, Verity Foster tended to be anything but vain. She had never displayed any arrogant sense of entitlement – not while Teddy O'Neill had known her. And you could see that now. Was it any wonder she had found herself elected head girl in the *Collegiate*, the Protestant school across the border in Balla.

Where she had been the object of much admiration by staff and students alike throughout the course of her five years studying. It was really going to be great – the two of them getting back on, he meant. It would be his reward for having been out of Ireland for a whole year and a half. Sure, his time over there, it hadn't been all roses – it had been goddamned lonely at times, to tell the truth. But now his reward was right there in front of his eyes.

He smiled as he remembered the night he had told Hubert Considine everything there was to know about his girlfriend. Everything about Verity and how much he loved her. But for some reason that Teddy couldn't under-stand, his friend had simply shrugged and said nothing – just lain there in silence, staring at the ceiling. Maybe the *black dog* had been at him or something. Anyway, it didn't matter now – it was all a long time ago. Teddy stretched and marshalled his resources – just as the blood began draining from his face. And he realised that none other than Verity Foster was actually hastening towards him across the floor. Was, unbelievably, standing directly in front of him, fingering her chain and smiling with those lovely sparkling eyes. In that truly lovely way, he thought. What was it she was showing him? He almost asked her to explain, staring dumbly at the small glittering diamond protruding from her extended finger.

– We're engaged to be married this autumn, she was saying – this is my intended, Austin Fry.

– I'm really pleased to meet you, said Austin. Verity, Verity tells me you've just been to London. *Great city!*

Teddy nodded and swallowed hard. As she continued:

– Maybe we can have a dance later on – for old times, Alphonsus!

Austin Fry nodded and mimed a pretend punch.

– OK then, Alphonsus – see you later!

– It really was wonderful to see you, said Verity.

– *Bye!* called Austin.

And with that, they were gone.

As the boys came barrelling in the door, boisterously – Duxass, Jo'burg and Winky, full of drink. As soon as Teddy saw them, he let out a whoop, tearing across the floor and leaping hysterically on to Winky's back, yelping as Duxass offered him the bottle:

– *Boys, but we are gonna have some crack tonight!*

The following afternoon, Jude O'Hara was making his way home from rehearsals – once again frustrated by the incorrigible manner in which theatrical affairs were proceeding. The truth was that he too was on the verge of throwing the whole thing up – for the cast, and not just Happy Carroll and Barney Corr either – they simply did not seem to be capable of accepting direction. Rarely a day passed without someone's sensibilities being sorely offended. He had badly lost the rag today, he reflected.

– Will you for the love of Christ stay in your positions, he had snapped, you're not at a cattle mart, you know. It's supposed to be Jerusalem, at the trial of Our Lord Jesus Christ. Behave like that this coming Easter and we'll all be the laughing stock of the town!

Yes, he was seriously thinking of abandoning the whole project altogether – and only for the disappointment it would cause Father Hand might have done so. So undermined did he feel because of the whole sorry business that just as he was passing the *Yankee Clipper* he was seized by an appalling anticipation of dread – becoming convinced that he was either sustaining a heart attack or on the verge of doing so. A cold dew covered his skin. For the life of him he couldn't comprehend what was happening now – for he had taken a wrong turning not once, but twice. It was as though he had inexplicably become a complete stranger in his hometown. He burst in the front door calling out his wife's name.

– Are you there? For Christ's sake, woman, do you hear me, are you there!

– Here I am, dear, replied his wife, goodness me, whatever is the matter? You look like someone who has just seen a ghost!

35

Which in a way he had – except that the spirit in question was his very own self – and his spouse, indeed, and all the people he had ever known. Who would, in time, find themselves every bit as disconcerted as Jude O'Hara on that occasion. Not knowing who they were and from whence they'd come – a situation which, when it happened, was destined to continue for some considerable time – eternity, in fact.

Although time, of course, means little to me – with both the future and the past being nothing more than the horizons that bound a flat and motionless expanse of sea. Which they happen to call *Time*.

Across which Jude O'Hara and all the others pass, rather sentimentally classified as the *faithful departed*. For it is they, of course, who do the actual passing – *Time* never does. It never goes forward and it never goes back, so when I refer to the 1960s or '70s or indeed the '80s, for me the same moon shines over it all, little farcical pageant that it is. So don't pay too much attention if you find yourself hopping, like poor Albert Craig, between the decades. For, I assure you, we shall end up precisely where we began – one always does.

* * *

In this case the gloriously triumphant *Holy Week* of Easter, in the year 1958, when Cullymore became as a beacon upon the border. The same year, in fact, when the unsuspecting Patsy Murray, that genial gentle barber – was about to receive the shock of his life. Not that anyone was ever to know that, in a time when everyone covetously guarded their secrets. They didn't dare risk the priest finding out about them – and have themselves publicly condemned from the pulpit. Or worse, incarcerated in some kind of institution. Not that these anxieties were confined solely to those of the Catholic persuasion. No, the Protestant citizens had their own store of clandestine enigmas. And late at night, like everyone else, they also would find themselves in flight – fugitives from both themselves and their neighbours.

And, in this, in spite of all her education and self-possession, Blossom Foster was no different to anyone.

Which was why her shadow, one particular morning, in March 1958, the year when the greater part of this narrative takes place, fell across the frosted glass of Patsy Murray's barber's shop window. It was 8 *a.m.*

Patsy had been perusing the paper when he heard the softest tap on the glass. The barber found himself taken aback, having just sat down to enjoy a quiet rest and to give his full attention to the crossword. But then he heard the tapping again, even more insistent this time. He crossed the floor hesitantly, gently tugging back the blind – descrying, to his astonishment, Blossom Foster on the footpath outside.

He swallowed hard, scarcely able to believe the sight that met his eyes. But there could be no doubt but it was her, the bank manager's wife – waiting on his barber's shop step, dressed in her leopard-print coat and stole, looking huntedly about her. Drawing back, he watched as she tapped the glass again – but this time more firmly, with her ring.

– I can't understand it, the barber gasped, it's hardly the kind of time you'd come looking for Golly. *Eight o'clock?*

His wife had only departed fifteen minutes earlier, bringing their son Boniface with her to Mass. Affording Patsy, or so he had thought, a rare opportunity to attend to his crossword and enjoy reading his newspaper without having to listen to his son's persistent questions. For Boniface, God love him, at times he could be a trial – an awful yapper. Was it any wonder that he got on Golly's nerves at times?

– That young fellow would try the patience of a saint, she often said.

But Boniface now was the least of his worries.

What ought I do? he wondered. He was in a quandary.

The truth, of course, being that he had always been uncomfortable talking to women – especially Protestants. Who always appeared to be in possession of a greater sense of assurance and confidence about themselves. In a state of mounting agitation, the barber hovered precariously by the latch and realised that he was perspiring uncomfortably. The shop door swung open and a blast of cold air hit him. He found himself staring into the face of Blossom Foster. He caught a glimpse of his own reflection in the glass – he was acutely pale. She, however, seemed quite at ease. Behaving as though she'd been expected all along.

– May I come in? he heard her say – a request which was quite superfluous for her foot had already crossed the threshold.

She smiled as she stood beneath the framed photograph of Manchester United, tapping her nails on her fox fur's vulpine head, in a steady even rhythm. As she said to Patsy:

– I was just up the town leaving Bodley into work when I thought on my way back that perhaps I might pop in and see Patsy. For it's been on my mind – yes, I have to talk to my old friend.

– Talk to *me*? replied the barber hoarsely. You kept thinking you had to talk to *me*?

– Yes, she retorted, yes, *you*, Patsy – crinkling up her nose as she exuded a little shiver, that's what I remembered – that I had to pop in and have a chat with my favourite barber.

She lowered her eyes – and then her voice.

– It's just that, you see – you're an expert hairdresser.

– An expert hairdresser? replied Patsy, in a tone which suddenly had begun climbing the register until it was almost falsetto – it embarrassed him deeply.

– Yes, I know it's unusual, Blossom nodded, but it's just that, you see, I had this extraordinary dream.

– A dream? An extraordinary dream, do you tell me, Blossom?

– Yes, Patsy dear – an extraordinary dream. That I was in *Monique's* – just chatting as we always do, as usual. But then, all of a sudden, I felt these strong warm hands on my

236

neck and I looked up to see – to become aware that it wasn't *Monique* who was cutting my hair. It wasn't her at all.

– Was it not? It wasn't Monique?

– No, dear – *because it was you!* Now isn't that the funniest thing? I really do think it is most extraordinary. But do you know what was even stranger, Patsy? Do you know what I was saying to you – as there you were, just clipping away?

– Maybe that you were in the wrong place. *I'm in the wrong place, Patsy*, maybe. Is that perhaps what you might have been saying?

– No, Patsy. I wasn't saying that at all. What I was saying was – Patsy you really are the most wonderful barber. The best. Top class. No one in Cullymore could ever hope to match you. Or anywhere else either.

Then, quite dramatically, she coughed and switched the subject.

– What do you think of this cold war, Patsy? she asked. What do you think of it at all at all?

– I don't know, replied the barber, I really wouldn't have much of an opinion of it, to tell the truth.

He paused as his face grew markedly flushed. To tell the truth it was now a deep scarlet.

– Why – what would your opinion, Blossom, of it be?

He formed the impression that this remark had amused her considerably.

– *O you men!* she chuckled, with a girlish impishness. You really can be such sillies at times, do you know that? You really can be the silliest of sillies! Honestly! *Prut!* But there's only one silly I care about, Patsy.

– Oh yes, gulped Patsy – and who might that be?

Blossom turned her back and lit a *Senior Service*.

– Patsy, she asked, would you like a cigarette?

– No thank you, replied the barber, I'm only after putting one out, so I am.

– Do you know something, dearie? his visitor went on, as a wreath of blue smoke lolled directly above her head, before I came down I was listening to the wireless. I was listening to the wireless and guess who was on?

– I don't know, Blossom. Who?

– *Alistair Cooke*. That's who – *Alistair Cooke*, all the way from America. Talking about the way things have gone in the world.

– Yes, it's terrible, Patsy replied – although the words had departed his lips before he could give them any proper consideration.

– He says that all over in these current times there are people who lie in their beds, awake – worrying. That they find themselves lying there at all hours of the night, fretting and agitating that it's all going to end. That everything they have worked for their whole lives will come to nothing. It will be like an X-ray world, he was saying. As, shadows of our former selves – we'll be *desolate*.

– People do fret, there's no denying that, agreed Patsy, you'd feel sorry for them, so you would, some of the things they get into their heads. It'd remind you at times of the *Stray Sod*.

– *The Stray Sod?* What's that, Patsy? I can't say I ever heard tell of that.

– Nothing, Blossom. It was silly of me to mention it. It's stupid. The *Stray Sod Country* – old wives' tales is all.

– You would feel sorry for those people – wouldn't you, Patsy? Worrying and sighing, night after night. About this silly old cold war.

– Yes, it's true, Blossom. You most definitely would. Yes.

There ensued a lengthy pause and then at last Blossom Foster slowly turned, with her eyes still lowered – contemplating her varnished pink fingernails. As she, with measured composure, slowly began to raise her head with a smile. Her voice was lower now – and huskier.

– But me – I'm different to them. I was wondering, perhaps – do you know what I mean, Patsy?

– Yes, Blossom. I think I do, he replied – falteringly, because it wasn't true. In fact he hadn't a clue what she meant. She sloped her foot and extended her toe to its full length and, having inspected it for a moment or so, began to move slowly across the floor – as though negotiating a path through the small and disparate hillocks of shorn hair. She was approaching steadily.

– I couldn't be bothered worrying – about atomic experiments or anything else, she informed him in soft and low, almost maternal tones.

– I couldn't even be bothered about *space*, she smirked.

– *Space?*, answered Patsy – quite dumbfounded.

– Yes, *space*, explained Blossom, on the wireless *Mr Cooke* said that some people, even people in high-up places, are of the opinion that the Russians and the Americans ought to leave space alone. And not be sending these capsules up there at all.

– Capsules? Those sputniks, is it, that you see in the paper?

– Yes, sputniks if you want to call them that. But I think he meant any kind of rocket, really.

– Any kind?

– Yes, any kind of rocket. Just rockets, Patsy.

– O I see. Yes, any kind of rocket. All kinds of rockets.

– I mean, let's face it, Mr Murray – space is enormous. I mean, what I'm saying is that it's absolutely vast. Who knows what they might find out there? Then there's always the other thing, as *Mr Cooke* says.

– The other thing? said Patsy.

– Yes, the other thing. The fear, I mean, that you might never get home. If you went out there. Into space. That you might never come home after all those thousands of millions of miles. Imagine that.

– I heard them talking about it on the telly.

– That you might be left there – for years, for centuries.

– If something went wrong with the capsule, maybe. If an engine blew up.

– Then you'd be out there – marooned. Why it doesn't even bear thinking about. Not for the likes of you and me anyway. The likes of you and me that have families.

– You'd be thinking about them all the time up there. You'd have to get home, at all costs, Blossom. Family is important.

– Of course it is – it's the most important thing in the world, dearie. And, Catholic or Protestant, it simply doesn't matter. For at the end of the day, everyone's the same. Of course they are, Patsy. For that is the way their Creator made them.

She exhaled some smoke, crushing a mote of fluff between her thumb and index finger.

– Patsy dearest – do you know what really makes me mad?

The barber shook his head, again averting his eyes.

– People saying unchristian things about the Pope.

– Things? What kind of things, Blossom?

– What kind of things? Things like – well, that he isn't a proper leader at all. That a proper leader is someone who represents reliable, decent, hard-working people – those, you might say, who are genuinely Godly. Have you ever overheard anyone saying that?

She lifted her cigarette and stared directly at him. The fragrance of her scent was making him feel faint. The only other lady's perfume he'd really experienced was that of his wife – and Golly never wore it now, not much. Its sheer intensity overwhelmed him.

– I wonder will we see him when we go over there – to Rome. His Holiness, I mean?

– *Rome? What?* stammered the barber. I don't understand, Mrs Foster.

Blossom flicked some ash off her cigarette and smiled.

– O for heaven's sake, don't call me that. O but I'm sorry – didn't I tell you? Myself and hubby are going there again this year. Do you think the Pope would mind if two old Protestants came to see him, in St Peter's Square? Ha ha, I'm joking – of course he wouldn't! Because none of that silliness matters any more. Now that it's the 1950s everyone's the same, no matter what their religion is. Of course certain people are still stuck in their ways. You'll hear some people going on about the coronation – praising Her Majesty to the heights and all the rest, there's no one better than the Queen, they'll say. Which might have been true in the bygone days of Empire. But not now. No, nowadays your people are every bit as good as ours, and if there once was an empire where people looked up to Her Majesty, the Windsors and all the other royals, well that, I am afraid, is all over now. It's all over, Patsy, because where we are living is in the modern world. Everyone now has got the same chance. As I was only saying to hubby last evening – all that's left of the olden days now are the odd little bits and pieces you might find lying about the house. Such as *Imperial Leather* soap, Patsy – or *Darjeeling* tea. She paused and teased some discarded hair with her toe, meticulously moving it across the faded linoleum.

– Tell me, Patsy, if you don't mind. Does Golly use *Imperial Leather*?

Patsy replied hesitantly that he really didn't know.

– *I* always use it, Blossom Foster informed him, to be perfectly honest I wouldn't even entertain the idea of using anything else. She tapped her *Senior Service* and paused, holding him fixedly with her gaze – elevating her right eyebrow.

Bewilderingly, Patsy found himself on the verge of erupting into laughter of a completely unrestrained nature.

– Would you not, Blossom? he asked her, before, red-faced, adding:

– I wouldn't know all that much about soap.

Blossom smiled as she plied her bracelet of white seed pearls.

– But of course you wouldn't, Patsy – especially not about *Imperial Leather*. Because that, of course, would be more of a woman's soap.

Now it was her turn to avert her eyes, still teasing the pearls as she said to the barber:

– Patsy, do you ever tell her that she looks like a film star? Do you ever say that to Golly, I wonder? To your lovely wife . . .

– Tell her she looks like – what? Like a film star? Is that what you said, Mrs Foster – a film st . . . ?

– Yes. Like *Jane Russell*, say, or *Lauren Bacall*. Do you ever look into your wife Golly's eyes and say to her dearest, if you don't mind me saying it, there are times when you remind me of the lovely *Jane Russell*?

Patsy Murray choked.

– *Jane Russell?* he said.

– Perhaps. But not necessarily. Not necessarily *Jane Russell*. *Elizabeth Taylor* maybe – or *Marilyn Monroe*. There are lots of other stars it could be. Stars of the stage and the Hollywood screen.

She hesitated before continuing:

– Would you mind very much, Patsy dear, if I told you something?

– I don't know, Blossom. I couldn't really say. I wouldn't really know – not until I heard it.

There was something deeply unsettling about her smile – as if, just for the briefest of moments, it wasn't Blossom Foster who was standing there at all.

As she said softly:

– Imagine if it was you and me who happened to be up there – right up there, on that silver screen. In a world-famous film – *Roman Holiday*, for example.

– *Roman Holiday?*

– Yes. *Roman Holiday.* With *Audrey Hepburn.* Sometimes I think that Geraldine looks like her.

– Does she really? I wouldn't know. I'm not even sure who *Audrey Hepburn* is, Mrs Foster.

– Blossom, Patsy. *Blossom*, please, dear.

She was standing right beside him now, her warm gloved hand cradling his elbow. Patsy Murray's heart was beating furiously and his cheeks might have been on fire. The curls of smoke from Blossom's cigarette went drifting idly in the direction of the frosted window. There was a certain remoteness apparent in his visitor now, but along with it a sense of determination and purpose – effortlessly freighting its manipulative cargo.

– Will you do me a favour, love. Will you tell her I called?

– Who, Blossom?

– *Who, Blossom, who!* Mrs Murray, of course.

– Is that what you want? Then of course I will, Mrs Foster!

– I told you not to call me that!

– Certainly, Blossom. Of course I'll tell her. I'll tell her that surely. If that's what you . . . the barber replied.

But never got around to completing the sentence. For his

morning visitor had already departed. As the barber's shop door suddenly burst open.

– *Damn you to hell!* screeched Patsy Murray, you put the fear of God in me, so you did!

It was Boniface and Golly – arriving home from Mass.

– Who's for tea and bickies? asked his wife, whipping off her headscarf as she strode cheerily across the floor.

At that very moment in her elegant, well-appointed bungalow *Dunroamin*, Blossom Foster was also feeling sick. For she could not believe what had just happened. She looked at the clock – it was just gone 8.45. Where had she been for the past three-quarters of an hour? She certainly hadn't been in Patsy's barber's, she told herself, she couldn't have been. Because it wasn't in her to do a thing like that. So someone or *something* must have made her do it. So sly and duplicitous, by times, are one's subjects – with no end of strategies by which they seek to exculpate themselves.

– *It wasn't me!* she cried, plunging her face into her hankie.

But it was her – it *had* been her. And wasn't it ever so fortuitous that I was there again to shoulder the blame? As I so often and so willingly tend to do, to the point of weariness on my part. So I mean, who wouldn't long for diversions such as picaresque hamlets like Cullymore can bring, when once again the dreary catastrophes of the globe are craving attention, whether it be the headscarved skeletons of *Bosnia* or the poor unfortunate waterlogged *Thais*.

But the idea of dear Blossom Foster as a curvaceous temptress, more than anything, that did amuse me. For I really was not sure if she genuinely had it in her, as I nudged her subconscious desires along.

Truth to tell, though, what one of them ever failed to comply with my quiet urgings – as they lay there in the nights, haunted by themselves and their secret possibilities, beneath those probing, interrogative stars.

36

Teddy and the boys liked to doss about the corner. Something which Teddy informed them he wouldn't be doing for very much longer, now that he was thinking about returning to England.

– Yup, heading back across the water, he sighed. To London and Piccadilly – far away from this town, it's fulla squares if you ask me.

He was giving his buddies all the *gen* about Soho – as they loitered outside Dagwood's snooker hall, puffing their smokes.

– Sure, guys, sure you got to be careful, ain't gonna tell you any different, like I mean it's a big city – ain't nobody gonna argue with that.

The boys were hanging on his every word.

– Way it is, lads, he continued, you take it into your head to get the ferry, head on over London way, of one thing you can be certain and that is that there's gonna be no end of flash boys, slags, spivs and geezers – each and every one of 'em with only one thing on their mind and that is rook you, baby, for every goddamn cent. Take it from me, fellas – they don't care, every one of 'em raised on the street.

His pal Duxass had his fingers hooked in his waistcoat, frowning concernedly as he crunched some gravel beneath his hobnail boot.

— What about the wogs? he asked Teddy, they give you much lip in your time over there? They say that the darkie can be a wild dangerous man.

— Nope, replied Teddy, vehemently shaking his head, those kinda people never given me any trouble, Duxass. Matter of fact, any of 'em as I happened to meet down the *Nimbus* – gentlemen each and every one. Trinidad, Tobago – you name it, fine guys.

— Trinidad, Tobago, repeated Duxass – captured in an exotic trance – mighty places, eh lads?

— The other side of the world, my man, laughed Teddy, aiming a pretend punch at his friend's considerable abdomen. Duxass had been talking about going over to London ever since they had left school. But, like the rest of them, always lost his nerve whenever the time came. Dagwood Slowey appeared in the doorway of the hall, his narrow head looking out as he squinted underneath his sandy-coloured quiff, looking the spit of his namesake from the comic strip *Blondie* in the *Sunday Press*.

— *Ah would you quit your auld boasting about London, O'Neill. It's only a hell full of whores and Antichrist Protestants!*

There had always been four of them in the gang. Initially they had planned to make the trip to London together – to start up their own Ted outfit over there. But Fonsey had proved to be the only one who'd had the nerve. Which, privately, had relieved his pals. For in their heart of hearts they didn't consider themselves worthy of London – not like Fonsey, who was always reading up about it. The great thing about their mate, though, was that he didn't brag. As Duxass said:

– Not like plenty of the other bastards. For there's plenty about this town who'd be only too glad to gloat if they got the chance. To laugh at the likes of us standing at the corner. Not Fonsey.

– No, sir, agreed the others.

He had told them about all his wild nights, sure enough. Had even admitted that in the beginning he had been intimidated.

– Of course I was. It's a big place, lads. I mean I'd never been in a city that size in my life! But you'll never believe what I went and fucking did, that very first day – didn't I go and get on the wrong fucking tube!

– *Choob*, mimicked Duxass, dropping a blob of saliva between his toes.

– *Choob*. Woh, boys.

– So there I am, continued Teddy, there I am way out in the middle of fucking nowhere – Elephant and Castle I think it was called – way out in the wilds of South London.

– *Elephant and Castle*, murmured Duxass, savouring the words.

– Farking 'ell, continued Teddy, you want to see them high rises, Duxass, I'm telling you – stretch for miles they do. And you're giving out about wogs? Well, let me tell you this – it was one of *them* showed me the way back to the station. So whaddyou think about that then, Dux?

There could be no mistaking the decidedly working-class London inflections which now had begun to inform Teddy's speech.

– Yup, there I am standing in the middle of bleeding South London, outside the station in Elephant and Castle with the traffic non-stop roaring in the rain. And what do you know but the next thing I look and there's this *doll* – got to be over forty, I swear.

– A prostitute! A whore! Did you meet a whore – no! Come on, you have to tell us!

– Looks me in the eye and says it out straight. Didn't so much as flinch, swear to God.

– Holy fucking Jasus. What did she say?

Rocking back and forth on his Cuban heels, Teddy O'Neill grinned mischievously.

– Sexual intercourse, mate, she says. All it would cost you would be *five pahnd!*

– Holy Mother of God – five pound! gasped Duxass.

– But I didn't take it, Dux. I'd like to be able to tell you I did but I felt such a bollocks after going and getting lost that all I wanted to do now was get home and lay down my head. I hadn't the faintest clue where I was.

Duxass, disappointed and perplexed, ran his fingers through his oily hair.

– Five pound, he repeated monotonously, as though in an effort to reduce the concept to manageable proportions.

– Yeah, that was the night I happened by chance to meet Hubert Considine, explained Teddy, that was the very first night that I met my great mate.

– I know them, the Considines, frowned Duxass, I heard they were a kind of mad crowd, and always were. There's bad blood there – none of them's right.

– One of them long ago brained his wife with a shovel, nodded Winky. Came home one day – and *bang*, slapped her across the head with it. They say that the *Fetch* had taken his mind. That where he'd landed was the *Stray Sod Country*.

Teddy made it clear he was having none of this.

– Nope, he continued as he shook his head, I don't care what they say about the Considines. All I know is – Hubert Considine went out of his way to look after me.

His eyes twinkled as he tapped his foot.

– The two of us one day – we must have been in nearly every pub in Piccadilly. Then off we went to the *Nimbus Club* in Soho. I'll never forget it as long as I live. I mean, can you imagine it, lads. Hardly there a week and where do I find myself? In one of the most famous nightclubs in the city. But then what happens?

– What happened – tell us! For fuck's sake, Teddy – don't stop, will you tell us!

Teddy chortled as he described the scene. Duxass by now was beside himself with excitement.

– You could hardly see with the smoke, Teddy explained, but wasn't the singer wearing nothing, only a slip.

– No! choked Duxass, as the others craned forward.

– And that's not all, Teddy chuckled, stamping out his cigarette.

– O jakers! What happened then? Teddy, what happened then?

Duxass's eyes were out on sticks.

– Well, down she comes when she's finished to join us. Can you believe it, lads?

– She does not! gasped Duxass, as Winky and Jo'burg rubbed their hands.

– That's what I said, comrade – them exactly is the words that I used. Except that, unfortunately, there's just one small problem – it turns out she's not a *woman*!

– She's not a – *what?* squealed Duxass in disbelief.

– *Auntie Flo* is my name, she says, I swear to fuck, but I'm very pleased to make your acquaintance. For she's a man, for fuck's sake, and it turns out she knew Hubert from his time on the sites. Did you ever hear the like?

In the end this proved more than Duxass could take, his mind completely overwhelmed by garish images of Elephant and Castle, and of a city where the words *sexual intercourse* blinked incessantly from neon boards. Not to mention scantily clad *hostesses* who appeared out of nowhere to confront him from side alleys. Promising:

– For you, Duxass sweetheart, it would be just a *pahnd*!

– I can't stand this – I'm going home! he growled, as Winky and Jo'burg cupped their hands and called after him:

– A quid and you can ride me all the way from here to Balla!, collapsing in a bout of prolonged hysterics – in which they were willingly joined by Teddy, before finally going their separate ways.

37

I have to say she looks pretty sitting there – Imelda. Resting there, reading, in March 1958, not long before Manus is due to be killed.

Although Imelda, of course, was not to know that. Quietly turning the pages of her *Picturegoer* magazine, with her ginger-red tresses falling on to the shoulders of her crisp white blouse. Now on her tea break, Miss Hoare the civil service copy typist is giving herself to profound thoughts and considerations, poring over the great philosophies of our time. I jest, of course. For what in fact she is thinking of is *Ralph Foster* – who else?

She is frowning now. Look at her flexing her fingers beneath her chin. To give herself to thoughts of an extremely private nature. There are so many things you can never ever bring yourself to tell another person, she was thinking – as she sat there on the grass outside the Marlborough Street Department of Education building. You just couldn't bring yourself to tell them – because you knew that you couldn't ever find the words. At least that was what she had been convinced of – before meeting Ralph Foster, that is. To whom, on the contrary, you could tell almost anything. She had even shared her feelings about his very own sister with him – Miss *know-it-all* Verity Foster, of course.

– Do you know, she had said to Ralph one evening as they lay together on the bed in her flat, do you know when I was young what I wanted to do more than anything?

– What did you want to do, my love? asked the young policeman.

– Don't laugh at this, Ralph, but I wanted to steal into your house, creep in there in the dead of night – and cut up all of Verity's clothes.

– But why on earth would you want to do that?, her perplexed boyfriend had enquired then – not without a little amusement.

– Because I used to think she was snooty, Ralph. Especially when I'd see her on that bloody pony!

– *Paddywack*, said Ralph, kissing her fingers one by one, that's what she called him – absolutely doted on that animal, so she did. How she doted on that pony.

– *Paddywack*, what a stupid name! said Imelda swinging her legs, pecking her boyfriend affectionately as she climbed off the bed and pulled his white nylon shirt over her head. Before going off to look for matches to light the gas.

Ralph Foster's shirt was the only man's shirt that Imelda Hoare had ever worn. And it made her feel good. Made her feel giddy and warm all over.

– Honestly, when I think of it! Protestant fanny, I used to call her, Ralph, and think to myself how I'd like to kick her stupid Protestant fanny!

Ralph laughed aloud and shook his head as he reached for the paper.

– Bigot, he chuckled, you're the worst bloody bigot of all – I thought it was supposed to be us Protestants who were sectarian!

– It wasn't that she ever really did anything, Imelda went on, blowing out the match as the gas plumped abruptly, it was just the way that she had of looking at you. Excuse me, please, get out of my way. Here I come, don't you know it, I'm so beautiful!

– That's women for you, sighed Ralph Foster wearily, now only half listening – leafing through the pages of the *Irish Press*.

– *A devastated Manchester continues with its mourning*, he read aloud.

A bright-eyed young player was smiling out at the camera – *Duncan Edwards*.

Imelda continued talking away to herself, rummaging around in the cupboards searching for butter.

– I'll sneak in very late at night when I know she'll be snoozing, she continued, then I'll crawl up the stairs and open up all the drawers. Out then they'll come every item one by one – and I'll cut them up, her hateful swanky clothes. Yes, her fancy expensive clothes, I'll take them all out and start cutting. And I won't even think of stopping till the whole *ha ha* lot are lying there in a pile of rags. That will teach her to look down her nose at me, Miss McProtestant, Miss Fanny Adams!

– Our Verity is getting married actually, mused Ralph, licking his thumb as he turned a page, for herself and this Austin Fry fellow are getting along like a house on fire.

– Tell her to go ahead – she has nothing to worry about. Tell her that at long last Imelda Hoare has decided to grow up. My mother's scissors are locked safely away in the drawer – and that, my dearest, is where they're going to stay.

– Would you like to go to the *Astoria* tonight?

– I'm afraid, Mr Policeman, that you have a short memory.

Imelda crossed the floor with two steaming cups.

– And why might that be, asked the policeman, as his beloved girlfriend flopped down beside him – tenderly caressing his neck.

– Because we're going to the pictures in Fairview, that's why. We're going to see *An Affair to Remember*, if you please! Then Imelda leaped on the bed and placed both her hands on the grinning young Sergeant's shoulders – facing him, as she quizzed him with two besotted eyes:

– Do you think your girlfriend's as nice as *Deborah Kerr*? Well – do you!

– Poor *Miss Kerr*, sighed Ralph Foster playfully as he wrapped her in his arms, she simply isn't in your league, I'm afraid.

Then what did he do, the gentle policeman? Why, kissed her first on the neck, of course, and then crushed his two lips to hers. Before moving down to her swelling upper bosom as she writhed and squirmed with delirious satisfaction. Thinking to herself there were things which you simply couldn't say to certain people. Then there were the other things that you very much certainly could. Things, for example, such as:

– *I love you. I love you madly.*

Before meeting Ralph, Imelda had never undressed in front of anyone. Not just a man – but anyone at all. Fearing she might die of embarrassment.

– I'd be ashamed of my life, so I would, she used to say.

But it wasn't like that now. It hadn't even been like that the very first time, as a matter of fact. When, standing in the half-light attired only in her plain white cotton bras-siere, she'd felt his hands beginning to gently massage her shoulders. As his deep voice whispered:

– You don't know how terrific it is to be able to come here to see you. To get away from that dreary old routine of the barracks.

But the fact was that she *did* understand and was just so happy that the man she loved felt able to say it. Here in her humble apartment, in an old Georgian house at 37 South Circular Road, Dublin.

– O Ralph, she said, these times we have. I look forward to them like nothing else on earth!

Sitting there in the little park outside her office, she couldn't believe that that was now over two years ago. She had tele-phoned him earlier – now that he was back from the TT races in the Isle Of Man – having acquitted himself magnificently once more. His parents, Blossom and Bodley, had always been proud of his achievements, he had confided in her.

– Not as proud as I am, she assured him.

And which was true – *so* true. Whether it was hard to believe or not, when one considered that that very same Imelda Hoare, once upon a time, if she'd been told by Verity Foster that her famous brother Ralph had won yet another accolade for his motorcycle prowess, would have been driven, quite literally, to the edge of distraction – remaining lividly hostile for weeks. But now any news at all of his achievements had the effect of driving Imelda wild with pride. In the very same way as it did when he courted her. And whispered breathily, as he kissed her neck, smoothing a strand of ginger hair back:

– *Entering you is like entering heaven.*

No sooner had Ralph left the flat later that same day than Imelda found herself longing for yet another fortnight to have gone past. She also wished that her brother Manus would finally see sense and vacate the flat – for already he had been staying with her far too long. But that was her brother all over, of course – just so *thick* when it came to certain things. He had been staying there for almost a month now. Which, in another way, she conceded, for his own sake was probably just as well. For the youth of late had consistently remained in one of his broodingly serious moods – one of near-morbidity, in her view, and certainly one that was both unwelcome and unhealthy. Not to say unsettling, in a person so young. For Manus had only recently turned nineteen – but acted like someone already twenty years older.

– Who was that fellow I passed on the stairs? he demanded to know on one occasion. Meaning Ralph, of course.

– How he could get under her skin, her brother, she would often seethe in the cramped kitchenette, as if he had any right to know her business. With that unswerving, self-satisfied attitude of his. *Mr Certainty*, she called him – often to his face.

– I don't see what my visitors have got to do with you, she had curtly informed him, before continuing impatiently:

– I mean, it's not like I enquire into your affairs, Manus, or ask you what *you* do with your time.

– Your own life is your own life, he had replied sanctimoniously, it isn't for me to judge. But marriage, Imelda, is a sacred institution. These are things we ought to remember. These are the values we were both brought up on.

It took all the resources Imelda had at her disposal not to insist that he leave the flat right there and then. But what she had, in fact, asked her brother, weakening shamefully, was:

– Are you all right for money?

– Yes, he had replied, I'm perfectly fine. But thank you anyway.

She appraised the youth in his shabby grey suit and greasy black curls – giving the impression of a man of forty. How she wished he would go back and behave in the manner which was appropriate to a boy of his age, loitering outside the snooker hall, laughing and joking with all his friends – like he used to. With Jo'burg, Duxass, Winky and Fonsey O'Neill – smoking away and making their big plans. Now however, it seemed, his former companions existed only as objects towards which renewed contempt could be directed.

– This skiffle and rock and roll and all the rest of it, makes me laugh to hear them blathering on, he scowled. I'm embarrassed, to tell the truth, Imelda, that I ever allowed myself to associate with them. And Fonsey O'Neill – if you ask me, lately, he's become the worst of the lot, strutting around like he owns the place. All because he emigrated to England! What does he want to be going there for anyway? After all, mainland Britain has consistently been the enduring source of all Ireland's ills. No, I haven't any time for their ways or their foolishness. Those days are past. I have more important things to do with my life.

To the best of Imelda's knowledge, her brother had never had a girlfriend. Not that it surprised her – he even disapproved of people going to the cinema.

– It encourages dissolute, weak behaviour, he often insisted, and it has no place in the Ireland of 1958. This country, more now than ever, needs to build itself up. The political struggle isn't over. The reasons for the cause are as valid as they ever were. Rigour and discipline are what's needed – not corner-boy small talk. Commitment is what is required – loyal dedication to the ideals of the men who have gone before us. Who have gone to their graves, sis, for the ideals in which they believed.

It depressed her deeply when she heard him talk that way. Sometimes she arranged to meet him during her lunch hour, close to the college where he studied three days a week. But they found themselves now with increasingly less in common.

– How is your course going? she would ask, rarely receiving any satisfaction.

And the two of them would sit there, eating chips and exchanging inconsequential chat as the gulf between them yawned ever wider. She would have given anything to be able to talk to him about things she loved – such as hugging Ralph's arm as they sat together in the cinema – mesmerised by the lovelorn antics of *Cary Grant* and *Deborah Kerr*, looking into one another's eyes on their ocean liner, promising to meet again in six months' time. Even though they were both married.

Except that, of course, she couldn't do that – knowing full well just how profound his disapproval would be. Not only of their gay and irresponsible behaviour, but any aspect at all of their relationship. Such exchanges between two people who were not married being, in his view, *coarse* and *vulgar* – not to say irresponsible and an *occasion of sin*.

But there was another reason too – the simple fact that, as he constantly protested, he would not be in a position because he did not have the time, being much too busy with his college lectures. Already having completed one term in the *College of Technology* in *Bolton Street*, Manus Hoare had been identified as something of a gifted electronics student – and not only by his lecturers. No, his talents and application in this area had also been noted by certain other anonymous individuals, whose admiration for his abilities eventually saw him commissioned quartermaster of the

Balla Brigade of the *Irish Republican Army*, with responsibility for the entire border area. A fact of which – in spite of persistent but unsubstantiated rumours – his sister chose to remain oblivious. A detail which, had she but known it, was ultimately to prove most unfortunate indeed. When he was cut to pieces only a week later. Not unlike Una Miniter's dog – ah, so you thought I had forgotten – who had met a fate not at all dissimilar, but in his case at the hands of a one-man unit, going by the name of James Alo Reilly.

38

The handcart was lying heeled-up on the sidewalk as the *Scrawkey Dawes* took leave of their senses. The offal was scattered all over the road, with *Toby's* brains splattered like custard. Yes, James's rifle had found its mark all right, his rehearsal for the murder of Father Hand had gone off without a hitch.

– So much for my weapon being unusable, he chuckled, making his getaway on the Enniskillen bus.

For the majority of onlookers, the final twitch of the Jack Russell's back leg was almost unbearably poignant. Hardly surprisingly, Una Miniter was hysterical – clutching on to Barney Corr's arm.

– Who else have I got? I have nothing else in this world, Barney! O God! What on earth am I going to do? she wept.

– That fucking lunatic! seethed Jude O'Hara, I knew he'd do it eventually – I just knew it. The poor dog!

But the real truth was that Jude *hadn't* known it. No one had. Who could possibly have anticipated such an outcome? The urchins continued to wail and screech – making a bad situation worse as usual.

– Youse is adding nothing to the whole proceedings!

snapped Barney. Gather up all that stuff and get away to fuck with the whole lot of youse out of here!

The *Scrawkey Dawes* collected the remains of their festering cargo and squealed from behind the shafts of their cart:

– Whether youse admit it or not the devil is back! The town of Cullymore is finished now for sure!

The small dead terrier was placed on the grass. The mute assembly of gathered mourners longed privately for retribution of the fiercest kind. The truth being that the long-standing threat to Father Hand now was being taken very seriously indeed – with a lot of them feeling guilty for having trivialised it in the past. Father Hand was beside himself. As he clenched his meaty fists and swept back his shock of white hair.

– *To think we've come to this!* he wailed.

– It's a terrible day, moaned Dagwood Slowey mournfully, a terrible fucking day, so it is. God forgive me for cursing, Father!

But Father Hand had more to concern him than the shortcomings of Dagwood Slowey. Or anyone else.

– To think a human being would sink so low! I swear to God I'll swing for the bastard!

The priest said he would drive Mrs Miniter home himself. As the pet's still-warm carcass was placed in the boot, wrapped up in a child's blanket. Not so much as a word was uttered along the way, by either pilot or passenger. But Father Hand vowed that this, beyond all doubt, was now the end. In a civilised country, such behaviour simply could no longer be tolerated. And where was the civic guard? Drunk, or out of town. Either way he had been no use to Una Miniter.

– *Fuck!* he snapped, and went white as a sheet, hurting his knuckles on the steering wheel as he struck it – shamed by his housekeeper's wounded, downcast eyes. Who managed to display her disapproval of his swearing, even in the extremity of her sorrow, aspiring to better things on his behalf.

In the *Yankee Clipper*, talk of a very serious nature began developing. There were suggestions of vigilantes going out to the hovel. To fix James Reilly once and for all.

– Whether we like it or not it's gone too far! And it's us that has let it! snapped Dagwood Slowey, bringing his fist down on to the weathered oaken counter.

– I'll snap an iron bar across his back! promised Barney Corr. I'll beat the effing homo to a pulp with my bare hands. I'll murder the cunt!

– Does anyone have any idea where the shot might have come from? Did anyone happen to see where he was hiding?

– No one knows, the butcher explained, for loony and all though he might be, he's still too cute to allow himself to be seen.

– Then maybe it wasn't *him*, this hesitant voice suggested, could it be that we have accused the wrong man?

– For the love and honour of Christ! roared Barney Corr, what do you think this is, do you think we're down in the band hall practising a play? What do you think this is – fucking *Tenebrae*? Oo I can find no wrong in him – bollocks! There's only one suspect in this case – James A. Reilly, the mental fucking teacher! That's all – that's the end. So keep your mouth shut, you effing well-meaning moron!

– It could be the devil is working through the poor unfortunate, the reasonable but somewhat timorous voice went on to suggest.

– You and the devil. You'd think the devil was to blame for everything. The devil has nothing to do with it. I say let's go out and fix the fucker now. He's only got this far on account of the cop. Whether the policeman and his father were comrades in the civil war or not, the fact is he ought to have been arrested months ago.

– If he isn't charged, announced the barman, I'll string the scoundrel up myself!

But they drifted home in dribs and drabs, with the great majority, far from acting decisively, finding themselves now quite sickeningly apprehensive. Which gratified me considerably, I have to say – there being something quite disarming about their forlorn exposure. Especially when, one by one, they emerged into the street, as though they'd just been been granted an end-of-the-war licence.

With even Patsy Murray, usually one of the more disciplined individuals, unsteady and bleary-eyed, fuming with inarticulate rage, standing in the town square with both his fists raised – touchingly challenging the immensity of the cosmos.

– I know that you're up there, and that you're playing with our lives! Who are you? Whoever you are, why can't you leave us alone? My wife Golly hasn't been well lately. I don't know what's wrong with her. She's been having turns. There are times when I wonder if her mind's her own at all. Have you taken it from her – is that what has been happening? Please tell me! She's not sleeping at night – she hasn't been sleeping properly for months!

He continued for some time with his lachrymose imprecations, at one point actually sinking to his knees.

Poor old Patsy. He really was at his wits' end, kneeling there head-down in the square. The personification of the dignified, courageous *common man*.

It was well after two when Patsy at last arrived home from the pub. Boniface was lying fast asleep beside his mother. Not wanting to wake them, the red-eyed barber crept down to the sitting room – throwing himself, exhausted, on to the sofa. Only to wake up unexpectedly a mere half an hour later – disturbed. Consumed by a dire agony, if the truth be told, his features in the mirror white with restrained passion.

He was never to speak of what he had seen that night.

He could have sworn someone was breathing in the room.

39

Golly had made an appointment with the doctor. Before leaving she made her husband a sandwich and gave him a kiss. Lots of times Golly and Patsy got on well and you would think it was just like the old days when they did. They didn't even talk about his getting home late or say anything at all about Una Miniter's dog. They simply wanted now to get on with their lives. But that wasn't always as easy as it seemed.

– *Yes, it's positive, Mrs Murray, there is no doubt but you are indeed pregnant* the doctor said to Golly, who when she heard the news became somewhat uncharacteristically irate and replied:

– *No, you see, I'm afraid you are wrong.*

But the doctor replied that he *wasn't* mistaken. He most certainly wasn't, he insisted, and for facts of the matter were that she was *definitely* pregnant.

– In fact by my calculations you are already three months gone.

It was a bad thing to happen, it most certainly was – as far as Golly Murray was concerned. Because she wasn't ready to have another child. In fact she was trying hard never to slap Boniface – ever again. And it wasn't proving easy. She was sorry she had ever allowed him to keep that stupid blowpipe. That stupid shooter that he'd got free with *Kellogg's Cornflakes*.

How many times had he blown the peas at that stupid cardboard carton? Over twenty-five at least. Was it any wonder she'd lose her temper? Not that she had actually meant to *slap* her son – of course she hadn't. Not even a little. And she wouldn't have – if he had stopped, that is, whenever he was asked. But no, he had kept on doing it. Kept on lifting the blowpipe and defying her.

– Give me that shooter, Boniface, do you hear? she had shrieked. As he made a face. A stupid face.

Then the boy had pointed accusingly at her, contorting his features in that awful way she hated – and loathed herself for doing so. When her husband came home he knew what had happened – that she and Boniface had been fighting again. He could tell. And gave her a look of near despair. Now this, she thought. What if this child turned out to be handicapped too, she kept thinking.

Patsy was at rehearsals but she resolved to tell him the minute he came home. It would be a whole new beginning for them, she had convinced herself. But when he arrived, she found the subject impossible to broach. Patsy kept going on about the play. For him, he insisted, it was touch and go if *Tenebrae* would go ahead at all.

– Another row, he muttered behind the paper.

As Golly Murray turned her head towards the window, gazing across to the far side of the street where a single amber street light was glowing. There would never be a right time to tell him, she thought.

I really will have to do it now, she persuaded herself. She would just have to share the doctor's news with her husband.

– Patsy love, I'm *puh-puh-puh*, she began – then faltered. She drew her breath and tried again.

– Patsy love, I'm *puh-puh-puh-puh* . . .

It wasn't any use. She couldn't manage it. Then Patsy said:

– Would there be any chance of a little cup of tea?

And she stood in the kitchen, feeling like *Laika*. Staring down at the sugar and wondering what it was.

40

The first major death wasn't long after that – Dagwood. Subsequently they all started going down like ninepins – *one two three four five*, some in the 1960s and others in the '70s. And, as I say, it made no difference to me. Yes, poor old Dagwood Slowey the pigeon man was the first of Father Hand's old *gang* to depart, collapsing from a stroke one cold winter's night. Large funerals were still the custom at that time so the whole town turned out to pay their respects. Father Hand was fulsome in his praise – as might have been expected for the popular snooker-hall owner.

– We will never in our lives see his likes again, for he represented all that is special about our close-knit community – where no one has ever been considered a stranger. This fond little place that defines us all. May Dagwood's immortal soul rest in peace.

His birds, baskets, clocks and lofts were put up for auction some days later.

After Dagwood, it was Dean Harry Gribbins' turn – crashing his *Morris Minor* through a window, if you don't mind. When – and I really must say with this it was difficult to suppress a chuckle or two – in the process of piloting the vehicle down the main street he found his attention momentarily distracted by the sight of a lady's black lace brassiere mounted on a mannequin and instantly lost control of the vehicle. There were a couple of others who went that same year, but I won't bother going into the circumstances. For, as I say, what is the ebb and flow of time to me?

Although I have to admit that there is and always will be something quite special about that glorious year of 1958 – principally on account of *Tenebrae*, I suppose. Never was a metaphor for the farcical pantomime called life so colourfully and convincingly enacted. But we'll come to that later – it representing, I suppose, our heroic and glorious *grand finale*.

In the meantime, modernity was fast approaching the town. Indeed it had changed more in the past twenty years than in the previous two hundred. And people began feeling that *something* should be done. To mark the passing of the old rural ways.

– Now that our community is changing, they said, it might be fitting to remember the old times somehow. Look around you – it all seems so different to the Cullymore of long ago.

And it was undeniable. Indeed by the time the decade of the 1970s came around, what with all the building and construction that had been going on, it was becoming more like the suburb of a city. The Cullymore of the old days was definitely fading fast, it was widely agreed.

*   *   *

And so it came to pass that in 1975, the year of Albert Craig's death at the age of seventy-seven, an art exhibition was mounted for the express purpose of celebrating the *old* Cullymore. Jude O'Hara had suggested that it would be a great way of preserving the memory of those who had *shuffled off their mortal coil*, as he'd put it. Patsy Murray agreed, but was at pains to point out that his involvement would have to be curtailed, considering the way things were *at home*. They'd been having a few problems securing Boniface a place in the sheltered workshop – he was acting up again. Everyone understood and assured them they were more than delighted to have him involved. Since the recent onset of *Parkinson's* in early '74, Father Hand couldn't assist as much as he'd like either. But himself and Mrs Miniter pledged that they would do their best and attend as many meetings as possible. Happy Carroll, of course, couldn't be asked – what with his having gone *odd*, as it was termed.

– Happy Carroll's his own worst enemy, Jude O'Hara insisted, any friends he had he made sure they turned against him. He's better off now where he is, away from everybody where he can't do any harm.

A lot of the younger people, including Imelda and Ralph Foster, now long-married, had become deeply involved in local activities – so they threw their considerable weight behind the project. In fact, Imelda and Verity proved of great assistance to Conleth Foley – who, being the curator, was the real driving force behind the *Faithful Departed Exhibition* – selected in the end as the most appropriate name for the special event.

Which included a portrait of Mrs Markey standing smiling outside her café on a sunny day and another of Dagwood with a pigeon perched on either arm. And many other well-known individuals who had since gone to their eternal rest.

To add a sense of atmosphere to the proceedings, the *Salvation Army* – although their numbers in recent times were much depleted – agreed to assemble in the town square and perform a rendition of *The Old Rugged Cross*. With the bandleader attesting that they were privileged to have become involved.

– To represent that unique sense of belonging we have always had in Cullymore – a place where everyone knows who they are, who they are and where they come from, whether Protestant or Catholic. And that's what *community* is all about.

– The opposite of the *Stray Sod Country*, Jude had smiled.

– That's a splendid idea, Bodley Foster had replied whenever he was approached, I'd be more than delighted to help in whatever way I can. After all, we're all part of the *Old Cullymore*! There will never be strangers in our little town!

Before returning to the parlour to attend to his wife Blossom – who, only recently, had been diagnosed with *glaucoma*.

In the heel of the hunt, the exhibition turned out be an extraordinarily worthwhile event, with the local paper dedicating two whole pages of photographs to it – carrying many images of those who had once so proudly walked the streets of the town. OUR GALLERY OF THE PAST, proclaimed the heading.

The opening night, in particular, had been particularly successful – as convivial an occasion as could possibly have been imagined.

– Which is just as it should be, Hope Fairleigh-Warburton had enthused in her much-praised opening speech.

There were so many pieces on show to admire, she suggested, not least the portrait of Dean Harry Gribbins. There was also a photograph of the Redemptorist *missioners* to which she drew attention – looking splendidly fierce in their black suits and collars. And a somewhat crude drawing of Manus Hoare, attired in his battle fatigues, against a backdrop of a giant golden harp – entitled *Manus Hoare, Son of Erin*.

However, by common consensus, the centrepiece of the show had to be Conleth Foley's extraordinary tonal engraving – a piece to which he had accorded the title of *The Stray Sod Country*. Which, although they might not have admitted as much, had deeply unsettled a number of people. The engraving had been described in the paper as *somewhat enigmatic*, depicting the figure of a young man with his head swathed in bandages, standing on the shore of a lake – with his countenance bearing an expression of abject terror. Not unlike Edvard Munch's *The Scream*, although this was not directly alluded to. With him indicating something terrifying just out of reach – hovering beyond the perimeter of the picture. The fact that the pale hunted figure was attired in a Manchester United football strip only served to deepen the sense of perturbation it invoked. For there were many present who still remembered *Duncan Edwards*.

The party afterwards had been quite fabulous. They were a long way now, they all agreed, from the ancient and innocent days of the 1950s.

– When something like Father Hand's little play could be the highlight of our lives!

Now colour television, fast food, the advent of the supermarket, not to mention affordable cars, air travel and the vast improvement in telecommunications had completely and utterly transformed their lives. And in the process, more or less rendered the old world obsolete – a world where, perhaps regrettably, fear and superstition had too often been predominant.

– When you look back on it now, they mused, as though discussing the affairs of strangers, doesn't it seem a little daft all the same?

– Why there's times when you'd have been forgiven for thinking that the town had lost its mind!

– Back in those funny old *Tenebrae* days!

Father Hand had sent his apologies – he hadn't been able to make it to the exhibition, unfortunately – remaining in the presbytery where, as always, he was lovingly cared for by the ever-loyal Mrs Miniter.

Ralph Foster had been standing at the bar with his son and daughter and wife Imelda, waiting on Verity and Austin to join them when, unfortunately, someone had gone and mentioned the accent incident across the border – the bombing which had taken place the previous night, in which seven people had lost their lives. Thankfully, however, and almost straight away, someone moved in swiftly in order to pour oil on troubled waters.

– This exhibition is just the kind of thing we need, isn't it, officer? Yes! he enthused, pumping the policeman's hand as he did so.

– Thank you, replied Ralph, it's a pity more people don't feel like that.

– These *men of violence*. Sooner or later they're bound to get sense.

Patsy and Golly dropped by for a short while. Conleth Foley professed himself delighted to see them.

– Goodness me but you're both looking well! I haven't seen you for ages – where on earth have you been hiding yourselves?

Patsy Murray smiled warmly and said:

– It's Boniface, you know. Him and our other boy Luke – it can be difficult at times.

Their second child Luke had turned out to be extremely intelligent – gifted, in fact, the doctor had said. But, regrettably, there had always been problems between him and their first-born.

– *Youse care about him more than youse ever did about me!* was his constant refrain.

There had been no talking to Luke, unfortunately, who, now in his teens, had also been getting into trouble at school – albeit of a different kind.

Just at that moment, Blossom Foster sidled up, linked by her friend Hope Fairleigh-Warburton. Even now, after all this time, Golly – to her shame – found herself entertaining familiar, quite unworthy thoughts: *even though she's going blind, she still thinks that she's better than me. She makes me* sick!

– Have you seen the *Stray Sod* picture – the one of the young man out by the lake? enquired Hope. What a remarkable work!

– I don't know much about paintings, replied Golly.

– Come with us now, Mrs Murray, and we'll tell you everything we know about modern art!

– It's wonderful you're here, chirped Blossom, I suppose you heard about my recent illness? *Glaucoma.*

I'm glad, Golly seethed inwardly, *I just can't tell you how overjoyed I was to hear about it. It really was the most wonderful news!*

Bodley Foster came over with a tray – tall and authoritative in his Harris tweed jacket.

– Isn't it great that we're all here together? he smiled.

– We're a wonderful little community, beamed Blossom, if only our old friend Albert was here to see it.

– It'd be like the *Foresters* in the years gone by, sighed Bodley.

Hope proceeded with her analyses of modern art. Golly set her teeth, drew a breath and looked away.

– *The Stray Sod*, apparently, explained Hope, is a concept deriving from Irish folklore. It's to do with being lost in what once were reassuring surroundings. Being intimidated, confused – by the very thing that once made you feel secure. You feel, or so they say, that you've been entrapped, deceived. Tricked and snared by a seemingly beautiful world.

– I *know* what the *Stray Sod* is, replied Golly, somewhat sullenly.

– Of course you do, of course you do, continued Hope, how silly of me.

As Conleth Foley, a little tipsily, leaned across with one eye closed as he told them:

– It's what happens, Miss Warburton, when the unholy gate closes. When your neighbours – or who you thought were your neighbours – have revealed themselves to be *the unknown*. Which is what they have been all along.

What exactly had happened to Conleth Foley the night of the exhibition nobody had been able to establish for certain. That the pace of his drinking had been giving cause for concern was not in doubt. Initially he had been feared drowned in the lake – but had eventually turned up the following day, unshaven and quite distracted.

– Ah well, there you have it, that's artists for you, laughed Barney Corr, shaking his head good-humouredly, sure who knows what goes on inside their heads?

Even as he spoke Barney's card was being marked and a few short months later at the close of 1975, a heart attack removed him also from proceedings.

As might have been expected in the case of a small-town butcher, the turnout at his funeral was equally impressive, with mourners numbering well into the hundreds. Which was laudable, considering the dreadful events which had taken place just that morning when two Catholic farmers had been dragged from a remote farmhouse and pitchforked to death – by whom no one could say as yet. In such circumstances it would have been perfectly understandable if nobody had wanted to leave their house at all. But such was the enduring popularity of Barney Corr that they obstinately insisted on paying their respects. Then it was back to the hotel to share stories – and talk about the old times and good old Father Hand.

– And those happy times of his *Tenebrae* play.

41

Yes, those long-departed *Tenebrae* days, those hazy, innocent and superstitious times when *Laika* the mongrel orbited the earth and the parish priest they had loved and respected showed the Mayo donkey Father Patrick Peyton just what Cullymore was made of. Back in the days when Barney Corr, and so many others like him, were far from dead and had not the slightest intention of approaching that state – because they were far too busy, just as the popular butcher was now, standing there behind his counter, threatening once more to suspend his thespian services. Once and for all to resign from the play.

– *Definitely this time! For it's caused me nothing but grief,* complained Barney.

As his customers nodded, no strangers, it seemed, to the peculiar demands of the victualler's artistic calling.

But as always in the end, just as it was for all the other similarly disgruntled members of the *Tenebrae* cast, somehow he inevitably seemed to relent. And find himself once more looking forward to – and boasting about – the wonderful, forthcoming day of Good Friday, when he would don his best suit and proudly remark, as he promised, to his wife:

– Whatever complaints I might have had are over, Mrs Corr! These ordinary days when we stand here alive – they're the best fucking days of our lives and that's what you and I should always remember!

– Hush! Don't be cursing during Lent. We don't want Father Hand to hear you! urged his spouse.

Barney smiled as he thought again of the woman he had married – and had treasured and loved for almost thirty years.

– A pound of chops? Right you be there, Mrs! he chirped behind his counter, as he went over the lines of *Tenebrae* in his mind. Wondering just what the *big day* would be like. Good Friday 1958.

A day that, when it eventually came around, as it inevitably would, would see Barney Corr not being the only person to find himself overcome. No – for a certain Father Hand was going to be even worse. Why, with only a few wet weeks to go, one March evening in '58, back in those fondly remembered times, he could see it all clearly.

– O man, he was repeating to his busy-bee housekeeper, I'm just like a child on *First Communion* morning! I can't sit still for thinking about my show. You know how I have always wanted to put our town on the map, don't you, Una? Of course you do – you're my oldest friend. And nobody, believe me, is going to stop me – certainly not the murderer of your little *Toby. Especially* not him! I'll see he pays for what he did!

– Yes, replied Una, sobbing as she looked away.

As Father Hand smiled and gripped his knife and fork, suddenly and without thinking elevating his eyebrows and exclaiming in an acute, shrill voice:

– Bejapers, I'd do jail for some more of that tasty cabbage!

One of the reasons he had been feeling so good was that rehearsals for the play had been coming along splendidly in the past few days. And, against all the odds, everything else seemed to be falling into place. The street banners looked great and the set itself had been quite magnificently constructed by Happy Carroll and his tireless team of carpenters. And as far as the performances of the *Tenebrae* players were concerned, no praise could be considered high enough – with Barney Corr in the role of Pilate lately having proven nothing short of a revelation. All that remained to be done now was to eliminate these accursed and persistent rumours once and for all – yes, all this nonsense about James Reilly and his declared intention to commit murder. Which had even seen calls for *Tenebrae* to be abandoned. From people who ought to have known better. Individuals – it beggared belief! – suggesting that, in the light of what had happened to Mrs Miniter's dog *Toby*, going ahead might actually be *tempting providence*. They wouldn't put anything past James Reilly, they said. Who knew what he might be capable of? After all, he still hadn't been arrested. No one even seemed to know where he was, for heaven's sake. There was no sign of him out at the lake.

– It's very possible that he will go ahead. And do what he's been promising to do all along!

– Let him try it – let him just fucking try it! snarled the priest, and it'll be his very last act on God's fucking earth!

42

Teddy O'Neill hadn't made it to the *Faithful Departed Exhibition* – he hadn't been feeling all that well – kind of depressed. He would have liked to, however – for he often borrowed books on art from the library. Alphonsus was now thirty-five years of age, and was still hanging on hopefully to his long-cherished dream, that of building an elaborate American-style gas station on a site he had earmarked for that express purpose. In 1970 he had married a local girl Tessie Greenan and bowled her over completely by his sheer enthusiasm for this project. He intended to install a juke-box and a coffee dock, he told her.

– Now that it's the 1970s, Tessie, he'd assured her, there are good times coming in this country and me and you, we are gonna make a go of it. Way I see it, Cullymore has no choice but to catch up, get stuck in there and embrace the new ways – no hiding behind the door with our mouths hanging open. It's all about progress now, Tessie, and if we board the train we can turn this town around real fast. As my old mate *Billy Fury* used to sing, we'll turn Cullymore into a *wondrous place*.

He didn't really anticipate any difficulty at all, he said – elaborating further. The basic plan was to extend their already existing humble outlet, which Tessie had inherited from her father, and move into all sorts of uncharted areas.

– I don't know for certain, he told the boys in the *Yankee Clipper*, I'll have to talk it over with my lady. But at the moment I see no reason why we couldn't run gigs there, concerts – you know? Nothing special maybe, in the beginning – but it could build and grow.

To this end he intended, he asserted without flinching, to enlist the services of some of the entertainment people he had met while working across the water.

– Did I ever tell youse about me and *Adam Faith*, one night we went drinking after being in the *Two I's?* I didn't? Well . . . !

They would act, of course, as though they had never heard it before – hopefully nodding in all the right places.

– Then we hired a taxi and headed down to Brighton. There we are in a dance hall called the *Palais*, when this bloody flash boy – and, believe you me, he was a sour-looking customer – what does he do, he goes up to *Adam* and out of nowhere starts giving him *gyp*. And if that's not bad enough what's he do then – pulls out the shiv. Pulls out the fucking *shiv*, for Christ's sake. I mean I don't mind – but it's fucking *Adam Faith* and I'm not having that. No, I said – I'm not having that. Not a chance, friend.

They had heard the story a thousand times. He had been telling it ever since he had returned from England, years before. But it wasn't until he married Tessie after getting her pregnant that all this talk about *gas stations* began. In the beginning it had been innocent enough. At times, though, it could become ridiculous – especially if he'd had a few drinks. Then it wouldn't just be *my mate Billy Fury*. But ludicrous accounts of nights spent drinking with the *Shadows* and God knows who else. As he rocked back and forth at the bar counter, snapping his fingers and zigzagging towards the jukebox.

For a period, however, it seemed as though he was seeing sense at last. He had decided to catch himself on, he announced – and start listening to his wife.

– The one pump will do us just for now, love, Tessie had good-humouredly suggested, for after all I'm ticking over quite nicely in the shop. So there really is no need for any of these wild plans, at least not just yet. Maybe later, when we've a bit more put by.

The more he thought about it, Teddy began to accept the reasoning behind his wife's analysis of the situation. Still, he'd often find himself sighing, it would have been nice, maybe even just once – to come strolling out in his petrol-blue overalls and lean over the side of Verity Fry's *Datsun*, chewing his gum the way he had imagined it. He had seen her a lot lately, driving her motor around the town. He wished she'd pull in – but she never actually had. He, in fact, longed for that to happen, so he could show her and Austin Fry just how cool he could actually be – when the situation called for it. Seeing himself crossing the forecourt louchely, approaching the car without a care in the world, completely ignoring husband Austin as he greeted Verity, enquiring as to whether she was busy these times.

– I've a mate coming through on Saturday, doll, he heard himself say, he's involved in show business – has just recorded a new single, as a matter of fact. Maybe you've heard it – it's called *You're A Dreamboat*.

She'd know what he meant by that. Or would have – if it had ever happened.

Which it hadn't, of course. For she had never pulled in. And anyway, he thought, more than likely he'd have lost his nerve, and have hid in the back watching Tessie as she served them, chatting and laughing about nothing at all.

For quite a substantial period of time, the somewhat extravagant sideburns had remained. And they still had great gas whenever Duxass or Jo'burg – both of whom were married now too – happened to drop by to *act the bollocks*. But they never stayed long.

Like Duxass had said:

– I guess in a way we're the old-timers now, old buddy.

– Maybe. I guess, Teddy O'Neill had responded, somewhat distantly.

– But we sure had the crack, didn't we, back in the '50s? I mind well the day that you came back from London. And me, like an eejit – I'd never been to England in my life! I used to think you could get the ride there for sixpence! But look, Fonsey – I got to go. The wife is up the town with the kids. See you then, old mate. I'll drop by, maybe, sometime during the week.

– Sure thing, pal. We'll have a beer, yeah? *Thaaang!*

43

No one in town had ever become privy to the potentially explosive information which had come into Dean Gribbins' possession regarding the private practices of the respected dentist Albert Craig and he went to his eternal reward – disappointed, certainly – but at least with his good name intact. But one night Golly Murray woke her husband up – not unusually, in quite a state. Insisting she had seen just the shade of Albert Craig.

– He was weeping and crying about Jenny Cartwright! she insisted. He kept on saying he never touched her. That he *loved* her. But Jenny Cartwright was just fourteen, Patsy!

Patsy reassured her as best he could – and then, thankfully, at last she went back to sleep.

After the passing of Albert, it had indeed begun to seem as if much of the old familiar world had disappeared for ever. Acquiring in the process the inevitable patina of charm. With James A. Reilly routinely now being described as a *character*. Every so often the older citizens who remained would find themselves reminiscing fondly about his antics, and how harmless they had been in so many ways.

– Compared to what's going on nowadays, they would

suggest, what with drugs and violence and God knows what!

– I recall the day well, the *Yankee Clipper* barman would affectionately smile, indeed how would anybody be able to forget it? I mind well the day James urinated in the holy-water font. Took out his todger and pissed away right there and then!

– But do you remember the blood on the sacristy door? That was the best of the whole lot – and us, can you believe it, thinking it was the *devil!*

– And it the blood of an ordinary farmyard rooster!

– A bloody farmyard rooster, for Christ's sake! O Lord above, weren't we the right crowd, the things we believed!

– It was nearly as bad as Mrs Markey's *Hotpoint!*

– Aye – do you mind that! The first electric mixer in the town – and Mrs Markey screaming blue murder like it was possessed! O boys, but it's embarrassing whenever you look back!

– Still, the only thing is – where did James Reilly go in the end? He was never heard tell of after the play. Was he put in jail?

This, as always, proved a conundrum. For no one seemed to know what his fate had been.

– Maybe there was more to him than we thought.

– Maybe he *was* an agent of His Nibs.

– Ah for the love of Christ now, don't start that. Here – give us another round there, and let's say goodbye to those old superstitious days, when us Cullymore bumpkins, swear to God we'd have believed in anything!

44

Teddy O'Neill was replacing a silver hubcap on the tank of an Austin 1140 and was standing back a little to wave goodbye to its owner when he heard his name being called by his wife.

– OK, Tessie! he replied, wincing a little – the truth being that Teddy was suffering from a severe hangover – one which saw his senses becoming alert to an almost unsustainable degree. As he leaned back against the petrol pump listening to the click of his wife's heels approaching across the forecourt, he observed that she was carrying something in her hands. Suddenly he found himself seized by a memory of startling clarity – one in which he saw himself as he once had been. Teddy O'Neill as a *young boy*. Gazing out from his own private world, across the still surface of the *Stray Sod Lake* where he had been lying, as he so often did, beneath the skies watching the birds as they skimmed the verdant slopes, luxuriating in the molten sunsets of childhood memory.

– *Now here we are*, he heard Tessie's voice interrupting his reverie, I've sewed the elbow so it should be all right. Just don't you ever go tearing it again, getting yourself into such a disgusting state.

With an alarming suddenness, he then began remembering it all from the night before – seeing the car door sharply opening as he looked up from the patch of gravel where he had been lying and saw, to his dismay, the face of his wife Tessie. Standing above him as he haplessly crawled along the gravelled road. Behind her he could just about make out the tattered awning, or what remained of it, directly above the boarded-up *Cullymore Café*. Where Mrs Ellen Markey had once entertained her customers – farmers, customs men, policemen, travelling salesmen – and dentists.

– *Get in!* Tessie had hissed – there could be no mistaking the fact that she was mortified. As the door closed with a firm click behind him.

But that, of course, had been the night before. And now it was OK. As she stood there holding his mended sports coat.

– *Look!* his wife declared, in quite good humour now, it seemed – as good as new, an almost perfect jacket!

Before pressing her body up against his, whispering softly that of course she loved him, yes she did but he was never to do the like of that again, did he promise, yes he promised, but even as he did so the thought passed across his mind that he would have rather that a kettle of scalding water had been impenitently flung into his face – as she pecked his cheek and returned inside.

Call them what you will but one will never be given credit for the signals and suggestions which, out of compassion or a quaint sense of justice and fair play, one on occasion has granted to one's subjects – prefigurements, I suppose you might call them, or cautionary intimations. A rehearsal, perhaps, for the *main event*. Not unlike the one experienced by the barber Patsy Murray as he lay beside his wife in the quiet of the small hours, sometime in the 1970s.

It had been a particularly difficult day in the shop, and he hadn't, in any case, been sleeping well of late. He then found himself disturbed by a rustling noise of some kind. Some time elapsed before he at last succeeded in identifying the source of the interruption. A moving pattern was making its way steadily across the wall directly opposite. Initially he took the spreading substance to be *horsehair* of some kind – it was creeping quite fast now, and had completely covered one wall's surface. Its arterial advance gave out a chilling, crackling sound. But it was only when he saw the head of Blossom Foster, standing out in *bas-relief*, as though some pale, immutable *trompe l'oeil*, that he realised what he'd been looking at was in actual fact a diffuse proliferation of pubic hair. Which continued its march, making an awful whispering noise, radiating out to the four corners of the room. Then – the dread the barber experienced as a consequence was profound – Blossom's lips parted and he heard her whisper, with nothing, only *his* solitary attentions in mind:

– Isn't it funny, Patsy? You think you know me – and then you look up and see me like this. Why it's just like that morning I came to your shop. Everything seemed so *ordinary* then too – but it wasn't, was it? No, Patsy Murray – it wasn't one bit ordinary at all.

The perspiration was rolling down his forehead. His wife was still asleep in the bed beside him. Perhaps he ought to wake her and tell her what he had just experienced. But he couldn't do that – it might just upset her. But *of course* it would upset her. Why, might even put her mad. She might end up in the hospital again. So instead he just sat there, frozen, wringing his hands, bolt upright in bed.

Thinking how once he had believed you could tell your wife anything. But you couldn't, of course. There were so many things you could never tell her – or anyone else, for that matter. People you loved and thought you *knew* well. People you had spent your whole life engaging with, laughing and chatting and talking to. And yet, in the end, what had you achieved? You certainly weren't closer to any of them, were you? It was a counterfeit correspondence, a charade, a simulacrum. One that might be necessary for survival but a chimera nonetheless. Why, it was as if they had all been living there already – in the X-ray world that was the *Stray Sod Country*. That was how the barber felt after nearly thirty years of marriage. He felt as though he had reverted to being a child again – terrified and helpless, marooned in the world, inside, beneath his skin, a complete and utter stranger to everyone around him. And they to him, behind the closed unholy gate.

45

The traditional Olympian position of the remote artificer displaying scant interest in the subjects whose affairs he purports to chronicle remains for the most part unchallenged throughout the decades that followed Father Hand's noble bid for international stardom in 1958 – one or two interesting cases excepted. Notably the occasion in the late 1970s when Cullymore Hatchery was burned to the ground. Not that I make any case for it representing a tumultuous event in the history of world affairs, comparable say to *Krakatoa* or maybe *Dresden* – but in the excitement it created it really was hysterical – bringing back, as it did, in a time of supposed modernity, all the old familiar excitement and superstition. Not to mention the attendant qualities of hubris and inflated self-importance. Which were supposed to have vanished into the mists of so-called *Time*!

It soon emerged that thousands of the unfortunate birds had been roasted – scorched to a frazzle, in actual fact.

According to Happy Carroll's account, their poor heads had been cruelly lopped off and their helpless bodies bludgeoned with axes. But to make matters worse – and this, of course, was familiar territory – their warm blood had been used to scrawl obscenities. Yes, by all accounts, their warm blood had been ferried in buckets and used for the purpose of painting the most heinous and barbaric obscenities, just like before, on the sacristy door. Where it remained for all to see:

SOON, WHORE FOSTER. MANUS R.I.P.

It really could not have come at a worse time – what with eleven people having been incinerated at a hotel conference that very morning – ninety miles away, in County Down. And perhaps it was unsurprising that fear and agitation would again begin to take root. But no one really expected the old forgotten rumours to start circulating with such a vengeance – that serious consideration would actually be given to talk regarding the supposed return of the *devil*, and assertions that his *hand* was at work yet again.

But just like in Father Hand's time, these rumours bedded in and began spreading thick and fast. For a while things were looking very grave indeed.

However, thankfully in the end, wiser counsel was seen to prevail. With it ultimately emerging that the guilty parties, far from being in league with paranormal agents, had been nothing more than a trio of drug-addled vagrants who had been making a habit of such escapades – from their base in the city embarking on a rampage of anti-social behaviour, targeting smaller towns around the country for this purpose. The judge suggested they remain incarcerated for a period of no less than eighteen months.

The relief in the *Yankee Clipper* that evening was palpable – not just as regards the old nonsense about the so-called *devil*, which they now dismissed, but because the outcome had put paid conclusively to initial suggestions that the affair had been in some way *politically motivated.* That possibility could never have been countenanced – otherwise it would mean that the old days were well and truly back – that the town had, unhappily, returned to the bad old times in Cullymore – when in March 1958 Manus Hoare, a youth of a mere nineteen years of age, had been cut to ribbons in a disastrous barracks raid, by none other than Sergeant Ralph Foster. Who had then gone on to marry the dead man's sister. It was just about the last topic anyone wanted to dwell on, especially since there had always been rumours associated with that operation – even if they remained unproven. Nobody wanted to entertain the possibility that it might well have been Happy Carroll who had informed on the raiders. Which was why they insisted:

   – Thugs and racketeers – *that's* who defaced the sacristy door. So shut up once and for all about it – and roll on the '80s!

46

He had been twenty years married when at last he decided to pay a visit to his doctor. There Teddy O'Neill was informed that his symptoms suggested *reactive depression* – a diagnosis to which he responded with an admirably mature and measured calm, at no point raising his voice, simply nodding his head as he processed the information. Quietly and reasonably wondering where it might be that his old self had gone – that carefree young teenager from the B & I ferry, who had once sat up drinking with a man twice his age. An old boar of a fellow who had smiled as he christened him *Teddy* O'Neill.

Try as you might to avoid it, he told himself, the reality was that those times were gone for ever. Yes, gone were those carefree days when Teddy O'Neill would have had them all in stitches, hypnotised really, with his stories of his various adventures across the water – and not all of them factual. But what harm had there ever been in that? He rarely even saw Jo'burg or Winky or Duxass now. The only one left who bothered about England was Happy Carroll, and that was because he was glad to have someone to talk to, living on his own by the lake as he had been doing now for years. And who, like all the rest of them, was showing the signs of age. As a matter of fact, looked far older than he actually was, slinking about the place with a crouched and hunted air about him – an unfortunate development which was the inevitable consequence of the years of innuendo and whispers which had become attached, some time after the death of Manus Hoare, when a newspaper report had seemingly identified him. There had always been suspicions, even around the time of the raid itself. But these had never been properly substantiated. All the same there were those who had their opinions.

– I don't know for certain if Happy Carroll is the informer or not. But I know this – he is one contrary man to deal with. God forgive me but I always hate him coming to rehearsals. Nothing pleases him, no matter what I do. No, to tell you the truth, Patsy, it would come as no surprise to me if Happy Carroll does turn out to be an informer, Barney Corr had suggested, one night in the *Yankee Clipper*.

– He gets on my fucking nerves at times too, so he does, growled Patsy Murray. I hate to see him coming around the place. You'd think he'd be ashamed of his life with all these rumours going around. But no – he keeps telling everyone he informed on nobody. Between you and me he's lucky I didn't clip him the other night in here. I never asked him to join my company. I had just been to the hospital with Golly – the last thing I needed was to have to listen to the likes of him!

On that occasion, Happy had kept returning to the subject of women.

– I remember thinking he didn't look right, continued Patsy, there was a look in his eye that was neither normal nor natural. As if he'd know anything about women – telling me how to live my life. What be's wrong with Golly, he kept saying, I seen her the other day and she seems to be failing bad. As if I could tell him the workings of a woman's mind! To shut the fucker up I said maybe, Happy, it's the change of life – could be that that's what's bothering my Golly. But even that wasn't enough – no, he has to know, even though it's none of his bloody business. In the end it got so bad that I couldn't stick it any longer. Right, I says, that is fucking it – fuck away off now from about me, do you hear – and he looks at me then with the eyes biting into me. O he wasn't so happy then, Mr beaming Happy Carroll. Looks at me with the auld lip trembling. All the same, he says, she had no right to say it. Your wife Golly shouldn't have said the like of that to Blossom Foster – even if she is a high and mighty Protestant. After all, she's *losing her sight*. It's not what you say to a person that's *going blind*. She shouldn't have said it, Patsy. *And on the steps of the Protestant church and all!*

In spite of himself, Patsy knew that there was no response he could make to this charge. For they were the very same sentiments he had been wrestling with himself.

The unseemly episode had taken place outside the gates of the Methodist church some days before – at the very beginning of Golly's most recent *turn*. His spouse – who never swore – had confronted Blossom Foster on the steps and said:

– O hello there, Blossom! I can't tell you how delighted I am to hear you're going blind!

Patsy had been mortified – as any God-fearing husband would be. But for the life of him he didn't know what to do about it. Especially when he heard her saying:

– Ha ha – that will teach her to try and trick me. I knew all along what she was up to with her fashion show. Believe me, Patsy – I did. And don't start telling me I was imagining it!

Things were to show no sign of improving as the years progressed. No, regrettably the barber continued to be at sea – utterly perplexed. Why had their lives turned out like this? Sometimes, of course, his wife would be perfectly fine. But then other times she would give you this look – as if it wasn't her who was observing you at all. But someone else – someone you had never clapped eyes on in your life. It was a dreadful thought – and he wanted to think no more about it.

47

Although he had heard Conleth Foley had been behaving uncharacteristically in the days immediately following the *Faithful Departed Exhibition*, Jude the director of *Tenebrae* hadn't given much credence to the gossip until he had called around and discovered his friend sitting upright in the bath, entirely naked apart from his bow tie. When Patsy Murray was informed of this, perhaps not surprisingly he began to laugh. A reaction which left him completely unprepared when, quite by chance, he met the artist by chance on the street. He was wearing the bow tie again – but kept repeatedly loosening it and whipping round, as though anticipating a confrontation of some kind.

– He's playing with us – that's all there is to it.

– Con, you sure do come out with some extraordinary statements, chuckled the barber, with not a little uneasiness evident in his voice as he added:

– And on such a beautiful day and all!

Before looking up to see that Conleth had already departed, calling back in a disappointed croak:

– I know that you don't believe me, Patsy. No one does. But I know what I seen. *I know what I seen, Patsy!*

*　　*　　*

Things had been hardest of all after Boniface's illness in 1978, thought Patsy as he sat there one evening in the kitchen. After which the boy had passed away. That's really what had tipped Golly over the edge. They had always known that it was most likely their son would die – the doctor had always been direct about that. But it hadn't made it any easier. Things had been bad for a long time afterwards. Words would rise to your lips out of nowhere. He didn't know why he said the things he did. Once he had said to his wife:

– You neglected our boy, Geraldine. Why don't you admit it?

Why had he uttered such words? He didn't know – because they weren't true. And he sat there wishing more than anything that he could turn back the clock – to a time when such words had not been spoken by Patsy Murray. For he knew they couldn't have done anything to help Golly – whose nerves had become more fragile than ever.

Her turns in recent times had been inconsistent and unpredictable. And the effect this had was that, however illogically and inappropriately, perhaps while chatting to his friends about local affairs, or purchasing cigarettes across a counter in a shop, Patsy would feel compelled to reveal his innermost fears – principally the one that had him thinking that his wife was in mortal danger of losing her mind altogether.

Patsy Murray plunged his face into his hands, and thought of his wife as a young woman standing before him – smiling as she stared at him from the kitchen corner, wearing the same dress that she'd worn the night they had met in the

Masonic Hall. But when he looked again there was nothing, only the television screen – blinking off and then on again. He was at his wits' end, really – not knowing which way to turn.

The truth was that, were it not for Luke, he didn't know what he'd have done. But it was hard on Luke too – having a brother who had demanded – and had received, over the years – more attention than the younger boy.

– But we'll muddle through, Patsy said to his son.

His only son Luke of whom he was so proud – and who, one day, would qualify as an architect, eventually forging an international reputation.

– Somehow, some way – we'll make our way.

– We will, Da, we will, the bright-eyed boy courageously replied.

I have made no secret of the fact, throughout, that of all the Cullymore citizens I have always perceived Golly to be disarmingly attractive – so wan and frail, so utterly hopeless in her vulnerability. There has always been something quite special about that quality – the sheer *pliability* of her supplicant soul. I arrived one night in her room dressed as Boniface. Looking fresh and smart for this, his *First Communion* morning.

She was found the next morning, standing on the lawn – pointing at nothing and laughing hysterically.

48

During her stay in the hospital, Golly had had time to think about many things – such as the only occasion in their married life that her husband Patsy had ever struck her. He had *threatened* to do it many times, of course, especially whenever Boniface was acting up, but would always manage to draw back at the very last moment. Until that Holy Thursday evening in 1958 when he, as he had informed her, was finally at his wits' end. No, his *fucking* wits' end, which was what he actually said.

– *I am sorry I ever had anything to with that play!* he had snapped. *There's been nothing, only arguments, right from the very start!*

On top of that, he had allowed himself to be recruited as one of Father Hand's so-called vigilante brigade, which had set about finishing off James Reilly – good and proper.

– We must ensure that nothing at all interferes with *Tenebrae*, the priest had bawled unrestrainedly from the pulpit, with the advent of *Holy Week* and the play coming up, there simply is far too much at stake!

Then he had marched them out to James Reilly's shack.

– Be prepared, he had counselled them, as soon as you enter this domicile of evil to find yourself affronted by something close to a demon. The moment you cross this evil threshold you will find yourselves in the abode of wickedness incomparable, a place where resides utter *badness* itself – a domain which insults all right-thinking mortals. Where vice and malignity lurk in every corner!

His voluble testimony suddenly seeming laughable, even shameful, as with the aid of Patsy and the others he eventually tore down the rickety door – and found himself confronted by a sad string of clothes drying above the fire. A cracked photograph of Reilly's mother sat poignantly on top of the television.

For the first time in living memory, Father Hand's standing was considerably reduced in front of his parishioners. And he knew it.

– Youse have got to believe me, he cried in a panic, he's Satan's man on earth, I tell you – *the Antichrist* – call him what you will! Where are you, Reilly? Is this another of your infernal schemes? Show your face, you devil's gillie!

But already the sorry-looking band of would-be vigilantes was making its hangdog way back to town.

– No, please! pleaded the priest, seeing in his mind Patrick Peyton sneering.

But he resolved not to let him – not to let Peyton, of all people, undermine his efforts. Not now, at this eleventh hour! Now, more than ever, he would make *Tenebrae* a success beyond anyone's wildest imaginings!

– And see that you hang your head in shame. Do you hear me, Peyton – you impertinent fucking Mayo mule!

49

Looking back on it now, with the benefit of hindsight, I can see plainly that the good priest managed to get himself into such a state over the incident that he could count himself lucky not to have been taken away himself – and maybe billeted along with Golly in the confines of *Balla Mental Hospital*. Not that anyone would ever mention his *mysterious disappearance*. For in those days such sensitive subjects were taboo. With the generally accepted practice being that if your wife or spouse – or in this hypothetical case, one's parish priest – happened to be committed to an institution, you simply declared that they had gone away *on holiday*. Or were perhaps visiting a mother or ailing relative.

In the case of Geraldine Murray, however, the most recent breakdown had caused Patsy a great deal of stress – he found himself tired of having to come up with excuse after excuse to explain his wife's absence. But now that she had returned, what did it matter.

They could act as if it had never happened, he reassured himself. Especially since her stay had proved such a triumph! Yes, what a success her stay had proved!

*　　*　　*

Or so Patsy had insisted to his customers. Thankfully now, he informed them as he clipped and scissored away, now that she was back at home and on the proper medication, his wife would be more than capable, the doctors had guaranteed it, of giving her family all the attention that they needed. Of going about her business like any ordinary wife.

She would routinely attend to all domestic matters, he went on, all the cooking and cleaning and such – just like she used to, before this infernal trouble had come upon them.

Patsy said it was really fantastic to see her back to her old self, smiling.

But, although of course he didn't mention the fact, it was even better to have her back in the marital bed – just like it used to be. Patsy became convinced that all their misfortune was now at an end.

And, as they lay there together the very same night, the old contentment had indeed returned as he meticulously scrutinised the football results in the *Daily Star*, tuning the TV handset until at last he located the BBC radio station, and the *Sail Away* theme came sweeping out as it always had. Followed by the soft caring tones of the announcer, so caring and benign that it might have been the voice of God.

– *Rockall, Hebrides, south-west gale 8 to storm 10, backing southerly, severe gale 9 to violent storm 11. Rain, then squally showers. Moderate, becoming poor.*

So reassuring that, just for the briefest of moments – as Patsy Murray folded his paper – he dared to contemplate the possibility that a period of sustained happiness now lay before the Murrays. Until he found himself dismayed as he turned and recognised the familar expression. As his wife enquired, in that glassily abstracted way:

    – I'm sorry to have to tell you. But I'll be leaving you shortly – for outer space.

50

Her tone of confounded impotence sounding not at all dissimilar to that of Una Miniter when on one never-to-be-forgotten morning in 1978 she had heard a small, almost childlike cry issuing from the master bedroom and rushed upstairs to discover the body of her adored employer Father Hand lying on top of the covers – his *Parkinson's disease* having finally claimed him.

– *He's dead!* she had wept uncontrollably on the landing. *O no, God help us – Father Hand is dead!*

– He died with the name of *Father Peyton* on his lips, she would often be heard murmuring softly to herself, for many years afterwards.

Trying as best she could not to sin in her heart – but it was difficult. For, although no one would ever have dreamed it, much less give voice to such an unthinkable possibility, Una Miniter had actually been in love with her deceased employer. Even if she never admitted as much – even to herself.

But now that he was gone, as she sat there alone in the bereft silence of her presbytery bedroom, scarcely a month after the funeral, she found herself once more thinking about *Gussie*, as she had called him, if only in secret.

Imagining herself kissing his robe over and over, unable to stop herself, actually covering his chasuble with little pecks and wanting, more than anything, Father Hand to return to life. Which of course was not possible – except that it was. For that very night she *saw* Father Hand – standing naked in the corner and reaching his liver-spotted hand out to her.

– *Why didn't you tell me, Una?* he croaked, *for the truth was that I loved you too.* Except that I didn't have the courage ever to tell you. O God when I think of the time that I spent upon this earth, and what I would do if I had it again. I would leave the priesthood, I don't care – I would! And I'd take you to see *Frank Sinatra* with me! We could go to *Pat Boone* in *Madison Square Garden* – and I wouldn't care about Father Peyton, so I wouldn't. And do you know why – because I'd have a woman who really loves me! A lovely woman who isn't my dead Mammy! *O God!*

Huddled there clad in her white elastane underwear, Una Miniter cried like she had never done before, pecking at his stole like a woman possessed. As Father Hand whispered:

– Sweet Mrs Miniter. My sweet and gorgeous Una. Why did I have to die, my precious pet? The wonderful times we both could have had – if only I'd known! If only we'd had the courage!

– I loved you passionately, o so passionately, she choked, but I hadn't the nerve to tell you either! I just couldn't find it in myself, Father Hand!

– Why do we have to die, lovely Una? Why must we become the *Faithful Departed?*

51

With whose legions *Blossom Foster* was also to become united, passing away peacefully in the mid-1990s. After which her husband Bodley was never the same again.

Patsy Murray had met him one evening by chance, looking hopelessly out of sorts, as though he had just drifted there in a daze, into the *Sky Sports Bar*, the fancy new pub which had recently replaced the *Yankee Clipper*. It seemed as if he wasn't standing there at all – but felt himself in some distant place . . .

– Maybe we've been strangers all the time, he said, and that, in spite of what we thought, that's what we were all along. Do you ever think that might be the case, Patsy?

The barber found himself stammering hopelessly – completely at a loss. But the retired bank manager was not bothered in the slightest. Because he wasn't listening.

– I miss my wife, Patsy heard him continue, but then maybe I spend too much time on my own. I go over all the times the two of us spent together. I just can't accept that the woman I loved is gone for ever.

– She's gone to join them, Bodley, she's taken her place among the ranks of the *faithful departed*. All the people we knew who once walked these streets.

– Yes, said the bank manager, as though unconvinced, I suppose that must be where she's gone.

Patsy had finished up his drink and left. Thinking, somewhat shamefully, that, having troubles enough of his own to contend with, he had provided little solace. And it made him feel guilty – surely it ought to have been his duty to demonstrate some form of fellow feeling with his fellow citizen.

Especially now that Golly seemed to be in much better form – had been now – *touch wood* – for months. She had even said that she loved him the night before. Relieving him immensely by telling him that, at last, those awful dreams which had been troubling her had stopped. Particularly the one about Boniface – wearing his white *First Communion* badge as he stood there before her with a perfectly made little basket of coloured plasticine eggs.

The only thing worrying Patsy being the possibility that this might be just another false alarm – another cruel and deceptive period of respite which would ultimately prove as short-lived as all the others.

And that then it would be back the very same as before. But somehow, he thought, this felt different. It really did.

52

*– Yes, in this grave hour, all Irish men and women, at home
and abroad, must sink their differences, political and religious,
and rally behind the banner of national liberation.*

Those were the words which had been spoken by Manus
Hoare, quartermaster and *IRA* volunteer, in the *Tenebrae
year* of 1958, a week before the performance of the play,
and not long before his unit set off to get themselves shot
to pieces. When they arrived in their commandeered truck
in the middle of the main street of the unsuspecting border
town. After the first volley of shots children started screaming and mothers ran out in an effort to whisk them off the
street, as a grenade was flung but failed to go off, rolling
back in underneath the truck – then exploding.

The automatic fire turned the van into a veritable slaugh-
terhouse, and Manus himself was already wounded in three
places. They clambered aboard and attempted to retreat,
but unfortunately never made it.

In the *Yankee Clipper*, violent retribution of all kinds
was pledged – by Happy Carroll no less than the others,
his perfidy not as yet suspected. On account of his relative
youth, the degree of sympathy exhibited for Manus Hoare
was considerable. Poor lad, they said, all he was doing was

trying to free his country. They then declared themselves hurt when they approached his sister and found themselves informed that she didn't want to know about any plans for commemorations or anything else. Ending up calling her a Protestant collaborator whose very own husband had been responsible for the carnage. These were the very same sentiments which would surface twenty years later when Father Hand's successor, at a specially organised commemorative *Mass for Manus Hoare*, felt compelled to make it clear that he had no intention of allowing his community to open old wounds.

– That's all in the past, my friends, he began persuasively, and that's where it should remain. Such terrible events belong to a different time. And that is where they ought to stay. Indeed there are occasions when I ask myself what sort of place we were living in in those days. One might be forgiven for thinking we had taken leave of our senses, some of the things that seemed to go on. Thankfully, I feel, we're more civilised now, and that the time has come to replant the garden.

The young priest may well indeed have had a valid point. For when that period is even cursorily examined, it does certainly seem over-represented by what might be termed individuals of a more than usually ardent caste. Hot-blooded, and at times irrational. Particularly on what might be called that long-awaited *Tenebrae* morning, to which we must now return for our glorious *grand finale*, as promised. Yes, on that *Good Friday* morning of *Holy Week* 1958, where there was quite an uncommon degree of excitement on display.

Why, already Father Hand had been up since the crack of dawn, pottering around muttering and fussing and organising. As indeed why wouldn't he, as Una Miniter had just observed, now that the holiest of holy days had arrived at long last. On this *glorious, glorious* day, as she put it – pursuing her employer, to no avail, with a clothes brush.

– Make no mistake, this is the most significant day of my life, the parish priest declared, yes, after today, Mrs Una Miniter, I'm afraid the game is up for poor old Father Peyton. When this is all over, he'll be afraid to show his face, so he will! As soon as word gets out that Father Gus Hand succeeded in putting on the show of all time, the show *by jiminy* to end them all, with no assistance whatsoever from *bobby-dazzlers* or *good-time Charlies*. No – for all he required was the assistance of ordinary, decent, hard-working people. So put that in your drum, Father Patrick, and *bang it!*

In spite of the prevailing spirit of excitement, it could not be denied that the preparations for the play had not been without their share of difficulty – difficulties of a not inconsiderable nature. That there had always been a certain degree of bad feeling between certain cast members needs no repeating here. And, to add to this irrefutable fact, it was now rumoured that James A. Reilly had been spotted the very night before – out by the lake again, polishing his rifle.

At the Holy Thursday ceremony, the parish priest had made one final dignified appeal.

– Please be reasonable, my dear people, he had requested, can't you see we have no need to worry about Reilly any longer. He isn't the agent of Satan at all, he's nothing more than a deluded malcontent. In any case, he's gone and won't be coming back. He's cleared off – didn't you see that the hovel he lives in was abandoned, empty? Won't dare show his face ever again, I should imagine.

But the teacher *was* seen again – not long after midnight, and not out at the lake. But scuttling down an alleyway, clutching his *Lee Enfield*. It wasn't any use, try as they might, the dread and anticipation – it simply would not go away.

As he emerged through his doorway now on this final Good Friday morning, out into the fresh clean air of the town, passing through the presbytery gates in his black-and-gold vestments, what infuriated Father Hand most was the obstinate damned endurance of this thorny disquiet. You just couldn't seem to get a hold of the thing – but it was everywhere. These were the thoughts that preoccupied his mind as he crossed the square with his white hair flying, all of a sudden seized by a sensation of deep resentment. Which he had not legislated for – it took him completely by surprise. It was as though Father Peyton were smiling from the shadows.

– *Get out of the way, you stupid cur!* Father Hand snarled at a loping abject mongrel, aiming a wild but ineffectual kick.

But, thankfully, finding his spirits relieved, elevated indeed, by the sight of the huge wooden cross that the men were carrying and the *Tenebrae* banner which now appeared around the corner, hoisted aloft by Patsy Murray and Jude O'Hara. The entire street was a riot of vibrant colour, the square itself a green roof of swaying palms. He made his decision there and then – to finish off Peyton once and for all.

– This, my friends, will be a day to remember! Today a beacon shines out across the glorious Irish border!

He sank his fist in his palm and gave the order for proceedings to commence immediately.

– *Everrrybody march!* barked Jude O'Hara through the raised loudhailer, proudly brandishing his head-steward's badge. As the *Tenebrae Procession of 1958* surged forward in an overwhelming and mighty wave.

Next to Una Miniter a Roman legate walked along in swishing white-and-purple robes. A Roman legate who, only seconds before, had been involved in an extremely bitter dispute – the residual resentment of which, unfortunately, showed no signs of receding.

– For heaven's sake, Barney, don't be like that, the diffident schoolteacher Jude O'Hara continued to plead, with hands parted, we've had enough of all that.

But the butcher made it clear he was in no mood for *détente*. Was, in fact, on the verge of removing his robes there and then. And, had it not been for the swift intercession of Una Miniter, the situation could have become very grave indeed.

– For heaven's sake, gentlemen – on a Good Friday! Behave yourselves! she had insisted.

But this made little real difference, and matters were not improved by the nervous and purposeless behaviour of Happy Carroll who kept murmuring behind his hand:

– *They can say what they like. I know Reilly is going to do it!*

Then another argument was seen to develop – this time between Dagwood and Conleth Foley.

– God's curse the day I ever agreed to be involved in this! All the time I wasted when I could have been happy with my pigeons! the snooker-hall manager had muttered. Only to find himself reprimanded, on Jude's behalf, by the artist. But to which he responded:

– What would you know about it, Foley? You know as much about acting as my arse does about shooting snipe!

– Stop it, please! implored Jude O'Hara. This infernal squabbling – it really has got to stop!

– *He's going to do it*, whimpered Happy Carroll, *I can see it already, o Jesus Christ and Holy Mary!*

Regarding manifestations of what might be termed one's *essentiality* down the ages there have, of course, been numerous claims advanced – the great majority of them unworthy of any serious attention. However, of this much let everyone – reader or casual observer – be certain I have no need of vulgar trappings whether brimstone or blue-burning candles. Such meretricious accoutrements are redundant and surplus – just as they have always been. So, as I awaited the procession's arrival that day, it was hardly ever going to be likely that I would find myself identified, much less apprehended, in the anticipated manner of some entity analogous to *Nobodaddy* or the *Fetch*. No, I remained there, as always, with my anonymity secure – as featureless and unremarkable as the marble pillar, in the vicinity of which I was modestly sequestered.

Meanwhile the serpentine assembly continued its way through the town, up hill and down dale, through the maze of winding streets, the tensions which troubled it more profound now than ever. At one point Dagwood punched Happy in the chest, and a glob of saliva narrowly missed Patsy Murray's ear. But, just at that moment, the church gates, hove fortuitously into view.

– *At last!* cried Jude O'Hara, with the massive double doors swinging open to admit them, and they found themselves swallowed up by the dark maw of the incense-fragrant interior. I smiled as I watched them sink to their knees.

– *What an exemplary, devout herd they make*, I sighed – examining my fingernails as in an orderly fashion they filed into the pews.

Beside a scarlet lamp suspended from a golden chain, Patsy Murray seemed lost in contemplation. He looked pale – the truth being that he hadn't been feeling well since morning. Had even, most uncharacteristically, found himself confiding in his neighbour Jude O'Hara that Golly had been showing those *signs* again – coming out with irrational things.

– God forgive me, Jude, he had said to the teacher, but do you know what I did? I swore at my wife. I called her awful names, so I did – my own lovely Golly whose love I treasure more than anything. There's times of late when I find myself thinking that I'm not inhabiting my own skin at all. That I'm being *manipulated*, Jude. That's the only way I can think of putting it.

The blue-swathed ranks of the *Legion of Mary* were already in position in front of the altar. As Mrs Miniter assumed her place in the organ loft directly over my head, her pliant, nimble fingers drawing sustained, plump chords from the tiered keyboard. With the tremulous notes hovering for what seemed an unreasonable length of time before dramatically descending on the solid, blocky figure of the white-haired parish priest standing before the great wooden cross. On which had been painted the single word: TENEBRAE – powerful, as always, in its resonance.

Heaped up beside it were mountains of pink and white and lavender blossoms, lovingly prepared by Mrs Miniter – who now, perhaps overcome by emotion, proceeded to launch into a series of unnecessarily flamboyant and elaborate octaves intended to elevate the congregation's spirits – but which, regrettably, exerted the opposite effect – chafing their already frayed nerves even further.

Ever so gradually then the lights began to dim, with seven candles continuing to burn along the aisles.

– *I can feel him*, hissed Happy Carroll, *I swear to God I can hear Reilly. O Christ! He's going to do it! Satan's agent is here, I can hear him outside the door!*

But Father Hand's powerful voice sharply silenced him, booming out through the floating grey clouds of incense.

– *Bless the Lord who forgives all our sins*, he bellowed.

And the congregation, with one voice, responded.

– *His mercy, Father, endures for ever.*

The priest ascended the stairs to the pulpit. Then, clearing his throat in the flickering darkness, he commenced with sombre authority:

– The service of worship tonight is taken from an early Christian service called *Tenebrae*. The name *Tenebrae* is the Latin word for *darkness*. Tonight we will experience only a small portion of Christ's pain and suffering the day of His crucifixion. One of the most conspicuous features is the gradual extinguishing of candles until only a single candle, considered a symbol of Our Lord, remains. As it grows darker and darker we can reflect on the great *emotional* and *physical pain* that was so very real for Jesus that evening. Towards the very end, when the tympani is struck, a loud noise will symbolise the earthquake at the time of Christ's death. At that moment, the temple veil was torn apart, making the *Holy of Holies* exposed to public view. Let us now reflect on the great emotional and physical suffering that was so very real for Jesus Christ Our Saviour as he hung on the cross on that very first Good Friday evening.

The priest's grave observations had a devastating effect on everyone present. For, almost without exception, they felt as though they, as individuals, were being personally held responsible for what had happened that awful day. When Jesus had been tortured and humiliated in the city of Jerusalem. Perhaps, they began to consider, they had been foredoomed all along. Maybe that was why *James A. Reilly* had been sent – for the purpose of punishing the community as a whole – possibly even to commit *murder*, they thought. As a means of making them atone for all their sins – particularly that of collusion in the *murder of Jesus Christ*. The more they entertained the possibility, the more likely it came to seem. Well then, that was it, they found themselves deciding – there didn't seem to be any way out. Father Hand was going to be murdered, that was all there was to it. And they themselves were responsible for it. The mighty bell tolled. As Father Hand turned a page and continued reading:

– *Most gracious God, look with mercy upon your family gathered here. This small community that has abided here for generations past.*

– *When he strikes the tympani! That's when he's going to do it!* squealed Happy Carroll, plunging his white, drawn face into his hands.

Father Hand coughed and solemnly continued:

– After the Christ candle has been silently and slowly carried from the altar then after approximately ten seconds of total darkness and silence the percussionist will start a quiet roll on the tympani. This will build in intensity and then decrease two or three times. Each time getting stronger and stronger. It will then slowly and quietly reduce to silence after several small build-ups. Immediately there will be one large crash of cymbals. This as you know will symbolise the death of Jesus Christ on the cross. Now I want you to show solidarity, to strike your missals with committed passion on the benches. Strike in memory of our dear Saviour's death. Do you understand me, my dear people?

– Reilly's definitely out there! O Jesus Christ, can't youse fuck-ing hear him! wailed Happy Carroll.

As the candles guttered in the heavy darkness, the ominous rolling of the tympani was initiated. Each fraught heart gave the impression of beating more loudly than that of its neighbour – *thump, thump, thump* went the missals and prayer books, as perspiration gleamed on every brow. Then a side door opened and Barney Corr stepped up to defiantly face Jerusalem's clamorous rabble.

– Youse are asking me to crucify him, aren't youse? But I can find no wrong in him! he declaimed magisterially.

Renewed blows rained down on the ancient wooden benches, as prayer books were raised and Barney Corr swept frantically towards the tympani once more, lifting the brass-headed beater in a mighty, two-handed grip. As the congregation bellowed:

– Crucify him! Crucify him!

– Louder! Louder! urged Father Hand.

– Crucify him! Crucify him!

– Louder, I implore you, in honour of Our Saviour!

– Crucify him! Crucify him!

– Who will you have – him or Barabbas?

– Yes, give them Barabbas, Hand you fucking cunt! For he's not half the criminal you are, you fucking bastard!

No one could believe the words they had just heard. As the doors at the back of the church were seen to burst open and every head in the building turning around. Staring in white-faced astonishment, with the clouds of incense momentarily obscuring their vision. Before, dumbstruck, they took in the figure of James A. Reilly – framed in the doorway in a square of blinding light and mounted grotesquely on the back of a donkey.

– *The time has come!* he announced, dismounting, raising his rifle as he began making a deliberate approach along the aisle – pushing back his tea-cosy hat.

– So all you Cullymore shitehawks, listen to me, he bawled, youse'd be as well to get out of this church right now – for death is going to be done here today!

– *Where's the lights?* Jude O'Hara shrieked hysterically. *In the name of God the Father, where are the lights?*

The schoolteacher kept running to and fro across the altar – to no apparent purpose. For his part, however, Father Hand demonstrated considerable presence of mind, grabbing Mrs Miniter's niece and bundling her out of harm's way. But James Reilly was already down on one knee – carefully pressing the butt of the rifle to his shoulder, patiently adjusting the volley sights. Closing one eye as he prepared to take aim.

– *O how I've longed for this precious day!* he moaned, his body shuddering in delicious anticipation – curling his index finger around the trigger.

When, with an abandon that seemed breathtakingly reckless in the circumstances, Barney Corr lunged forward, in the process demonstrating an agility quite extraordinary in a man of his girth, swinging the heavy beater and striking James Reilly violently on the side of the head. So sickening was the sound that the congregation moaned and shrank away, as one.

– *Take that, Reilly, you troublemaking cunt!* he bawled.

325

The butcher redoubling his efforts and repeatedly striking him, as the former teacher stumbled and reeled, clutching haplessly on to the altar rails. Before being felled by a mighty blow, even more merciless than before.

But it wasn't to end there – as the butcher continued to rain down ever more savage strikes, until his victim had been rendered hopelessly inert. Had relapsed, in fact, into what can only be described as a kind of ethereal slumber, and making no discernible effort to rally.

His attentions, although no one present was, of course, ever to know this, being compelled by the appearance of a figure which had just emerged through a side-altar door – gliding slowly towards James where he lay prostrate along the centre aisle. It was the student *Jerome Brolly* – looking more beautiful than ever, James thought, with his hair back-combed, in a white frilled blouse. But with no sign of any vaporous cloud hovering in front of his mouth. No – you could clearly see his lips. You could even see them parting as he enquired of his former custodian:

– Sir, if you don't mind me asking, what were you doing on the back of an ass? It's just that it seems so unusual – one's teacher riding a donkey, I mean.

– I'm sorry, Jerome, whispered James, now trying valiantly to raise himself up, I don't know what came over me that day in Junior 3. My mother was dying in the hospital, you see. Maybe that had something to do with it. I had been to see *The Spiral Staircase*. My mind was all confused. I think I might have been having a breakdown. I'm sorry for interfering with you.

When he looked again, an immense sadness consumed him, for he realised Jerome Brolly was gone – and that the figure towering over him was that of a fearsome, wild-eyed butcher. Who was glaring fiercely, murderously challenging him:

– To even *think* of moving a muscle, Reilly!

53

That the much-heralded play of *Tenebrae* had ultimately proved to be something of a burlesque, a near-degrading laughable farce, if the truth be told, was something no one could even begin to think of denying.

But, as is so often the way in these small, unremarkable out-of-the-way places, it was not so very long before the tried and trusted forces of mythology once more began to do their work. And within a few short months, indeed by the beginning of the summer in 1958, far from being a calamity of colossal proportions, it began to be suggested that what had actually taken place in Father Hand's church on that wonderful Friday during *Holy Week* had been nothing short of a miraculous event — yet another great occasion of which the little town could find itself proud. Indeed the more it was discussed the more it came to represent the veritable high point of Father Hand's illustrious career.

— *We've gone and done it again!* they boasted, *we have showed the world what Cullymore is capable of. Here's to our old friend Father Hand — boys, what a performance!*

After that, everyone professed themselves pleased with the way the whole thing had gone, the extraordinary way everything had come together in the end. Especially when the police car drove out to the lake. Where James A. Reilly was unceremoniously bundled into the back and taken away. To where no one ever really knew – or cared, for there was never to be any court case. In fact he had been ferried off to *Balla Mental Hospital* and signed in without ceremony. The civic guard, everyone agreed, had been *damned fortunate* not to lose his job – for not having taken action long ago.

– But no matter. All's well that ends well.

This was more or less the general consensus – and nothing more was said about the policeman after that.

James Alo Reilly was never to be seen again. In actual fact, he died two months later – by his own hand. Just as he had predicted – with the words of the Roman poet *Horace* on his lips:

– *Odi profanum vulgus et arceo – I shun and keep removed the uninitiate crowd. I require silence. I am the Muses' priest and sing for virgins and boys songs never heard before.*

Irrespective of whether the case against him had been proven or not, Happy Carroll continued to be the object of oblique scorn, and on one terrible occasion had found himself the recipient of a merciless beating – administered by friends of Manus Hoare. Subsequent to which he became almost completely withdrawn – taking up residence in James A. Reilly's vacated hovel. Attired, indeed, after the manner of his predecessor, in a navy-blue belted gabardine raincoat and knitted woollen hat

– spending hours squatting by the lake, feeding nuts to a fox cub he had tamed. On rare occasions he might appear in the doorway of the *Yankee Clipper*, and later the Sky Sports Bar, for the purpose of delivering yet another *warning*.

– He's coming, *Nobodaddy* – you mark my words. He's coming for youse all! He going to going to close the unholy gate!

His fearsome pronouncements, of course, ultimately becoming nothing more than a joke – a little bit of harmless local colour, just as they had been in James Reilly's time.

– He was in here again last night, laughed Patsy Murray, he's every bit as bad as James, and worse!

– What a character! laughed Jude O'Hara. It takes all sorts!

Which indeed it does, with everyone inhabiting the private, clandestine world of their own story – one never to be shared with friend, neighbour or even lifetime spouse. Making their way as best they can, slouching myopically across the broad white plains of *Time*.

Just as Hubert Considine had been doing, one otherwise unremarkable evening in London city when he found himself arrested. You remember, of course, Teddy O'Neill's old pal. Poor old Hubert – always had been edgy and apprehensive.

Haunted by the dread apprehension that, one day, for no apparent reason, simply because it happened to be in his blood, he would find himself malignly bearing down on someone with a shovel. He had dreamed the scenario so many times. Observing himself as he brought down the implement – on to a defenceless woman's head. Even as he entertained the idea, he continued to be convinced of its essential absurdity.

But there was nobody who knew myth and superstition better than Hubert Considine.

And how the world could deceive you – by logic and reason. By making you feel both secure and unthreatened – all the while preparing some hideous snare.

Which was why he would find himself waking in the night, sensing some foreign presence in the room.

Hubert Considine wished that he had married. In fact he wished all sorts of things. You remember that Hubert had already visited Teddy in *Skegness* and was due to come again one Sunday afternoon in late August. But had not arrived. His young friend and associate Alphonsus was never to become acquainted with the actual reasons for this non-appearance. Which is perhaps fortunate, considering the circumstances and the nature of what had actually happened. When, on the 28th of August 1957, Hubert Considine, having attired himself in his familiar two-piece charcoal suit and affixed his thin grey tie, set off for his place of work – a city-centre office in Holborn.

However, on his way, he had decided unexpectedly to make a detour. To pay a visit, in fact, to a gentlemen's convenience – in Holloway, North London. Subsequently finding himself standing by a brick-tiled wall, exchanging furtive glances with a middle-aged man. Before the truth dawned on him, it was already too late. When it transpired that the gentleman in the shadows was, in fact, a police detective, and Hubert was summoned to the station and charged.

In the months that followed, Hubert Considine was often to think that, in that terrible moment just before the policeman had displayed his badge, someone – or *something* – had emerged from the toilet cubicle – just beyond his range of vision. And had remained there, throughout the course of that awful event. Watching impassively, as he had done when his forebear had wielded the spade.

– It's *him!* he had choked, but the detective had just pushed him gently.

– Come along, please, he had urged – somewhat wearily.

Hubert Considine had been correct, of course – I *had* been there. Just as I have been on so many other similar occasions – such as that frosty October night in 1990, when *Detective Inspector Ralph Foster* opened his front door and found himself confronted by two masked men. Who enquired, somewhat deferentially, as to his identity.

– *Are you Ralph Foster?* one of them asked.

– Yes, he had replied, before they pumped five bullets into his chest, adding a sixth for good measure as he fell – just as Imelda arrived home with their grown-up son and daughter. Thereby fulfilling James Reilly's prediction.

– *That was for your brother Manus, you turncoat bitch!*

the assailants called back, before leaping on to a waiting motorcycle.

After witnessing that, Imelda Foster knew she'd need all the help she could get. And she was right, as she discovered one night when she woke up, just before dawn, and saw something forming, she thought, on the mirror. Which eventually turned out to be some words she recognised: *Entering you is like entering heaven.*

Patsy Murray had been similarly disturbed one night, much later on in the year 2009. When he had found himself relieved that the source of his anxiety had been nothing other than the rattle of a downstairs blind. Which he now realised. Before retiring to the kitchen – with the intention of making a cup of tea for himself and his wife. Then changing his mind and deciding to opt for cocoa. Which Golly, as he knew, had always preferred. It might put her in good humour, he thought, as he stirred the milk, cheer her up a bit.

He smiled as he carried the tray along the hallway, climbing the stairs as he hummed his favourite tune – *The Old Rugged Cross*, the plangent hymn of any close-knit, traditional community like his own.

When he entered the room, he saw that Golly was getting ready for bed – raising her long cotton nightdress over her head. Sympathising as she did so with the plight of poor Bodley Foster, who often played music long into the night – with *Three Coins in the Fountain* now faintly audible as it drifted through the open windows of *Dunroamin*, on the Enniskillen Road.

– He lost his wife and then his son, she sighed, life can be so unfair and difficult. At times it's hard for the likes of us to understand.

– I heard he polishes Ralph's motorbike every day, observed Patsy, setting down the tray.

His wife made no reply – just gazed vacantly into her cocoa. Until eventually, most of the steaming beverage consumed, she lifted her head to smile at her husband. Who gave her a little nod as she abstractedly clutched the pink hot-water bottle.

– Patsy love, have you seen my *People's Friend?* she asked, I could have sworn I left it on the sideboard.

– It's right over there, by the bed, he said, adding:

– Where you left it, dear.

– I'm such a silly, he heard his wife reply, turning back the covers and climbing into bed.

And Patsy flicked the flat-screen remote control which their son Luke, now a highly successful architect in Boston, had given them as a present for their golden-wedding anniversary, tuning in to the radio facility.

As the BBC shipping forecast began to float soothingly, with not so much as the faintest hint of static.

The wonders of modern technology, thought Patsy, so far ahead of the old times we grew up in.

– *Atlantic low 991, expected 130 miles west of Rockall, 1011 by 01.00 tomorrow. High Faroes 1028. Viking variable 3 or 4.*

As Patsy leaned over to lower the volume just a little, it seemed the most peaceful domestic scene imaginable. But, as is so often the case, perception can often prove so illusory. Which, as I observed them from my place of concealment, could be said to be an accurate appraisal of the situation in this case. As I watched Golly slowly turn the magazine's pages.

– A penny for your thoughts? asked her husband, smiling.

– I wasn't thinking anything at all, his wife replied.

Which of course could not have been further from the truth. For even in one's early eighties, secrets are fated to remain locked in the heart – destined never to be divulged.

This was not, of course, what Golly Murray might have wanted. But she had long since come to accept the situation. As in his own way too, so had her husband.

She turned another page, tapping her mouth as she began to yawn.

– It says in here that the American President might be coming to Ireland, she murmured, that there's rumours of *Barack Obama* coming, perhaps, next spring.

– What, love? asked her husband, what was that you said just now?

– *Barack Obama*. It says in here he has Irish roots.

– Oh yes, *Obama*, sighed Patsy Murray – not really paying very much attention. But Golly didn't mind – at least, she thought, she had been able to tell her husband *something*.

Which was more than she could when it came to other things which, even yet, persisted in crossing her mind. Such as the little badge on *Robinson's* jams, for example. No, she knew – the day would never come when she would be able to lay down her *People's Friend*. Commit herself to weeping her heart out and reveal to Patsy what she really and truly yearned most to say:

– When I was in *Balla Hospital* what I wanted to do most was to harm myself, Patsy. And do you know why? Because I remembered that little black fellow on the pot. You know who I mean – the *golliwog*, Patsy. With my stupid curly hair, that's who I've always looked like. I remembered all the names that the girls used to call me and more than anything I wished I had the courage to hurt myself. With scissors or a needle – I didn't mind which.

No, obviously of course you couldn't say that. Just as there were so many other things in your life you would never be able to say. To anyone. Even your husband. *Especially* your husband. There were other things too. For example, the day she had wanted Blossom Foster to be disfigured, maybe in a horrible accident. And the nights she had stood by their bedroom window, longing to be out there with *Laika* – far away from her husband and son.

But if it had been ordained that Patsy Murray was never to become acquainted with the most intimate secrets of his wife's mind, then so too must it be acknowledged that she, equally, was fated never to gain access to the deeply buried longings of her husband's closed man-heart. How could he ever admit to his own unworthy longings – that he, in turn, had wished her out there: lost and insignificant out amongst the constellations. No voice could ever be given to such base and ignoble desires – of which he had been, and remained, ashamed.

Which was why, having been awakened yet again in the night and finding her husband sitting bolt upright in bed, clearly in a state of extreme distress, Golly Murray continued to be oblivious as to the cause of these intermittent night-time episodes. Even though she did her best, consoling her husband and massaging his neck, sympathetically mopping his tense, anxious brow. Until, thankfully, sleep once more overtook her spouse.

But by which time she herself was now wide awake – extremely and uncomfortably alert, in fact. Which her doctors, of course, had counselled could signal the onset of one of her *turns*. A possibility which she was still considering when her attentions were diverted by the sound of childish chanting in the street – *Three six nine the goose drank wine the monkey chewed tobacco on the streetcar line* – and she was drawn towards the window where, quite miraculously, a magical scene was now proceeding. With a simple ordinary day about to begin – why, it seemed as though no one had passed away at all.

With some of the younger boys playing marbles and the girls in a ring reading comics and sewing, as the *Vauxhall Saloon*, with Bodley Foster at the wheel, pulled up to discharge a smiling Albert Craig. Through an open window a gramophone was playing – *The Old Rugged Cross*, as it happened – as Dagwood Slowey popped his head out of the snooker hall, with young Manus Hoare standing at the corner.

Already, she could see, the post office was packed, and Barney Corr, as usual, didn't seem to have a minute – run off his feet as he chatted to all the housewives. Then along came the baker in his van all the way from Balla, jauntily whistling as he flung the doors open, drawing out the steaming silver trays. And o look, there's Happy Carroll, mused Golly, as the carpenter went by with his pencil behind his ear. And Conleth Foley with his easel under his arm, making his way to the lake to spend the afternoon, no doubt. But I say, who's this – it's Jude O'Hara swinging his cane, on his way to rehearsals, I suppose – as Father Hand waved, calling to the schoolteacher from the presbytery across the street. Dagwood smiling as he tossed away his cigarette, turning around and going back inside the hall.

Just as the door of the café swung open and Mrs Markey appeared with her hands up to her face, releasing an ear-splitting scream and bringing the whole street to a standstill in the process.

At which point I myself decided it appropriate to draw proceedings to a close – Golly initially, of course, frozen with fear. When she found herself confronted by what has been classified historically as the *wanton* and *unutterable*. Her trepidations, however, happily abating when she saw who I had become. Not the appalling *Fetch* of antiquity, or the threatening, ethereal *Nobodaddy* but none other than *Little Bonnie*, her first-born son – got up like an angel on his *First Communion* morning. Visibly warming as I flashed her boy's lovely winning smile, before opening my hand, in which reposed six coloured plasticine eggs.

– *They're beautiful!* she choked. *O Boniface, I'm so happy!*

As I firmly closed the gate behind us, assuring her that this was how it would always be, in this courteous region where no strangers abide.

Our own unassailable Stray Sod home.

The text of this book is set in Adobe Garamond. It is one of several versions of Garamond based on the designs of Claude Garamond. It is thought that Garamond based his font on Bembo, cut in 1495 by Francesco Griffo in collaboration with the Italian printer Aldus Manutius. Garamond types were first used in books printed in Paris around 1532. Many of the present-day versions of this type are based on the *Typi Academiae* of Jean Jannon, cut in Sedan in 1615.

Claude Garamond was born in Paris in 1480. He learned how to cut type from his father and by the age of fifteen he was able to fashion steel punches the size of a pica with great precision. At the age of sixty he was commissioned by King Francis I to design a Greek alphabet; for this he was given the honourable title of royal type founder. He died in 1561.